John Birmingham is on the run from some mistakes he made in Queensland. He doesn't know how those drugs came to be inside his shoe. He grew up in Ipswich but asks you not to hold that against him. He writes for a wide range of publications but finds that porno mags pay the best rates and most promptly. Some of his best friends are lesbians. He used to work for the shadowy Office of Special Clearances and Records within the Defence Department but has also loaded boxes on to trucks, pulled a few beers, and read newspapers for a clipping service. He is kind of lazy and watches too much television. He recommends flu tablets for hangovers.

Also by John Birmingham in Flamingo

He Died With a Felafel In His Hand

THE TASMANIAN BABES FIASCO

John Birmingham

'And I hope I die in the night time
with my tv on and a beer in my hand
and you by my side.'

Blake Babies

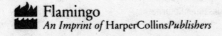
Flamingo
An Imprint of HarperCollinsPublishers

Flamingo
An imprint of HarperCollinsPublishers
77–85 Fulham Palace Road
Hammersmith, London W6 8JB

First published in Australia
by Duffy & Snellgrove 1997

Published by Flamingo 1998
1 3 5 7 9 8 6 4 2

A catalogue record for this book is
available from the British Library

ISBN 0 00 655130 0

Set in Frutiger Light Condensed mainly

Printed and bound in Great Britain by
Caledonian International Book Manufacturing Ltd, Glasgow

Illustrations by Darren Roach

CONTENTS

ACKNOWLEDGEMENTS
The Unusual Suspects

All the guys in alt.flame.roommate who gave permission to use their stories; Michael Barnes (who does not really own that Lamborghini); Simon Bedak (who now sleeps with a fire extinguisher, knows the value of audacity, and can say 'clitoris ring' in three different languages); Luke Berry (who amazed us all by getting that security clearance!); Sam Boucher (who tamed the bats, raised the dead, and finally got her favourite black vinyl pants back); Sandra Bridekirk (who should stop publishing Australia's Most Studly and go for the high-class chick market instead, perhaps by letting me do a tracky-dacks-down cover shot?); Kirsty Brooks x 2 (who missed out last time and who is doomed to blonde hair, big eyes and great rides on the freeway of lerv); Launz 'Flinthart' Burch (who has to keep moving because the Townsville Chamber of Commerce will not rest until he is brought to justice); Jon Casimir (who goes bump in the night, can leap from first floor balconies in a single bound and has not, to my knowledge, ever actually imprisoned any children under the stairs); Brett Cheney (who is still splitting tens like a motherfucker); Matt Condon (who has never sold real estate, except in Port Stephens); Matt Corks (who had no say in the trellis incident); Vicki-Anne Craigen (who always wears her pyjamas); Mandy Curties (who can ask me for a reference any day, and probably will); Michael Duffy (who leaves me alone and only calls to send over cheques, drugs, alcohol, tips on the gee-gees, etc); Jon Dwyer (who seems very pleased with himself); Alex Egarton (who keeps tabs on his cushions nowadays); Kate Evans (who is missing in action and missed by all); Larysa Fabok (who is engaged in valid scientific experiments on my behalf, with white coats, tree faeries and everything); Sam Hately (who probably has much better taste, if not balance, these days); Bob Heather (who is not really to be trusted with a bottle of tequila, or your sister, and definitely never with both at once); James Hine (who very wisely never paid that crazy girl's bill); John Horner (who should wear underpants in future); Shelly Horton (who is a story finder extraordinaire and whom you should ask about the stripper and the beer bottle); Emma Jackson Lauxcouteur (who has since been scrubbed until her belly button shined); Linda Jaivan (who just loves to get a nice cold piece of fruit into her);

Jane Lye (whose name is whispered in terror by real estate agents everywhere, but especially short ones with bright pink shirts); Steve le Marquand (who does a much better JB than I do); Pete McAllister (who got me out of the Nimbin Dope Harvest Festival alive … well, clinically speaking that is); Corina Mackay (who should write that goddamn book); Tony Molina (who introduced me to Frisbeetarianism); Sarah Mulveney (who moves around a tennis court remarkably well with that baby strapped to her back); Scot O'Keefe (who has been very good about all this, and I really think it's time you fat karate dykes just laid off); Danny Punch (who really doesn't want you wandering around his place in the nuddy); Jemma Purcell (who is not at all concerned about the price of greasy wool); Bronwyn Ridgeway (who saw the flying ducks hit the wall); Craig Roach (who is a very good cook now); Darren Roach (who braved another night with those ugly guys Wayne, Jimmy and Chris – the one true Milko from Acapulco); Mikey Robbins (who has lived with much stranger people than me, and really, you gotta worry about that); DeAnna Scott (who should have pulled the plug); Howard '5 Fingers' Stringer (whose absence was sorely felt on those long brutal red wine nights when all good publishers were abed and the Sandmen of the Terror Data stalked the Earth); Karen and Martin Turner (who are probably slobbering up a storm thinking about my mashed taters on toasted white bread); Joe N. Turner (who has also suffered at the hands of a 'nutter'); Heather and Jasper Vaile (who were always there and never let me down, which is more than I can say for myself); Clinton Walker (who is a dangerous man with a broom in his hand); and Julie Whitlock (who can't believe it's not real hair).

Professor John Frow would also have me acknowledge Douglas Coupland, Hunter S. Thompson, the impenetrable folk at Art and Text, F. Scott Fitzgerald, half a dozen weird news web sites (especially the ones dealing with dumb criminals; God, how I love them), Simone de Beauvoir, Warner Brothers, George Lucas, John Irving, Joseph Heller and, well basically, a cast of thousands. But really, what does he know? As Elroy would say, 'Fuckin' pointy-head!'

Baby versions of some bits in Tassie Babes have previously appeared in Rolling Stone and three anthologies; Hot Sand (Penguin); Men Love Sex (Random House); and Smashed (Random House). I thank everyone involved for letting me work out my ideas on their bar tab, especially the guys at Random for indulging me when I should have been hard at work on my Sydney book.

FIASCO? WHAT FIASCO?
Confused Author's Note

Hey there. How you doin'? Probably better than me I'll wager. I'm sitting here, hunched over this Jurassic laptop the good folk at HarperCollins have lent me, wondering when all these powerful painkillers I've been gobbling down are going to kick in and smother my headache. It's a choice little number I tell you. Part jetlag, part hangover, frontal lobes and back. Like someone's jammed a couple of rusty skewers in through my eyeballs and the nape of my neck.

Still, it's nothing like the baby I had the morning after I finished writing Felafel. I put that sucker together, with a lot of help from a lot of friends, in something like five or six weeks. It's all kind of a blur now. The night before it was due to go to the printers I was hammering away at the last chapter when, about four in the morning, in this delirium of sleeplessness, red wine, hot chips and amphetamine abuse I somehow deleted a couple of chapters. Just zapped 'em. Gone. No back ups. No hard copies. Nothing.

Oh man, let me tell you. It really was darkest just before the dawn. I was sitting there, alone in this little flat, underpants on my head, eyeballs hanging out by their stalks, shrieking like a banshee and pounding the computer screen. Eventually I calmed down and I did manage to stitch one of the chapters back together. The last one. But it was an ugly, Frankenstein's edit of a job. Paragraphs missing, anecdotes trailing away into nothing, through-lines all fucked up. Thankfully, the rest of the book looked like that anyway so I don't think anyone noticed. The other file however, chapter four, disappeared without trace.

 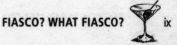

It was a ripping little yarn, based on a short story I'd knocked out for a student mag years earlier; the story of this disastrous party to which I'd invited my neighbours, these dopey, horny young babes from some pissant little village called Penguin, somewhere in Tasmania. As I recall they weren't all Tasmanians, one was a pom or an Enzedder or something but I wrote them up as Tasmanians because down in Oz we find Tasmania inherently funny. It's like a whole island full of cousins who love each other. The night of this party I was hoping maybe one or two of these barefoot, nine-toed beauties might get drunk or stoned enough to treat me like family, but it didn't work out that way. I ended up on their floor, pants around my ankles, vomiting into the shag pile and ... well, I'm rambling again.

The point is, that story didn't make it into Felafel in Australia. I reconstructed it from my notes a bit later, with some drastic changes, and it came out in a collection of drinking stories called 'Smashed'. Then, happily, HarperCollins picked up Felafel in the UK and I jumped at the chance to rewrite the bloody thing a third or fourth time and slip it back into its rightful place. The Tasmanians became Londoners and I got to make a couple of gratuitous Barmy Army and English gentry jokes into the bargain. Cool.

So, what am I doing, rubbing my throbbing temples and staring at this blurry computer screen at some hideous fucking hour on a Bank Holiday Monday in London? Well, you recall I wrote Felafel in about five weeks or so. That wasn't my choice. I had a crazed publisher with a deadline and an open cheque book. I did as I was told. But it meant that when I staggered off to the printers with my mangled, incomplete manuscript, I still had a missing chapter as well as a pile of unused stories and interviews. I decided to turn these into another book, this time in novelised rather than diarised form. You're holding that book right now. But as with the British edition of Felafel, you're holding a sleeker, shinier, somewhat sexier version than the one avail-

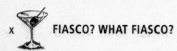

FIASCO? WHAT FIASCO?

able down under. Jokes and stories which I thought of as real thigh-slapping classics in the frenzy of a deadline two years ago, I can now see as, well, crap really. So I cut them out or changed them or whatever. I've also fixed up some inconsistencies and filled in some plot-holes.

The major change of course comes from Felafel having been published in its complete form in the UK. You got the missing chapter which the Aussies didn't. That also means, of course, that your edition of Babes is slightly different. Basically, there are no babes in it. No Tasmanians, no Londoners, no Kiwis, no nothing. The Fiasco of the title then has nothing to do with any horrifically undignified episodes of pants-down shag pile vomiting. Rather it refers to the gigantic God-awful fucking mess I got myself into four years ago, in the wee hours before deadline when, with a head full of cheap red wine and dangerous drugs, I carelessly tapped the wrong keys and deleted a huge whack of my first book. And people ask me why I've never had a real job.

Finally, one for the trainspotters. I often get asked how much of these books are true. Generally, it works like this. About seventy per cent of the stories happened just as you read them, except with the participants, identifying details such as names, locations and sometimes their nationalities changed. (For instance Hackett, the prostitute-loving American in Felafel actually hailed from London.) About twenty per cent are based on true stories but have been twisted right out of shape. About ten per cent of both Felafel and Babes is total bullshit. The interesting thing though, is that the weirdest stories are usually those which have changed the least – the tent-dwelling bank clerk in Felafel, or the attack of the giant possums and roaches in Babes. The attack of the roaches actually did take place, except in real life it happened in the middle of an Australian desert at a spy satellite facility called Pine Gap. And in real life Jordan disappeared after a couple of goons turned up at the door wearing balaclavas and toting machetes, wanting to know when he was going to come good with the forty thousand bucks he owed their boss. Nobody's seen him since. But I thought that was a bit melodramatic for a novel. I hope you can dig it. Because I'm going back to bed now.

John Birmingham (London, May 1998)

FIASCO? WHAT FIASCO?

THE FRAUDULATOR

Aristotle said that if you hold your farts in you die. I'm not sure where he said that but some big university guy told me so it's probably true. Kind of wished I'd kept it to myself though. Our place wasn't worth living in after word got around and I had to take a long and eventful road trip to get away from it. When I ran out of money and came back I discovered that we had resigned from the street's fruit and vegetable co-op and we'd had a spy in the house.

The co-op had sounded like a good idea, fifteen bucks a week for all the roughage we could handle. Unfortunately the co-op hippies only ever brought around these stupid left wing vegetables that nobody wanted to eat. They piled up in their damp recycled cardboard boxes, gelatinous hillocks of buk choy and witlof and plantains, all mouldy and rotting and just waiting on a lightning strike to zap them into a giant blob of sentient protoplasm which would eat some teenagers and attack the town and so on.

We were a mixed bunch in this house, which sat just off Swann Road in Taringa, near the two big hill-top high rise towers all my friends dreamed of living in for a while. If you'd wanted to visit us while we were still there you would have navigated by those towers. You can see them from all over the city. You'd drive towards them from Toowong, tracking along beside the train line and turning to cross

over the bridge just after Taringa Station. That's the start of Swann Road and we were the first street on the right, York Street. The house was a slumping, tired old Queenslander, its wooden stilts leaning drunkenly, all the verandahs walled in for extra bedrooms and there were . . . let's see, ten of us living there to begin with.

There was Taylor the cabbie and Jabba the Hutt. You've met them before. Taylor had the hot box, the glassed-in sleepout at the front of the house. He didn't mind the ten degree slope of the lino floor or the fact he had to string an old blanket up to get any privacy. He figured at least he had an actual room in this place, instead of just floorspace, and he liked it because he could come and go at all hours without disturbing anyone. Not that he was likely to. With so many folks living there we ran a twenty-four hour facility. Jabba, for instance, did not have a room because he did not seem to need one. Jabba wasn't like other people. Whatever the rest of us drew from a few hours nightly REM sleep his brain seemed to make up from the radiation pulsing off a warm TV screen. So Jabba had a couch, not a room, and on that couch he left a permanent impression of two hairy butt cheeks which are gonna have archaeologists of the future scratching their giant lightbulb-shaped heads in befuddlement.

In the two rooms directly off the big lounge lived Thunderbird Ron and Brainthrust Leonard. The T-Bird was a guy who'd gone deep into the cult of body building, so deep we used to paint him orange and make him wear blue undies at Superhero parties because he looked a bit like the Thing from the Fantastic Four. Next door to him was Brainthrust Leonard, this hypergeek propellorhead doing some sort of combined compsci-engineering degree. Leonard's dream room was an airlocked command centre in a geo-stationary spacelab with a fully reclineable Captain Kirk chair, a super computer which spoke in the voice of Gillian Anderson and a crew of horny space chicks in revealing Starfleet uniforms to pop grapes into his mouth and dance in laser

beam cages. In his real room he slept on a broken army cot beside a huge pile of slightly soiled underpants, a bigger pile of old magazines and an awesome, teetering mass of computer wreckage – TRS 80 monitors, defunct CPUs, tools, wiring, long dead motherboards, disks and cables, all sorts of shit. His turn-ons were Power PC upgrades, hot female newsreaders and eight-packs of generic underpants (one for each day and a spare just in case). His turn-offs were the monolithic dominance of the Microsloth Corporation, oily Internet business gurus and budget cuts to NASA's search for rogue asteroids.

The old dining room out the back of the house had been partly fenced off with a bunch of carpet-covered vertical dividers bought for ten dollars each at a government auction. They provided a sub-sistence level of privacy for Missy, a Malaysian nightclubbing queen with poor taste in boyfriends. Five foot three, with big brown Bambi eyes, boobs out to Wednesday and no sense of decorum, she was the secret lust object of most of the housedudes, who all thought they were in with a chance, given the sorry sort of loser she generally came home with. We called her fenced-off sub-division Area 51, because of the alien life forms which often landed there mysteriously during the night.

Past the bathroom and around a bit from Missy dwelled Elroy, who styled himself as the Milko from Acapulco, which was half right. He was a milko, with a van and a milk run, but he actually came from Gladstone. He and Taylor were like blood brothers. They worked the graveyard shift and had a disastrous history of sharing other flats and houses. They'd dined together at every late night greasy eating joint in town and were always neglecting their duties to sneak off for a quick spliff. Sometimes after a longer spliff they liked to drag race their work vehicles. Four in the morning on a still, moonlit night, if you're droning along the Great Western Freeway and suddenly everything explodes as an old cab and a milk van kick in the nitrous and peel out

in front of you in a big ball of flame, you know you just met my flatmates. Their all time favourite thing though was to sit and fester in
the Megamall, ranking every female who walked past on the basis of
how many beers they would need to drink before they tried to sleep
with her.

'Definite six pack.'

'No, maybe a dozen.'

'Never happen.'

'Or a dozen with regrets?'

'Whoa! Lookout! Stone cold sober coming out of Cookie Man!'

The master bedroom lay across the hall from Taylor at the front of York
Street. It was the seat of government for the house. The room of Stacey,
who wanted to be a war photographer but who, for the moment, got
all of the life-threatening action she could manage as den mother to
our cosy little Gen-X community. She wasn't the oldest or the biggest
or even the scariest one in the house, but she was the most grown up
and without her to boss everyone around, to collect the bills and make
the rules and dole out her harsh brand of frontier-style justice, York
Street would quickly have degenerated into a burned-up, post-
apocalypse landscape of urban destruction and flesh-eating zombies.
In that very Brisbane way, I had known Stacey (and most of the others)
for a long time before sharing this house with her. Our paths had
crossed when she was padding out her student grant taking happy
snaps for the same student newspapers which were paying me for

stories in misappropriated food vouchers and handfuls of single shot condiment sachets.

I liked hanging with Stacey because she was a take-charge babe who didn't seem awed or intimidated by anything. We'd caught a bus to Canberra once to cover a huge protest outside the exhibition centre. This military arms fair called Aidex was being held inside and about two thousand deeply offended greenies and lefties had turned up to try to stop it. They were camped in tents and caravans under trees in the car park across from the centre, a really mediaeval sort of scene with a lot of colour – banners and open fires and stuff like trumpets and drums going all through the night. Unfortunately, being the Left, they couldn't organise a piss-up in a brewery and spent most of the time arguing among themselves, all two thousand of them, in an enormous daily fishbowl conference. Would they don cricket pads and boxes and storm the police lines? (The International Socialist Option.) Sit quietly in the road and block traffic? (The non-violent, lentil loving Brand-X green/left option.) Build some pyramids out of big pine logs? (The feral forest collectives option.) Or light bees wax candles and chant some Druid prayers? (The two middle-aged weird chicks in white hooded gowns option.) In the end, much to the spastic fury of the I.S., they settled on linking arms in these crop circles of ten or twelve people and sort of merry-go-rounding on to the road leading up to the main gates. They even told the cops they'd be coming on to the road in three minutes and it would be really cool if they didn't, you know, oppress them or anything. Naturally the police beat the living shit out of everyone. People were screaming and crying and getting their heads cracked by batons. It went on for days. There was no real focus, no centre, just a raw, violent energy. And there, vectoring through it all was Stacey with her camera, following some invisible pattern only she could discern, a high soundless tune which carried her through untouched and unscathed. She was so cool.

After that, when she said she was going to America to work for one of the big newspapers, I figured she probably would. And it made me kind of sad because back then the only business I'd had with any newspapers was avoiding the accounts guys who were always chasing payment for my backlog of 'flatmate wanted' ads.

Stacey's room was the best in the house, befitting her role as Supreme Commander. As you'd guess if you knew her it was also kept the cleanest and most comfortable. A lemon tree grew just outside one window, close enough for her to lean out and pick off the fat yellow fruit as it ripened. But it wasn't her dream room. I asked her once what that was and she said, 'Oh, a loft, somewhere high up in Manhattan, with a wall of windows and exposed timber and brick everywhere. A bed, a darkroom, a comfy chair and some wall space to hang my pictures. That'd be close I guess.' At York Street she had a futon and malarial yellow asbestos board walls. And her brother, Gay Phil, camped on an inflatable mattress tucked away in one corner.

Phil was a virtual rather than actual flatmate. He'd fled from Jeff, his last boyfriend, a vicious redhead on methadone maintenance. Just turned up under the lemon tree at two in the morning with a massive cardboard box full of personal effects, a Hot Buttered boogie board and a Sunbeam wok. The house had a loose arrangement where everybody was allowed one refugee per year, six to eight weeks rent free, but I think Stacey was harder on Gay Phil because he was family. She made him cook and clean for us, which was cool because he was a fuckin' wizard with that wok. He was okay in himself too, loved a cone and TV sport, so he slipped sideways into the house routines. Even Taylor coped and he was a back-to-the-wall kind of guy on homosexual issues.

A Kodak moment: Taylor, tired but wired after pulling an allnighter. Gay Phil unpacking his big box of tricks in the lounge. CD player, books,

runners and baseball cap with Homer Simpson smacking himself in the head going 'D'oh!'

'You mind?' asks Taylor, trying the cap on for size. Nope, shrugs Phil.

'Watcha got there?'

'Magazines.'

'All right!' goes Taylor. 'New toilet reading.' And starts sifting through the stack of *Muscle and Fitness, Inside Sports, Bodyboarders* and *Riptides*. He grooves on the wave porn in the surf mags and digs into the box to get a few more out. Phil doesn't care, he just keeps on unpacking. Then Taylor comes up with a quizzical look and a short piece of string. Bobbing about at the end of the string is a small object shaped like a champagne cork, possibly with an internal power supply.

'Hey, Phil, what's this?' asks Taylor, with a quizzical frown.

'That, my friend, is a vibrating butt plug.'

For a week after that everybody went 'bzzzzz' whenever Taylor entered the room.

We'd lost our downstairs flatmates, the goth mediaevalist crossover couple Elvira and Damien (as in *The Omen*) when their whole Black Death retro routine spun out of control. Damien was this self obsessed character, hair going everywhere, clothed in nothing but scrappy old black clothes with 'wanker' written in whiteout fluid all over his jeans. He used to attach little bells to his black pointy boots – which were the most ridiculously pointy boots you could buy at the time – and the bells would jingle to warn of his approach. Damien really loved Christmas because he had visions of little kids coming down the street, hearing the bells and thinking that Santa was just around the corner. Then they'd be confronted by a horror like him.

Elvira was a spider woman.

They kept to themselves in the little flat downstairs, using one power

point to run a kettle, a microwave and a vintage Marantz stereo system of dubious ownership. They hardly ever ventured upstairs, coming and going by a well beaten track down Elroy's side of the house, sneaking in to leave their rent contribution when nobody was looking. It would have been a perfect set-up if only it weren't for the rest of their merry men. See, Elvira and Damien weren't just your common variety goths, they were part of this intensely weird mediaeval-revival society. The Dead Meds, Taylor and Elroy called them. Come five o'clock Friday dozens of these Meds would pull on chainmail and armour and get together for a weekend of jousting and roistering and generally trying to pretend they'd been born as heavy dudes of the Round Table rather than just a bunch of pathetic losers in Brisbane. Without warning, two dozen of them would descend on our backyard and then you couldn't go out there for fear of losing an arm or an eye as collateral damage during an Agincourt re-enactment. These guys really went for it. They were tricked out in full body armour made by their own blacksmith and they didn't hold anything back. Sailed into each other with broadswords and studded clubs and the noise would keep you awake for days, especially after they all got fucked up on mulled wine and amphetamines (one of their few concessions to the late twentieth century).

It was interesting to watch the first couple of times, but it got real old real fast and when a stray crossbow shaft exploded through the back wall and embedded its metal head two inches into the side of the fridge, Stacey decided enough was enough. She'd been deeply suspicious of the way the mediaevalist women embraced the Dark Ages' primitive gender roles but she'd kept that disapproval to herself, just narrowing her eyes and grinding her teeth as the ditzy Maid Marions ran hither and yon with bowls of fruit for their black knights. When it all came to a head I was sitting in the lounge, half watching *Get Smart* with Jabba but mostly arguing with Taylor about how and

why the coward of the county redeemed himself in the end, and why everyone considered him a coward in the first place.

'Because you know, Taylor, it don't mean he's weak just 'cos he turned the other cheek.'

BOOM!

A shriek. Then Stacey's voice pouring out a stream of oaths.

'What the hell was that?' asked Taylor.

'Exploding buttplug,' murmured Jabba as Stacey's footsteps came hammering up the hallway.

'This is going to end,' she said, storming past us to the front steps where she reefed open the fuse box and shut off the power.

'Oh, hey now,' said Jabba impotently as his wide screen Sony winked off and we plunged into semi-darkness. There was also a discernible drop in mediaeval background noise as the Marantz stopped pounding out mandolin music. Stacey marched back to the kitchen. Taylor and I shrugged and followed to investigate, finding her with both hands wrapped around an arrow which was stuck fast in the side of our dying fridge. It was groaning and hissing and clouds of cold steam were rushing out of the wound as Stacey placed one foot on the side and gave an almighty tug. The arrow head came away with a metallic tearing sound. She examined the missile and glared at us. 'Back me up.' Well, we knew that glare. That was her liver-frying glare and you didn't want your liver on the wrong end of it, so we fell in behind as she stomped off downstairs.

'Gonna be some real dead Meds round here now,' Taylor muttered to me. I just shook my head. There was confusion in the back yard with a lot of Sir Kevins and Lady Tricias milling around the stereo fidgeting with the controls. They all turned as Stacey scoped them out before settling on a couple of suspicious looking archers lurking down the back near a slowly rotating pig-on-a-spit. Off she sailed again, clutching the evidence in a tight little fist, Taylor and I trailing behind

feeling very exposed. We strode up to a dumpy, dark haired Lebanese looking guy in a bright yellow tunic, holding a crossbow.

'This yours, dickhead?' demanded Stacey, waving the damaged shaft in his face. I saw Elvira detach herself from a group of women in long dresses and gloves and move towards us.

'Sorry,' said the fridge killer, almost grinning, his eyes shifting about looking for any sign of support.

Stacey nudged into the red. She had lost any semblance of cool, which was kind of unheard of, not to mention uncool. She whipped him in the stomach with the shaft, which must have hurt because his eyes stopped shifting and started bulging and he gasped in pain.

'Yeah well, sorry doesn't cut it, you fucking tool! Sorry doesn't bring our fridge back to life or patch up that hole in the back of the house!' She hit him again and again, started whipping into him like a mad jockey. 'You think you're sorry? Well I'm fucking sorry that sorry isn't good enough!' And with that she wrenched the crossbow off him, fitted in the arrow, turned a slow, deliberate circle to take everybody in, then aimed and loosed the bolt into the engine driving the pig rotisserie a few feet away. Everybody flinched as it hit home with a loud bang and a shower of sparks, which brought the machinery to a screeching stop.

'Jeez,' mumbled somebody. 'That's a bit excessive.'

Elvira tried to speak but Stacey just rode in over her.

'Your friends have got fifteen minutes to clear off and you've got one week. Don't bother asking for your bond back because we'll be using it for repairs.'

When the sun next rose over York Street Elvira and Damien were gone, fled, with their microwave and electric jug, their Marantz and their coffins full of soil from the Olde Country. Which is all a kind of off-topic, round-about way of explaining how we came to be advertising for a 'gay-friendly' flatmate.

MONDAY

No, explained, Stacey, it didn't mean they had to be gay, they just had to be cool about it with Phil hanging around.

Big mistake.

We tried our luck in the *Courier Mail* and straight away every crank in south-east Queensland was on to us, most of them middle-aged truck drivers and labourers. They'd say, 'Oh, you don't mind if the first thing I do when I get home from work is take me clothes off, do you? It's just that I like to walk around in the nuddy.' And they'd all assume that because Phil was Gay Phil he'd obviously want them to bugger him at every available opportunity.

'Sounds pretty fuckin' friendly to me,' said Elroy, but Stace was having none of it. She pointed out that we wouldn't let white supremacists in on account of Missy, which was kind of tangential because we wouldn't have let one of them fucking pointy heads in anyway. But she started up with the old jaw gnashing business and everyone quickly agreed that no, there would be no new freaks or homophobes allowed. Taylor and Elroy didn't count since they were more clueless boofheads than genuine hatemongers. And indeed, after everyone stopped going 'bzzzzz' at Taylor, he and Gay Phil got along famously, Taylor becoming quite the bogus California surf Nazi after a stoned late night run to Surfers where we all got fucked up on 'shrooms and San Miguels and Phil taught Taylor how to catch smoking barrels on the boogie board as the sun came up. Taylor, a fickle sort of chap who was famous for his 'phases' suddenly took to wearing Mambo T-shirts and Byrning Spears boardies and hovering over Brainthrust Leonard's shoulder when he was online, pestering him about downloading giga-bytes of file threads from *alt.surfing*.

Anyway this was all going down in October, with exams looming at uni to be followed by a long, punishing sub-tropical summer when most renters fled home to their oldies' in-ground pools and well stocked fridges. There weren't a lot takers around for our vacant bat cave. We interviewed one hydroponics enthusiast, who said he'd need to draw about thirty thousand watts off the grid for a 'project' but assured us it'd 'pay for itself in the end.' And we had this other guy, turns up, knocks on the front door, Brainthrust Leonard and Stacey emerge from their rooms to answer it at the same time, see this ridiculous pretender standing there in his Ray Bans, no shirt and five inches of white Calvin Klein boxer shorts hiked up over the rim of his baggy new jeans. Stacey doesn't even speak to this guy, just turns to Brainthrust and says, 'Leonard, I've seen you dressed like that, but I think this man is doing it on purpose.' And slams the door in his face.

After that blowout, we tried Triple Zed, the street mags, and finally this gay paper called *Brother Sister* (although Stacey popped that one in without telling anybody). It was this last, unauthorised advert which brought us undone by delivering Jordan into our midst. Within a month or so of his sneaking in under the radar our nice anarchic comfort zone had become an angry swirling maelstrom of death metal junkies and Drug War narcs, stolen goods, hired goons, vengeful dykes, evil yuppies, dopey greens, heartless dole fascists and . . .

Well, my guess is, you'll be wanting all the details.

A black, dusty EH Holden swerved precipitously into York Street, clipping a wheelie bin which tipped over with a hollow plastic thump. 'Whoops,' said Fingers, rubbing a hand over his puffy, colourless face. Neither of us had shaved in a week and the gesture made a thin, raspy sound.

It was noon. Monday. Fingers grunted and eased the heavy, lumbering sedan across the centre line to the other side of the street where he parked, facing the wrong way outside my place.

'Game over,' he said, exhausted, tugging at a filthy, grease-covered black bow tie. I stretched around to wake the Decoy who'd been sleeping under a constantly shifting pile of McDonald's refuse the last two hundred miles. I grabbed a handful of lank, greying pony tail and yanked, 'We're home. Let's go.' He emerged like the trash creature in Star Wars except a lot slower and unsure of himself. I mean that literally too – he was dressed as a giant cockroach.

'Surfers?' he croaked.

'Too dangerous. They know where you live. You can crash here for a while.' I turned to Fingers, stuck out my hand and we shook. 'Fingers, my man, an excellent adventure.' He yawned and shrugged and I climbed out of the car, hot cramping waves of fatigue travelling up and down my back. The Decoy staggered on to the footpath carrying my dinner jacket. I collected it, slung it over one shoulder, nodded to Fingers as he pulled away and we trudged up my cracked concrete path. Our door was open which wasn't unusual. As we reached the end of the hallway, I pointed the Decoy through to the bathroom. I turned off to the kitchen for a cup of tea but pulled up when I found everyone gathered there.

'Hey,' I waved, drawing a desultory round of nods and heys and howdies as the banging on the front door got louder and louder, then stopped abruptly.

'Have a good time Double-Oh-Seven?' asked Stacey in that tone of voice which means 'better not have'.

'Well, you know,' I shrugged. 'Battled evil, cheated death, that sort of thing.'

It didn't raise a smile. They were a sad looking crew, most of them sitting in a rough circle, eyes down, heads hanging low or chins on

the table top. Stacey and Thunderbird Ron were the only two standing. The T-bird meditatively pushed himself off the wall with one arm,
slowly, again and again. Stace stood at the head of the table. A stack
of bills, the rent book, a small mysterious plastic bag and a rather
feeble collection of crumpled banknotes and coins sat in a pile in front
of her. A dark, worrying line of thunder clouds was building in back
of her eyes. Missy was propped up on a bench top, painting her
toenails. She was wearing a short orange skirt and a tight white top
with an inscription stretched over her bodacious taa-taas: THIS INSERT
HAS A PROTECTIVE COATING.

'So, what've we got here?' I said.

'While you were away Jordan ripped us off for at least five weeks'
rent,' said Stacey. 'Plus the electricity and gas money and all the phone
jar change.'

The house backed her up with a few nods and mumbled 'fuckin'
right's'.

'And, he had cops here too,' said Elroy.

'What, looking for him?'

'No,' said Stacey. 'Working with him.'

'Oh,' I went. 'That's interesting.'

I squeezed my eyes shut a few times, the road trip catching up with
me.

I didn't understand what was going on and I didn't know whether that
was because I was too tired or because the events themselves were
not amenable to understanding. A weird flatmate had done a runner.
Okay, sorted. And yes, the phone jar was a heavy hit but Jordan's share
of the rent and bills, even five weeks worth, wasn't much, 'We could
rip it out of the next guy's bond,' I suggested.

'Look,' said Stacey. 'This house ain't the fucking Tardis. We can't
keep shovelling in new flatmates every time we have a financial crisis.
Anyway, you're missing the point.'

14 **MONDAY**

And the point, the very sharp, scary tetanus injection of a point was not just that Jordan had skipped owing his rent. He had made off with the rent for the whole house for more than a month. It had been sitting in the biscuit tin along with the other bill money, waiting to be paid. 'He fraudulated us,' said Elroy.

'Oh,' I said, finally getting it, sinking into a chair and joining the collective gloom.

Stacey grabbed a pitiful handful of cash. 'This is what we came up with to cover the shortfall,' she said, rummaging through and picking out the plastic bag. 'And what the hell is this anyway?' she asked.

'Uhm . . . I was wondering if I could pay my share in marijuana,' Elroy suggested sheepishly.

Stacey fixed him with a withering stare, 'I don't think so, milk boy.' She tossed the bag back at him. It bounced off his forehead and landed in front of me.

I shrugged, opened it up and started rolling a joint.

'Couldn't we all go out and get extra work?' suggested Missy, who had finished buffing her tootsies. There were some wry grins at that and, thankfully, a lightening of the atmosphere.

'Oh, Missy,' sighed Stace, pinching our house babe's dimpled chin. 'You should know by now that's not how things work around here.'

'Maybe we could run a raffle or something,' said Leonard.

'Or grow some dope?' added Elroy. 'We could sell those magic mushies in the back yard.'

'Too late for that,' said Stacey, nodding at Taylor, who had been strangely silent, just sitting, staring intently at the bright red tartan contact paper which covered our fridge door.

I lit off the joint, drew it in deep and passed it around before rolling another. Stacey took a drag, which meant we probably weren't going to go to core meltdown.

'God,' she sighed. 'I'm gonna have to raid my oldies' fridge again.'

I tamped down the second spliff, suggested maybe we could clean up under the house. We could squeeze a whole bunch of rich, dopey foreign students in there. Strictly temporary, 'til we got back on our feet. If we found some Japanese we could even charge them the whole hundred and fifty and then some. This was a big house after all. But the guys just weren't sparking today.

'Where's Jabba?' I asked, noticing he wasn't there and remembering I'd missed him on the way past the lounge too.

'Gone out,' said Leonard.

I shook my head in surprise, 'But Jabba never goes out . . . Jabba hardly ever stands up.'

'Jordan stole his TV,' explained Stacey.

'Fucker's a dead man,' said Elroy emphatically.

The Decoy appeared at the kitchen door, freshly scrubbed and looking perkier than anyone there, but still wearing his giant cockroach costume. 'Sorry, didn't have a change of clothes,' he said. Most of the house didn't jump too much as they adjusted to the sight. Except for a badly hallucinating Taylor. He got one look at the giant roach leaning up against the kitchen door, screamed and fell off his chair trying to get away. Gay Phil and Elroy chilled him out, calmed him down. I asked the Decoy if we had any takings from the Casino left and he said about fifty bucks. I nodded to the pile on the table. 'Toss it in, and get some clothes out of my room. Decoy's gonna be hanging here for a few days if everyone's cool,' I said. 'He's on the run.'

'Cool,' said Elroy, impressed.

Leonard sucked the life out of a burning roach and made a slow, obscene, lip-smacking sound, 'Man, I could really go for a run right now . . . to the Donut King!' Lots of stoned people nodded in fuzzy agreement. I swooped down on the money. 'Right then, let's go.' Everyone hesitated, glancing at Stacey. She still wasn't happy, but the Jordan debacle was down to her. She'd leveraged him into the

MONDAY

house in a rare lapse of judgement and now we were all suffering. 'What the hell,' she said at last. 'This isn't going to pay for dick anyway. Let's go say hello to Mr Fuckin' Donut.' Everyone cheered and suddenly the oppressive blowout in our domestic accounts receded a bit. With a head full of smoke and a sugar binge in the offing we were the invincible Team York Street again. She was smart that way Stacey.

Funny then, that she didn't spot Jordan coming a mile off. I mean, I hated that guy soon as I met him. I tell you. He was one edgy little rodent-boy. A bisexual Singaporean-Chinese, with an alleged ex-wife and a kid, who was conducting a transcontinental phonesex affair with an Adelaide sugar daddy. He had long, feline claws for finger-nails, which I've never really trusted in a bloke, and he rang on the last day of the semi-secret *Brother Sister* advert, with a garbled cover story about being an accountant and having to move right away because he'd woken up that morning and found his female flatmate climbing into bed with him and he was gay and she was naked and it was horrible and did we mind if he couldn't get the bond to us right away because he didn't think she'd cough it up when he split on her and on and on and on it went, down through this frenzied spin cycle of bullshit and PR. He was a fast talker, really emphatic, really keen for the place. Was it a nice place? He had to find somewhere right away. It's like a nervous breakdown scenario, 'I've got to move today, it has to be today. This Very Day. My God she was NAKED!'

Stacey had answered the phone on her way out to a lecture so she didn't have time to talk. She handed him on to Gay Phil who wasn't really integrated into the house command structure and so didn't feel he had the authority to say yes or no. He asked Jabba, who didn't want to talk to anyone while *The Tick* was on; Missy, who was trying to get rid of some ball-scratching oik she'd met on the dance floor;

and finally the T-Bird, who was frightened of Gay Phil because he was a big confident gay fella with a lot of style and panache while the T-Bird was just sort of stiff and wooden and frightened of girls. The T-Bird could not even look Gay Phil in the eye without blushing. So he just mumbled, 'Yeah okay whatever,' and before we knew it Jordan walked among us.

He arrived at four in the afternoon with a hard, overstuffed loveseat in this cheap, thoroughly vile, florid material; this hideous, piebald, white shag carpet which looked like someone had skinned a sick polar bear; and an extended family of actual bears, you know, teddy bears, from this big plush fucker the size of a grizzly down to dozens of little decorative Valentine's Day Winnie the Pooh bears with miniature heart-shaped honey pots clasped between their paws. Hateful, sick-making stuff the lot of it. But most disturbing of all? He built a shrine in his room around pictures of some baby, with all the other people torn out of the photographs. Brainthrust Leonard and I snuck in there on recon patrol a few days after Jordan moved in. We shook our heads and whistled in awe. 'If you go down to the woods today ' sang Leonard under his breath.

The first indication that Jordan was seriously unbalanced came when he started in on his renovations. Two days after settling in downstairs he decided the collapsing black hole atmospherics of the previous tenants were not for him. Six tins of bright white super-gloss paint appeared from the ether and he went at it twenty-four hours a day, for three days solid. He was the merciless, amphetamine-powered Terminator of house painting. He would not stop. You'd come home from work or uni and he'd be painting. You'd go to bed and he'd be painting. You'd wake up and he'd be painting. He ate speed, drank Evian, played bad music and painted and repainted and repainted again.

Missy broke out in hives, from the fumes down her part of the house.

Taylor fell into a stereo war, his *Don Dudley's Truckin' Hits* versus Jordan's entire Celine Dion discography, pounding through the floorboards until Stacey pulled the plug on them both. She was even-handed about it but you could tell she had her doubts about Jordan by then. Weirdos had begun to visit and they were much uglier, more disturbing weirdos than anything the Dead Meds had thrown at us. One crying girl appeared with a washing machine, tipped it off the back of a ute and said she hoped Jordan was satisfied. Jabba made a rare trip from the couch to the back steps to find two seedy, strung-out smack dealer types deep in conversation with a chunky red-headed bloke in a loud sports jacket. They just stopped talking and stared at him.

Another time, Missy, home alone, answers a knock at the door and finds the lead singer of this infamous and yet not very good death metal band the Dream Fuckers swaying there, clutching a plastic bag full of these pills and asking to use the bathroom. She goes 'Uhm ' but he's not really asking, more levering and gradually pushing his way past her, then searching from room to room till he finds what he wants.

'He goes in there and stays for a fucking long time,' she told me furtively that night. 'I'm like, what the fuck is going on? When he comes out he's got blood all over his face. I go in there and there are little capsules all squeezed out, blood everywhere, tissues with blood everywhere.'

She'd lost it, screamed at him to get the fuck out of there, gloved up and disinfected the bathroom. 'I don't like him,' she said, meaning Jordan, not the Dream Fucker. 'He never looks you in the eye. His eyes are always slipping all over the room. He never finishes a sentence. He always leaves things hanging.' If Missy didn't like a guy, chances were there really was something wrong. She was a doofus magnet. Her last boyfriend had picked her up outside some rank suburban beer barn. She was standing around with half a dozen girlfriends when he pulled up in a stolen, grey Datsun – grey because it had been stripped back and undercoated but never properly finished. The window wound down and a spotty face, framed by short spiky black hair, emerged. 'Hello, girls. How about a shag?' They broke up after he lost his licence, busted for hooning along at Warp Factor 8. He told the cops he'd just bought a hot pork sandwich and had to get home to eat it before it got cold.

The day of the Dream Fucker we were drinking beers and talking at the foot of the back stairs, just a few metres from Jordan's room. It was early evening, his third week in the house, and the summer sound of crickets was loud enough to cover a quiet conversation but we were almost whispering: Gay Phil, Taylor, myself and Missy, who'd had three showers after cleaning the bathroom, and would back up for another two before going to bed. Nobody had called a formal scrum-down on Jordan's case, but one was evolving as the twilight leaked out of the day. Small irritations had blistered and burst into running sores. Resentments had led to whispers and whispers now fed more resentment, which threatened to metastasise into a full-blown share-house Bosnia.

'Don't feel you have to let him stay on my account,' said Phil. 'I think he's a creep. Keeps hanging around our room rubbing his nipples and telling me how people are always telling him how youthful he looks.'

'You know he's been married?' I asked. 'Had a kid with this girl in Melbourne. He's got this weird fucking altar devoted to it in there, candles and shit.'

'He told me he'd run an escort company in Melbourne,' said Gay Phil. 'One of the big licensed brothels. Said he'd been filthy rich but he'd blown a hundred thousand in a few weeks.'

We nodded like a bunch of ancient beer-drinking sages presented with a particularly interesting bowl of burned pig innards. None of us

doubted he could kiss off a hundred big ones without raising a sweat. At least as long as it was someone else's money.

'I think he's stealing my clothes,' said Missy after a while. 'My black vinyl pants are missing. He's always been asking to borrow them.'

Taylor, disgusted, tossed his empty stubbie way down the back of the yard where it landed with a muffled tink. 'I say we get the boys together, give this fella a good whuppin'. Nobody would think less of us for it.' We gazed over the yard to the spot where Taylor had landed his shot. Without the mediaevalists to keep it down the garden was reverting to its natural old growth forest state. Before Elvira and Damien it had been left for so long that elephant grass climbed up over the Hills Hoist, big yellow-green stalks of the stuff, fatter at the base than Missy's wrists and so thick you couldn't penetrate it without a machete. We used to roll empty kegs down there after parties and they'd never be seen again. Part of the Meds' appeal was that they volunteered to hack through the savannah. Said it'd give them a chance to practise their broadsword technique, and damn if they didn't all turn up one Saturday, blow 'charge' on their trumpets and start swinging. A fair job they did too, with only an occasional clang and inarticulate curse to let us know they'd discovered one of our old party kegs.

'Guess I'd better cut that grass,' mused Gay Phil. 'Stacey's been on about it. That and those damn vegetables.' And with that we rolled our eyes and fell to cursing the hippie fools at the co-op and trying to decide who to blame for joining it in the first place. And after we'd had another beer and Missy had gone off for another shower and Gay Phil had told us all his surfing war stories, Jordan was momentarily forgotten.

Late night tableau, Monday. Jabba tossing and turning on the couch in the lounge room. He won't tell anyone where he's been, but Taylor insists he spotted him down at the Megamall, watching the sales display TV sets. A few feet away from Jabba's couch, Leonard padding around in the gloom, tapping the walls. Light from Thunderbird Ron's desk lamp leaking out under his bedroom door, behind which he is cramming for a sports science exam. Missy and Phil cruising the Valley together, probably checking out a drag show at the Wickham. Taylor driving the cab and trying to write an assignment for his Ag Science course, which means he can probably be found at the Windmill Café eating a double-decker veal-and-cheese toasted, washed down with beer. Elsewhere in the house, Elroy stacking some zeds before his milk run. Downstairs in Jordan's old room, the Decoy, our fugitive house guest, recovering from his ordeal. And in the kitchen Stacey and I drinking powdered coffee and making ourselves sick on donut refuse, with me still wearing my ruined dinner jacket.

'Aren't you hot in that thing?' she asked.

I smoothed out my lapels and shook my head. 'Some of us prefer to sacrifice comfort for style, babe.'

'Well, you gonna at least clean it before cocktails?'

I picked up the last iced donut and broke it in two. 'Tell the truth,'

I said. 'I didn't think there'd be any cocktails this week. Figured Jordan would have made off with the bar.'

Stacey shook her head, 'No, he took some weird shit besides the teev. Old rags, tins of polish, that broken egg whip. You know that weird speed mentality. He took the lids to our pots but not the pots. And he didn't touch the bar.'

I dunked my donut and crammed the mushy remains into my mouth. I'd given up trying to impress Stace a long time ago. When I had the sickly sweet mess safely down I asked her what we were going to do about the money.

'Well, we might get it back off him,' she said. 'I could beat it out of him myself. Ratboy's gotta learn. You fuck with us and our vengeance will be swift . . .'

'*And terrible to behold*,' we both finished loudly. Kind of a house motto.

We were quiet for a while as I rubbed my eyes and tried to read the time on our Felix the Cat clock (*Its eyes go tick tock!*) before Stacey gave me an odd, quizzical look.

'John, if you weren't hanging around here, playing video games, drinking Elroy's home brew . . .'

'Compiling life experiences, you mean.'

'Whatever. If you weren't, what would you be doing?'

'Dunno,' I shrugged as a cockroach flitted across Felix's face. 'Never saw much point in thinking about it.'

'But if you had to,' she said, leaning forward and picking at the donut box.

'My dream pad?' I smiled.

'Whatever. Your perfect batch pad.'

I mulled it over for a few seconds. 'Maybe a high rise apartment, in the city, with a sunken lounge pit, and a hot tub too . . . to entertain an endless parade of giddy blonde soap actresses.'

'Who'd find the lure of your lava lamps and deep shag pile carpets completely irresistible?' smiled Stace.

'Of course. I'd wine and dine them out on the terrazzo. Dizzy them with my masterful command of a dozen regional cooking styles. Ply them with obscure little numbers from my collection of vintage champagnes. All the time wondering how long it'd take to get them out of that low cut Versace dress and into my evil clutches.'

'Be a lot quicker if you didn't dunk your donuts.'

I realised then she'd walked me into that one. 'Jeez, you're a snob,' I replied weakly.

'Night, John-boy,' she beamed, pushing back from the table.

I nodded as Stacey left. I stayed at the table for another ten minutes or so, turning over the scraps of the day. Wondering what sort of hard rain was about to fall. It had been less than a week since Gay Phil had sat right here, scarfing down a bowl of Fruit Loops and looking up to find a very fidgety, nervous, distracted Jordan standing in front of him rubbing his nips and asking what Phil thought of cops. Phil just shrugged, noncommittal.

'The thing is,' muttered Jordan, 'shoulda said this earlier, shoulda mentioned it and . . . it's just . . . well . . . I'm working for them . . . for the cops . . . and they want to run a bit of an operation . . . out of here . . . uhm . . . tonight . . . but don't tell . . . you know, Stacey.'

BEACH BLANKET MASSACRE: THE GIANT ROACHES ATTACK!

Tuesday morning. I surfaced slowly. I dreamed I was a haunted, long-lost German submarine, a *Geistenboot* rising through cold layers of poisoned green water, blowing noxious gases, my skeleton crew of tongueless dead men listening to the pressure hull clang as we climbed through the depths and the rusting metal expanded. The clanging became banging, which resolved itself into two distinct noises, hammering from the lounge just outside my bedroom door and someone enthusiastically working the knocker at the front door. I tried to hide my head under the pillows but I was awake. I had broken surface and there was no sinking back to the cool, dark ocean floor.

True to my word I had slept in my crumpled shirt with the big ruffles. At least I'd managed to crawl out of my pants before I face-planted on my foam slab, intending to sleep for two days. Now, groggy and dizzy, I fished a pair of grey running shorts from amongst the hairballs and dust dunes under the bed. Fell over once getting into them. Recovered my balance and tottered out to seize the day. The hammering and knocking continued. Leonard was in the living room. He had pushed Jabba's couch back against the bar we had rescued from the tip twelve months back. Jacked into a Walkman and mysteriously engrossed in measuring, drilling and hammering the wall outside his own room, he seemed not to notice the noise at the front of the house.

I could see two figures through the dirty glass panels on the front door. Nobody else seemed to be around and as I shuffled past the clock in Stacey's room I saw why. It was already noon. The knocking stopped as I approached. Mormons, I figured. Well, I'd show them. I flung open the door, ready for combat.

'Good morning. My name is MacMillan,' the taller of the two said. 'And we're from the Department of Social Security.'

Now, I could probably deal very quickly with the issue of how the Decoy's hideous problems became entangled with ours. How his tormentors became our tormentors and how, in the end, he saved the world. But you and I have a bond, punters, worth at least £6.99 (rec. retail) and I'm not going to short change you. So . . .

You might remember my friend the Decoy, a lightning rod for bad vibes and harassment. It was mostly from guys with badges and guns and an attitude surplus, but pretty much anyone who felt like it was free to kick in. You'd be walking down the street with the Decoy when he'd suddenly jack-knife over and fall to the ground because some lunatic had slammed a fist into him as they passed. This madman would be all over him, dancing a hobnailed cha-cha on his ribs and screeching like some space alien with Tourette's about how the Decoy might have thought he could get away with it but this guy knew all about him. And his plans. Oh yes, he knew! He fucking knew! And the loon would continue until he got tired or distracted and wandered off without ever having laid a finger on you.

You shouldn't get the idea that the Decoy would go around look-ing for trouble, though. It's more that trouble came looking for him with sniffer dogs and a death warrant. The Decoy, you see, is this fully preserved Flintstones-era hippy. Got himself a greying pony tail and this little pot-shaped belly and, unlike most of the boomer scum he grew up with, the Decoy never actually got with The Program. Never

wised up and sold out. Never came on board for the big win, as they say. Worse still he speaks in this soft Canadian accent and presents with a sort of wounded Bambi demeanour which affects cops and psycho-killers in pretty much the same way. Like a bucket of fresh chum thrown into a tank full of hungry Mako sharks.

The Decoy and I had first crossed paths during one of my slacker periods, when I was just spooking round the campus video game room and kicking back on the veranda at the Student Club for nine, maybe ten hours a day. This was the dreamtime when the System really did love you and want to be your friend. A time before job search diaries, intensive individual case management and – I shudder to even write the words – work for the dole. It got to the point, however, around about the seventh or eighth time I registered as unemployed, that the goons began to see things a little differently and to express this difference of opinion in very muscular terms.

That's how I came to team up with the Decoy. We'd briefly shared a place over in Auchenflower and haphazardly kept in touch afterwards. When he heard about my troubles with the bureaucracy he rang up and offered me a job with this news clipping agency he worked for. Man, that was the cruisiest part-time job I ever had. Reading the fucking papers for money. Who'd have thought I could get paid for that? Working for the Decoy I had to browse all the metro dailies and put little Xs next to the stories which were interesting enough to warrant filing. They had a list of topics we were supposed to follow, mostly politics and war and stuff like that, but I liked to throw them a curve ball every now and then, mark up something like the obituary of this totally bogus Irish soothsayer who invented the practice of Mammarism, also known as 'chest clairvoyance'. He figured to read a female client's future by painting her boobs and pressing them against a sheet of paper to get an imprint which he could then study.

My personal, unclassifiable fave, though, was this little piece about

a factory which cranked out generic brand prefab frozen pizzas until the local council realised it had clogged the sewage system with about 18,000 tonnes of pizza sludge. They couldn't even bury the stuff in case it 'moved' in the ground and, say, swallowed up a whole housing development or something.

I'd copy the best ones, like these, and Blu-tac them to the fridge at home. Although I had to be careful about that. Our soda siphon went missing after I pasted up a clip from the *Japan Times* about this bizarro sexual practice called 'pumping' which was out of control in Thailand. These crazy Thais would stick the nozzle of a bicycle pump into their arse, then give themselves a blast of air and a cheap thrill. If you wanted a turbo-charged hit, I guess a soda bottle was perfect, although it'd want to be empty, because otherwise you'd get a carbonated fizzy enema. Elroy might have been up for a piece of that action, but he was more likely to get drunk and try it on as a party trick in front of a room of horrified visitors. So I put the disappearance down as yet another black mark against Jordan, our downstairs nemesis. Taking a clandestine shot in the bot with somebody else's soda fountain was just about his speed.

Anyway that clipping job really was the sweetest set-up. It really let me explore the whole man of leisure scenario. There was a drawback in that I had to get there early in the morning, but they always put on gallons of thick, tar-like, scalding hot coffee and a jumbo feast of sticky buns and sugar hits. I'd come roaring out of that place about lunch time, completely wired on Colombian Roast and jelly donuts, a free man looking for trouble. Mostly I'd have a swim then head to the Student Club for a couple of beers and a burger with the works, some hot greasy meat and a soothing ale to smooth the jagged edges of my massive pre-dawn stimulant binge. All of this and a hippy for a boss. It was too cool. The Decoy was an anarchist, you see, did not believe in hierarchical structures at all, and would take the most

egregious slackness and back-chat from his self-centred, ungrateful work Gen-X force.

Sadly for us drones, however, the Decoy kept poor company. He lived in a decaying, eighteen-room house with an outlaw cabal of public broadcasters, drug addicts, losers, drunks and political activists. Make a long story short, he had to flee after the Special Branch came through the windows before sun-up one morning and threatened to execute every fucking one of them who didn't get a haircut and start driving trucks for their country. So the Decoy takes the hint – sort of – loads up his Kombi and makes a midnight run for the coast. Plans to hang with some ageing hipsters he knows down there. Got themselves this commune going in the Gold Coast hinterland. A very low-profile affair up in the rain forest. Great views of the sea and all approach roads.

The Decoy got word to me back at the clipping room that he'd legged it out of Dodge and asked if I could bring down some stuff he'd left at the office; his string bag, spare sandals, and half a box of Jamaican cigars. (His one vice. He liked to toke up with a black coffee after his lunch.) On one hand, I'm thinking: Bummer, now they're gonna put some fascist dickwad in charge of this place. On the other hand I'm thinking: Excellent! A new pad to crash for Schoolies Week or a casino run.

The house he'd fled to was this old place in the rain forest, set way up on stilts, with a tree growing up through the middle of it. What had happened was that some old guy had originally slung this canvas arrangement about two or three feet off the ground under the house. It was much more complicated than a hammock, more like a hanging tent with separate rooms. He'd also planted a palm tree at some stage so he could stick his head out and pluck dates. But of course the tree wouldn't grow under the house. So the hippies had cut this big square out of the lounge room floor, then another one out of the ceiling, and

then the roof. This whole house had been opened all the way through so this joker could grow his sticky dates. When you walked into the lounge room there was a four-foot wide path around this big hole. You'd sit around the edge of the wall and watch the top of this little tree trying to make it to freedom. First time I went round, to take the Decoy his stuff from the office, I saw this big canvas thing hanging from the underside of the floor. I'm standing there scratching my head, thinking, *What madness is this?*, when this old guy swings out on a rope, completely starkers. Nuts hanging free and everything.

'Hi there!' he goes. 'Beautiful day.'

You got used to it, though. You'd often go around for a visit and find the place full of naked hippies. You'd have to be cool about it too. Instead of gawking and running off at the mouth you'd have to sit there, pretending to chill while the breasts of some totally nude forest nymph smacked you in the head as she bent over to top up your peppermint tea or Eccocino. I guess this place was the Decoy's Dream House. The only downside was he had to share it with Naked Tree Guy and Roger the Hippy. Tree Guy was okay, just a little strange, but Roger was a pain, one of those sanctimonious 1960s idiots who grew old without growing up, who just couldn't let go of the idea that their decade was the coolest, most interesting, noteworthy and relevant decade in the history of the world. A proposition I had some trouble with since it produced legions of dudes like Roger who did not believe in washing — he insisted that vigorous rubbing of the body's natural oils would keep the skin clean and lustrous. He was a confirmed rebirther, performed a salute to the sun every morning and ate only raw cabbage. Nobody could eat meat at their place because 'it gave you a smell' according to Roger. He said he could smell meat eaters inside the house. Even with all this Woodstock-fired bullshit I still thought of him as more your Charles Manson-style hippy, since both he and his weird girlfriend slept with knives

under their pillows and regularly attacked each other in the night.

The Decoy was hep to that. Long as they kept it to themselves he'd be a cool banana. Trouble with Roger was, he couldn't keep things to himself. When I ran into the Decoy with his eyebrows and half his ponytail burned off I obviously had to ask what the story was. He sighed and said that Roger had almost burned everyone to death the previous night. He'd started seeing this woman and they were rooting like rabbits. 'And I mean that, all the time,' the Decoy assured me. 'I mean they get home and they *sprint* into their room.' Anyway, he'd awoken about three in the morning. All this chaos and panic at the end of the hall, like 'Shit, shit, shit,' and a sort of *whoomping* sound. 'What the hell's that?' he thought groggily, got up, went out in the hallway, and there was Roger with this huge burning doona he was slamming into the floor. They had been having tantric sex by candle light, because that's the authentic way to do it, and afterwards they'd fallen asleep and let the candle burn down. It was sitting on top of Roger's stereo. Burned all the way down, hit the plastic cover, melted into the electronics, exploded and set the doona on fire. When the Decoy emerged to investigate, Roger, who was frantically windmilling the doona into the floor, reacted by throwing the burning bedspread at him and charging back into the bedroom to save his Bob Dylan collection. When the Decoy had clawed his way out from under, he was on fire too.

I'm telling you all of this so you can put the Decoy in context. The basic thing you've got to understand is that the Decoy is a very gentle, very non-confrontational sort of guy. A live and let live, to each his own, whale-watching, soy-bean-eating, tuned-into-the-cosmic-concert sort of guy. I said before he had only one vice that I know of. The cigars? In fact he had two. The Decoy's other deadly sin was cards. The man was a demon for blackjack. He loved the game, and that love nearly finished him. But not in any way you're likely to imagine.

*

Jupiters at Surfers Paradise was, far as I can recall, my first legit casino, and I've seen some desperate action at their tables. I'm not one for the cards myself, you understand, but I've known some in my time. The Decoy for one. And the Man, Howard 'Three Fingers' Hunt for two. Fingers is in Thailand now, hiding from a bunch of Lebanese builders who were compounding fifty points on the dollar for short term loans to hapless card-counting losers who couldn't keep track of their sums. One of the last times I saw him he'd been down at Jupiters, doing okay, when he hit his groove and shot two grand up in about half an hour. Man, we shoulda took that money and run. But we didn't, and in not doing so we set out on a journey of nearly three thousand miles, to madness, deliverance and back.

I hadn't planned on a big road trip. It's just that the house was really getting me down. Partly the ever-increasing stockpile of rotten vegetables but mostly Jordan. Apart from him – and Elroy, of course, who was a moron – I was the only one at York Street who didn't have some commitment to assignments or exams as November rolled on. One thing that fucking graduate tax achieved, it got me out of the university system. I probably would have hung around campus till I died but that sucker came down and I was out of there like a bat out of Hell. Thirty grand for an Arts degree? Oh yeah. For sure. I'd pay that. HahahahahaHaHaHAHAHAHAH. *HAHAHAHAHAHA!!!!*

(Crash!)

(Oops.)

Sorry, fell off my chair.

Okay, as I said, I'm not much of a gambler. Haven't got the nerve for it. But Fingers does. He's played most of the tournaments around the country and he wanted to crack the knuckles and get a little practice in before signing on for a monster Pro-Am at Jupiters at the end of the month. He dropped around to York Street just before things turned really evil and asked if I wanted to come hang at the casino

for the day. I figured what the hell. My hours at the clip joint were flexible and I had a bit of spare change so I did what I almost always do when confronted by an ugly house situation – I ran away.

We gave Gay Phil a lift down the coast. He said he was going to work on his Japanese but I think he was really going to work on his barrel rolls. He and Fingers hit it off right away. Phil climbed into the back of the EH, Fingers tossed him a cold Corona and asked, 'So, you always know you were fag, Phil?'

'Ever since my dick got hard,' he replied, sending Fingers off on a half hour recounting of the first time his dick got hard and how complicated life had become from that moment on.

'I wish you could take a pill to chill that sucker out,' he said. 'Just for short stretches, you know. Like when you got to deal with lady cops or magistrates. Don't know about you fellas – well, I guess I do know about you Phil – but nothing makes my dick harder than a powerbabe. Man, I only got to get a glimpse of a shoulder pad and I got hair on my palms. I'm like rolling my eyes back to whites and running round with a rail spike in my pants looking for something, anything, to nail it into.'

Fingers shook his head and stared off up the freeway. 'The whole Hillary Clinton Health Care thing was a very difficult time for me. Three or four months there I just sat in my bedroom ripping the top off it.'

It was a useful trip for Phil and me because we hadn't done the late night bonding over coffee business and I'd been a bit unsure of him moving in. It wasn't with him being gay and all, it was to do with Stacey. She was just about the best friend I had and I didn't like anyone subtracting from the amount of the time or attention I could demand of her. I figured when she took off overseas one day we'd write each other a few letters, maybe spend some money on phone calls. But eventually she'd meet some thin European aesthete with a regular income and decent personal hygiene and I would slowly recede from the centre of her life to the borders and then over the edge into the darkness of lost correspondence and neglected photo albums. Gay Phil, who had already travelled across four continents, who'd met and understood some nutjob called Derrida, who ran with an outlaw Rasta gang in London, who'd had an affair with Jackie O's private secretary's brother, who spoke Italian and French and was learning Japanese, well, he seemed to be a herald specifically dispatched to bring on the day of Stacey's departure.

'Rastafarians, Gay Phil?' queried Fingers, hoisting one sceptical eyebrow skywards.

'Yeah,' he shouted over the roar of the wind and the car's engine. 'My boyfriend back then was working as a recording studio engineer. He worked in a very dark and dubious studio run by these Rastas who produced the heaviest dub music you could imagine. They were always falling out of the studio stoned and going to the 7–11 across the road to explode cans of baked beans in the hot dog microwave.'

Fingers lit a thin cigar and used his rear vision mirror to follow Gay Phil's story. I craned around in the front seat. He sucked back another beer and continued.

'One time I was at the studio when this visiting South African group who sidelined in guerrilla warfare arrived. They'd been searched at Heathrow airport, but within five minutes of arriving in London they were armed with submachine guns. This was a bizarre time for me. I was quickly considered a part of their posse. Or their mascot or something. I never really understood. They just liked Australians. The West Indies were flogging our cricketers back then. Maybe that was it. Anyway, there were five of us, backpackers, dossing in this typical London terrace, all brave sons of ANZAC and good friends of Dorothy.

'The Rastas were always coming around for bongs and beers. They liked the way there were lots of disappointed, slightly desperate white women hanging around. Some of us went to the local one night and

half a dozen skins started hassling us. Pretty badly too. But my boyfriend got on the bat phone, got word to the studio, and about five minutes later these terrifying black guys appeared, armed and dangerous, and promising the skins they would go to any length to protect their posse . . . or their pussy.'

So you see what I mean about Phil?

During a break for burgers and beers, he skewered his last boyfriend, Jeff, on the spike of a great first date story.

'I'd just extracted myself from a very confused situation with a married man,' he told us. 'He was way back in the closet so we'd had to sneak around town whenever we wanted to see each other. After him, I thought going out with someone as out and politically gay as Jeff would be a cool change. But I didn't count on his drug habit. We were clubbing on our first actual date. This is down in Sydney and we were staying at his brother's flat in Coogee, minding it while he was overseas. We danced and rub-fucked for hours, drove each other mad with it, then tore off home in his little black V.W. Jeff dropped me at the front of this old Art Deco block, said he was just going to get some more drugs. Said he'd be back in ten minutes. Two hours later I'm still sitting out the front in a pair of black boots, white Calvins and nothing else.'

There was no sign of this prick and Gay Phil said he didn't fancy sitting around like that until sunrise, but he had no keys or money. They were in the V.W. The only way inside was to scale across a drainpipe, across a twelve foot drop, and break in through a window. So there he was, some time after midnight, in this ridiculous outfit tightroping it across the pipe.

'I did get to the window,' he said, 'but then I looked down and froze. I was stuck on the side of that building like a dumb piece of modern art for three fucking hours before Jeffrey came back and let me in.'

'Goddamn!' said Fingers. 'Why'd you hang with him after that?'

'Well,' answered Phil a little wistfully. 'He was interesting. You can forgive people a lot if they're interesting.'

That was something Stacey had said more than once and I sat upright in recognition. I suddenly wanted to bear down on Phil, to extract the secret of making myself interesting so that I too could be forgiven a lot. But instead I just ate my burger and drank my beer and kept everything bottled up and buried deep where it could never do anyone any harm.

Twelve hours later, we're at Jupiters and I'm wasted. Fingers had been buying drinks all night. He flipped me a hundred dollar note and told me to go wild. The moment with Phil had passed away, and with a head full of booze the reverb hardly raised a blip on my radar. I drunkenly threw Finger's grey nurse at the dealer. Three quick hands. The house bust on two of them and I made blackjack on the last. The tiny crowd which had gathered to watch exhaled in excitement. Damn! I figured. I'm walking with the King. I must have been up five or six hundred by then, all in the space of a few minutes. The quiet but annoying voice of reason – kind of a whining little Johnny Howard at the back of my mind – kept nagging at me like a ratbastard to take the money and run, to be comfortable and relaxed with what I already had. But the roaring plastered Visigoth of my greed smacked him down, yelled to a waitress for another hog's head of ale, and told me to keep my arse where it was until I broke the house and had a pit full of casino goons at my feet, squealing like stuck pigs and howling for mercy.

Fingers had quit the table by then, but he couldn't stand hanging around and not playing, so he decided to ghost me, started pushing out bets on my bets. I chipped up and went for the max. I got a split and a double down Bam! Another four hundred unearned dollars. All right! I'm thinking, This is meant to be! This is where we make the big league. Where we become rolled gold Masters of the Universe.

Where the horny casino babes appear at my elbow and ask breathily, *Is zis zee only game you like to play, Mistah Birmingham?* If only I'd heeded little Johnny Ratbastard. Perhaps then everything would have been okay. We could have driven back home. I could have made the Jordan shortfall up from my winnings and been the big man on campus. I could have been interesting and forgiven. I could have been a contender. But I didn't and I wasn't. I just pushed those chips out again.

And then our luck turned rancid. Instantly. We started going down in flames on these excruciatingly big bets, gave them back every cent we'd won in the space of three heart beats. We walked out into the hot close night, both of us completely busted, both cursing the casino and ourselves and saying it's a mug's game, never again, you know. It was four-thirty in the morning. We kissed off the idea of a consolation six-pack down in the dunes. Just jumped into Finger's car and drove off. I'm laughing at him. He's laughing at me. We're like Never Again. We spent the entire drive shitcanning gambling and gamblers. Then, when we made the tollway on the outskirts of Brisbane I discovered ten bucks in a shirt pocket. I couldn't believe it. It was so late. I was half blind. I felt like shit. But Three Fingers' face just lit up. He put that car into a screeching, smoking powerslide, howled through degrees one hunnert and eighty and thundered back towards the coast, into the rising sun, chasing our lost three thousand with this ten dollar note. We marched in, laid it down, two minutes later we're back in the car park having the same conversation. Never Again.

We just could not face another drive to Brisbane and we were shit out of luck on the Strip so I say to Fingers that we should hit on the Decoy for bed and breakfast. He's like, 'Excellent idea, JB.' So half an hour later we're bouncing over a rutted dirt track, past the hand painted sign which points the way out to hippy valley. The Decoy's Kombi wasn't around, but blue smoke curled out of the kitchen chimney so I figured he might be making an early run into town for some leaf and twig bread or maybe some soy milk.

'Don't sweat it, Fingers,' I said, catching a flicker of concern which flashed across his face as he came to terms with the top of the tree growing out the middle of the old house. I headed up the front steps and through the distressed fly screen door. 'Yo! Tree Guy!' I shouted into the unnaturally well-lit house. I moved through to the rear of the place, skirting the parapet in the living room. I heard Fingers mutter something like 'Sweet Jesus' as he stumbled, literally, across the renovations. Naked Tree Guy was out the back with a sleepy-eyed nymph stoking an old wood-fired stove.

'Decoy around?' I asked, entering the room.

'Nope.'

Naked Tree Guy, normally generous with his hail-fellow-well-met routine, just shook his head then and pointed at their battered answering machine. The wood nymph keyed the play function and Decoy's voice — shocky, disjointed and panicked — filled the kitchen.

'What's goin' on,' asked Fingers, who wandered in at the end of the message.

'Fingers,' I said. 'A brother is hurtin'. Quickly, to the Batmobile!'

'But . . . uh,' said Fingers, sort of nailed to the floor and heedless of the small tendril of drool dropping slowly from his lips. Nude wood nymphs before breakfast will do that to a guy.

'Be v-e-r-y careful,' went Brainthrust Leonard. 'Don't do anything to startle them.' Leonard and I were huddled together just outside the kitchen where the two *Gruppenhaussturmführers* from Social Security had settled themselves in with a very worrying pile of files. 'We might have been datamatched,' Leonard muttered.

'Data whatsis?' I squirmed, not at all happy with this. He grabbed my arm and leaned in to whisper.

'Eight, nine times a year all the paying agencies – social security, DEET, V.A., all of them – they core dump their records into one central processor.' He checked over my shoulder to make sure we weren't being monitored. 'They use a Terradata, a massively parallel computer, can run about a thousand billion floating point instructions per second. Terraflops they're called. They cross match the data from all the core dumps,' he muttered softly but with the mounting excitement of a true geek. 'So if Tax know you earned money that Austudy or the dolies never heard about, well that data will match, or rather, it'll mismatch and a red light will go *ping*! and in a secret dungeon somewhere beneath the disappearing lake just outside Canberra a door rumbles open, a faceless sandman shuffles out and he walks the Earth until he finds you and eats your soul . . .'

I stared at him, aghast.

'Okay,' he said. 'The sandman system is still in beta but the rest of the software is really elegant.'

We both risked a peek in the kitchen. They were pointing at our tartan-door fridge. Leonard continued. 'They can scan the whole country in a few hours. It's like having a national I.D. system without letting on that you've actually built one. As an engineering solution it's exceptionally cool . . . 'cept in this case I guess, 'cos the Gestapo out there are probably gonna do terraflops all over us.'

I bit my lip and shook my head and generally stalled for time but there was nothing for it. They had to be fronted. I was thankful for

small mercies. At least most of the cheats and fraudsters were out of the house cheating and frauding things.

'Okay. This is the plan. I'm going to talk to them . . .'

'What you gonna say ?'

'Well, I, uhm . . . I thought I'd start with evasions and memory lapses, a few bald faced lies . . . maybe work my way up to a twister of outlandish bullshit. Whatever happens, you get downstairs. Under no circumstances are you to let the Decoy out of his room. They must never know he's here, understand? I don't want to even think of the consequences of getting him mixed up in this.'

'Okay,' nodded Leonard. 'Can do.'

He started to move away but I pulled at his elbow.

'Thruster. I wouldn't tell the Decoy about those Sandmen if I were you. Let's keep that on a need to know basis . . .'

'Hi there!' said the Decoy, who had appeared at the back door and was making his way towards us. We were shaking our heads furiously as he drew level with the kitchen.

'Oh great,' he said happily. 'Visitors.'

Stray morning mists held soft against the land as we boomed down through the Tweed Valley. Not much traffic at that time of day so Fingers pushed his beloved, black sedan through a fantastic rippling world which climbed steadily up into the ranges of northern N.S.W. We were both tired, wired, unshaven and dirty. We hadn't had time to change from our formal casino rig but they're used to a little weirdness around these parts and the Drive-Thru crew at McDonald's did not so much as blink at the two crazed and vaguely criminal types in black tie ordering up six egg McMuffins, a dozen black and super sugary coffees and half their back room stock of McDonaldland Cookies.

'How's the Decoy fund holding out?' asked Fingers around a mouth-ful of McMuffin.

I flicked through the big, creased envelope we'd picked up from his room in the tree house. Inside were an unemployment benefit claim, a piece of note paper with an address and phone number, about two hundred and seventy bucks in notes and a top-up from the phone change jar. We'd tipped that in as we were leaving. Said it was an emergency and Naked Tree Guy agreed.

'I think we got enough. You ever been to St Kilda?'

'Nah,' said Fingers. 'I once stood next to Jeff Kennett at a Bears' reception though. Got close enough to stab him in the heart with my stale sandwich . . .' He drifted away on the memory of opportunities lost and roads less travelled. '. . . Anyway, I figure we keep the ocean on the left-hand side of the car we got to hit it eventually.'

'Sound thinking,' I said. I loosened my bow tie and cummerbund and settled into my meal on wheels. I'd catch flashes of the morning sun on the Pacific as we ripped through the scenery. I wondered if we'd get there in time. Wondered how the Decoy gets himself into these things. But I already knew the basics of that and although the details only came later I figure you may as well know too.

The Decoy had met this girl, Jesse, on the rebound and after they'd been going out for a week or so she suggested they go to Melbourne for a holiday. Said they could stay with friends of hers who had this big old place on the beach at St Kilda, just across from Luna Park. This huge white Victorian terrace with about a million bay windows she said. They could hang out in Acland Street, get drunk at the Espy, and perhaps drop down on the sand after dark for a little waterfront nookie. Now, the Decoy hadn't been to Melbourne before so he carefully answered yes, wary of the sort of trouble he could get into such a long way from home, but thinking that anything which took him out of Queensland had to be good and thinking, but not saying, that he might even be able to get away for a little blackjack action. Nothing serious, you understand, just a little low rolling diversion for a couple of hours. A chance to smoke a big cigar and lay his accent on just a little bit thicker.

Well, it started on the bus trip down. Jesse was drinking from a small bottle of brandy. She'd insisted they sit down the back of the bus of course, because that's where your born-to-run badass road warrior types prefer to hang out when they have to take a Greyhound instead of a chopped hog. Somebody snitched, or maybe the driver had psychic powers or a really strong nose for cheap hospital spirits, because they pulled over about three in the morning and he powered up the intercom to wake all the passengers with a booming announcement.

'Somebody's drinking.'

Well, forty or fifty of them turned as one and stared at the Decoy. Jesse wouldn't fess up. She just sat there, quite happy to let the driver tell the whole bus what a bad influence the Decoy was and how he should be ashamed of himself and how he'd be walking the rest of the way if it weren't ten below out-side and he, the driver, would probably be charged with negligent homicide for turning him out. And the only thing for the Decoy to do is nod and mumble and 'yessir' at the driver because he's a path of least resistance guy and he knows that if he ventures from that path he'll be spending the night under a bush in a ditch by the side of the road because that's just the way the universe is.

Anyway, they get to Sydney, where there's a two hour delay. They get off the bus and wander around and it only takes a few minutes before the Decoy realises he's left most of his money back on the Gold Coast along with his unemployment form and a covering letter from his local dole fascists allowing him to temporarily sign on down south. He'd given them some frantic bullshit about going to Melbourne to

look for work and they'd shrugged and signed and stamped and thought 'fucking hippy' as they handed the paperwork to him with the blank, dead stare of the deeply indifferent. He told Jesse he needed to get to a phone to deal with this hassle, otherwise he'd run out of money before they even got there.

The coach had pulled into the Darlinghurst depot and they'd walked out into the grittier end of Oxford Street, the end where the sex shops and Yeeros bars have got it all over the fashion boutiques. Jesse, who seemed to have plenty of money, said she'd wait in a coffee shop while he went in search of a phone. The Decoy meandered around, wary of getting lost with no money in a new city, finally spotting an old blue phone in the foyer of this gaudy little cinema. The guy in the booth looked like Jack Kerouac's demented older brother. He was tricked out in a tweed jacket that had every known form of human grease and snot wiped over it. A wet cigarette hung out of his mouth and a matted curl of pepper grey hair obscured one eye. The Decoy smiled at him, said, 'Just here to use the phone,' but he didn't even move. He could have been a wax model with a real cigarette stuck in his mouth for effect.

So the Decoy gets on the phone to the dole fascists, makes his way through their defences. He argues and begs and whines and cajoles and he finally gets on to somebody with the authority to help him out. But as he's babbling on to her about leaving his money and papers back in the Deep North this terrible moaning and groaning starts up, then this shouting, 'Oh, yeah, do it to me. Do it to me. Harder, baby. Harder. Do me like a horse.' He cringes and tries to cover the mouth piece. He ploughs ahead regardless, hoping it will die off. But it doesn't. It keeps going. Louder and louder and more perverse than before. The dole fascist is going, 'I beg you a pardon. I beg you a pardon.' To this day he remembers the odd way she said it. 'I beg you a pardon.'

She hung up when the horse fucker reached a crescendo. Left the

Decoy with a dead phone in his hand and about eight cents to his name. He stared at the phone. Just leaned against the wall with his eyes bulging and a thin greasy sheen of sweat on his face, stared at the scarred and battered body of the phone, stared at the burns and slashes, the deep wounds and gouge marks. After a few minutes of staring and breathing and feeling his sanity drain out through the soles of his feet like ice water, the Decoy pushed himself off the wall and shuffled numbly out into the day. Grandpa Kerouac hadn't moved once.

The Decoy found Jesse, told her what had gone down. She shrugged, said it was a drag and all but at least she had some cash. She suggested they just head on down to Melbourne, crash for a few hours, get over the trip and then charge into the guns of the D.S.S. again. The Decoy thought that was an outstanding suggestion. Jesse bought him a health food bar, they hopped back on the bus and pretty much dozed through the rest of the journey.

They get to Melbourne. They do some walking, catch some trams (which the Decoy really digs), do some more walking and arrive at a seedy but sort of charming seaside strip about an hour later. There's a big mad grinning Luna Park face just across the way. Some place called Greasy Joes just around the corner. Trams everywhere. Seagulls. Food smells. The water and a sunset. Okay, thinks the Decoy, cool.

They stood out front of this big old dump which had been turned into a boarding house about twenty years ago. All the Decoy had been told was that it was a housing co-op and the world he came from, anything with co-op stamped on it had to be good because co-ops were going to Smash The State (or at least bury it under a mountain of stinking vegetable matter). Okay, good, thought the Decoy. A co-op. Sounds fab. Jesse told him they'd be staying on the ground floor with a friend. Great, he said, your friend in the co-op.

They knocked on the door until it became obvious nobody was home. They walked around the back. Nobody home there either. So they broke

in after Jesse assured him it would be okay. Been there, done this, been told it was cool, or something to that effect.

All right, let's cut to the good bit. Loosen your belts. Pop a beer. Comfy now?

G-o-o-o-o-o-d.

It had been a long bus ride, a day and a night. The Decoy was on the rebound. Hadn't had sex for six months or more. There was a mattress on the floor in the co-op. This girl was keen. So he was quickly talked into a shag on the floor of somebody's room in this strange house at the beach in St Kilda. Long as they changed the sheets afterwards it'd be fine, she said. So they are naked on the floor. Naked as the day they were born. They're doing the wild thing. They're getting right into it. There's bumping, grinding, biting and scratching. There's moaning, groaning, grabbing and jabbing. And then there's a scream.

'Jesus fucking Christ!'

And the Decoy knows it's not Jesse. A grenade goes off in his head, searing white light and pain, followed by a wet high-pitched ringing. He goes right up into the air, spins around like Wile E. Coyote, comes down, lands next to her with a thump and sees the intruder, an intensely angry-looking bald woman, in a deep, exaggerated karate stance, one fist clenched and tucked in at her side, the other hand held forward to ward off a retaliatory strike. She was wearing boots, dark purple leggings and a leather jacket.

'Hi. It's only me,' Jesse pipes up.

'And me,' adds the Decoy hopefully. 'We're friends.'

The woman exhales all of the air in her body, a sound like the air pumps on a garbage truck fully decompressing. She draws one foot back, changing her guard from left to right as she withdraws to a safe distance, then barks that he's no friend of hers and if he doesn't get his filthy hairy hippy carcass up off her mattress she'll be wearing his balls for earrings. Gee, thinks the Decoy, no need for rudeness. But he's

reassured as she relaxes out of the defensive posture and the two women, who are friends thank God, embrace and greet each other warmly. The purple legs woman, whose name seems to be Brie, gives Jesse a sarong to wrap herself in while they touch and talk and excitedly catch up on each other's lives. The Decoy wasn't offered a sarong, and after standing around being ignored for a few minutes he quietly covered himself with a small square of seagrass matting before skulking off into the other room where he'd left his back pack. He hurriedly put on some clothes and returned, a little red-faced but being as brave and English about everything as possible. 'So this is your place, eh?' he ventured during a lull in the chatter. But Brie just glared at him, said she didn't know Jesse was going to be bringing somebody with her. They would have to talk it through to see if it was okay. Fantastic, thinks Decoy. What happens now? He goes back to Brisbane with eight cents in his pocket?

Well, it took a while but Jesse did smooth things over. They agreed that yes, the Decoy was a jerk and yes, it was a horrible, impossible imposition, but if he kept his mouth shut and his dick stowed he'd be allowed to stay. He could send them a rent contribution when he fixed up his dole back in Surfers. Okay. Fine. He was keen for a shower and figured nobody could object to him cleaning himself up, so he asked for directions to the bathroom. They were collective facilities, of course, and they were on the second floor. He had to walk around to the front of the house to get access. So he grabbed his gear and made the trek and was starting to unwind under a strong, hot shower when there was a really loud knock at the door, actually more of a thump, and someone yelled, 'Would you get the fuck out of there! Other people have got to go.' He cursed softly under his breath, but it wasn't his place and he didn't want trouble so he got out and dressed quickly and emerged from the bathroom to be greeted with another, 'Jesus fucking Christ!'

A different large woman stood blocking his way, yelling at him, demanding to know what the fuck he thought he was doing. He hastily explained the situation. That he'd been on a bus for two days, and he left his money behind and . . . and . . . But she cut him off with a backhander to the solar plexus. Said she didn't give a fuck. Said to get the fuck out. Said if she caught him in there again she was going to cut his balls off and so on and so forth. He made one last attempt to win her over. After all he wasn't a bad guy. But she screamed. Not a victimised, cartoon lady on a chair being menaced by a mouse scream. But focused, a war shout, a karate scream like in the movies. She screamed and launched a round house kick at his ear, snapping it short, just one inch away. The Decoy hammered down the stairs with her threats and war cry ringing in his ears. He had begun to suspect there was something amiss with this co-op. What was it with these women and his balls? They were nothing like the gentle beach people he'd been expecting. No friendly forest nymphs around these parts it seemed. Just a lot of bellicose karate experts. The Decoy scarpered around to Brie's room again, running out the front door, onto the street and around the back of the house, mortified by the stares of passersby and terrified lest some ravenous seagull swoop down to tear off his vulnerable, freshly scrubbed genitalia. It seemed to be all the rage around here. He came in all breathless and flushed, asked if there was a large, angry woman resident upstairs. Brie turned aggressively, 'Yeah, lots of them. What's the problem? What have you done?' The Decoy thinks, Oh shit, lots of them, so it's not just this dragon. There's a whole house full of these ugly angry women with their bad vibes and short hair and I'll probably have to . . .

. . . Oh! . . .

All became clear. This wasn't any old co-op. His dopey girlfriend had brought him to St Kilda to spend the weekend in a lesbian separatist co-op. A place which had an absolute rule of no men under any

circumstances. And so, in fact, it was explained to him it was probably best if he didn't go to the toilet or the bathroom at all during his very short and uncomfortable stay here. He'd have to urinate out in the back alley for a couple of days. And number twos would have to wait until he found a public toilet. Perhaps at the Esplanade Hotel up the road.

The Decoy had to have a long sit down after that. He sat, swallowed up in his own private world for a good half hour or so, until Jesse suggested they go out and find something to eat. And he didn't have to worry about having no money. She'd lend him some. She was gentle with him, didn't want to dump any more surprises on him. Said he'd really enjoy eating out in Melbourne. It was a world-class city. Not like Brisbane. You could get anything you wanted here. Pasta, vegetarian, Albanian, Chinese, Cajun, African, anything. He slowly regained his composure. It wasn't so bad. He could avoid the lesbians, keep out of their way, avoid the house altogether in waking hours. Jesse could lend him some money. He didn't need much. He was used to being poor. And he was hungry. His tummy was actually growling. Yes. A big hot feed was all he needed. He started to cheer up. He darkened briefly when Jesse mentioned that some of the wymyn might be tagging along, but as she explained, they knew the area and it was their van they'd be riding in. Okay, he mumbled. He would sit down the back and practice becoming invisible, a skill he planned to call on a lot during the next few days.

Half a dozen of them piled into the van a bit later and drove around to Fitzroy Street looking for some new place Brie had read about. Riding up and down the restaurant strip was torture for the Decoy, who'd had nothing more than a couple of Tic Tacs and a health food bar since leaving Brisbane. He could smell what seemed like thousands of spices and exotic bouquets wafting out of dozens of different ethnic eateries. His mouth watered so much he could have gargled with his

own spit but when the van drew up outside some rustic café and the doors slid open to allow everyone out, he found his path blocked by some shaven-headed Suzie who asked him, predictably, where the fuck he thought he was going. He said, without too much hope, 'To fill my tum?' But she shook her head and told him she wouldn't step out if she was him. This was a Wymyn's Restaurant. So the Decoy sat in the car for a couple of hours, a bit too scared to get out and walk around. After all, he might be in the middle of a whole separatist neighbourhood. What would that be like? Streets full of lumpy, excitable wymyn shrieking and charging around after him with samurai swords?

Best to lay low.

They came back after a while, climbed into the van smelling of garlic and red wine, announced they were off to a party. He pretty much knew what sort of party, but hope springs eternal. There's often food at parties. Maybe Jesse would bring some out to the van. Sure enough, they rolled up to an old warehouse with boarded-up windows but lots of noise and light coming from inside. It had some name like The Place painted on a sign out the front. This 'Place' was jumping with people and lots of aggro-sounding music. The Decoy was sure he could smell food. So sure he forgot himself and made to climb out.

He jumped in terror as three angry wymyn screamed their scream of power and blurred the airspace right in front of him with fearsome backfist/crescent kick combinations. He stood quaking in the fractured silence which followed.

'Where the fuck d'you think you're going?' one of them asked.

'Lesbians, you say,' muttered Taylor, stupid with beer.

'Yes. We've had trouble with them before,' nodded Elroy, just naturally stupid.

'They took over our last house. This place was almost perfect. A big, cheap, three bedroom place. We lived with Toni, this great chick. Every night she pulled twelve cones and drank enough beer to kill fifty bastards. But she moved out to become a soapie star.'

'We found her sister on a bus.'

'Yes,' said Taylor. Slowly. Significantly. 'We got talking to this Rachel girl. About five minutes into it, we clicked onto the fact she's Toni's sister. Small world. So we start shooting the shit. Rachel's looking for a place. We give her our address . . . She's Toni's sister, she's gotta be cool. Well, that afternoon she turned up with a ute and moved herself in while I was down the pub. She bulldozed Elroy . . .'

'She was like Xena's big ugly step sister,' said Elroy.

'He came down to the pub and told me she'd moved in,' Taylor continued. 'I shrugged, a woman who doesn't fuck around. Nothing wrong with that. Or so it appeared at first. For two days. She swept, she cleaned, she cooked. Then she comes back with a friend of hers, Janelle, the sumo wrestler. Tells us she's been thrown out of home, needs somewhere to stay for a few days. *Okay*, we say. Just a few days, though. So another ute turns up and in goes Janelle's gear. Remember, Rachel was the newest flatmate, she had the smallest room. There weren't going to be too many cat swinging events held in there.'

'Yeah,' agreed Elroy. 'Couple of days later we're in the pub. We decide she's gotta go. We drink a dozen beers for the courage.'

Taylor leaned forward dramatically, confidentially.

'When we get home, Rachel's door is closed. All this girly laughter inside. We stare at each other. Don't get me wrong . . . neither of us is lesbophobic.'

'Just check out our porno vids.'

'It's just the thought of those two . . . I mean . . . Oh don't go there!'

'It's a freak-out, man.'

'We sit there despondently,' said Taylor. 'Two very sorry diggers. Okay, so they're lovers. The sumo still has to go. Then the door to Rachel's room opens and out she troops.

'"Oh. Hi," she says. "Didn't hear you come in."'

'Out stomps Janelle and grunts in our direction.

'Then a third, even larger, even uglier monster crawls out of the Black Lagoon. "Oh sorry," says Rachel. "This is Gloria, a friend of ours. She wants to know if she can stay for a few days or so. Just got evicted."'

Elroy tapped the kitchen table. 'You see the pattern forming here?'

'Well, it wasn't a question, her moving in,' said Taylor. 'Because they trundled off to the bathroom for a sexy post-growl shower without waiting for a reply.'

'Ye Gods!' shuddered Elroy.

'A week later, they're all still there. All three sharing the one tiny room. All three going to bed at seven thirty at night. Dining at the Y . . . No no, please, bear with me. . . They're giggling and romping away until the wee hours. Meanwhile we're spending fifteen hours a day at the pub. The house began its death spiral. Nothing was being cleaned. The carpets were just a mash of muddy footprints.'

'Things started to get broken,' said Elroy. 'These fat dykes were also clumsy dykes. Things started to go missing . . . Klepto dykes.'

'Shocking art works were hung on the walls.'

'Bad taste dykes.'

'We went insane,' confessed Taylor. 'I stormed home one night. Hammered on the bedroom door. The giggling stopped. Rachel came out with my Fosters beach towel wrapped around her. I spoke before I could think. "Rachel," I said, "The lesos have to go." She closed the door and stepped into the hall, never taking her eyes off mine.

'"They . . . are . . . not . . . lesbians!"

'"Aah, come on Rachel " I said.

'The door burst open and Janelle, the middle-weight, stepped out screaming, "How dare you! We are not fucking lesbians!"'

'I dunno what they were fucking if that's the case,' laughed Elroy. 'They couldn't have fit anything else in that room.'

'Gloria followed them out,' said Taylor. 'To put her two bob's worth in.'

'They must have been anti-matter lesbians,' said Elroy. 'You know, from the Reverse Universe. Where everything is the same but in reverse?'

'Right,' nodded Taylor. 'They stared me down, sensed my weakness. Waddled back into the bedroom and slammed the door. I was completely fucking flabbergasted. That was the end of it. They were too big, too scary to defeat. Time to pack up and move on. A great house for two years, a neutron star of blazing horror in two weeks. Next morning we packed our meagre belongings into a van. We were set to go about eight in the morning. The anti-matter lesbians were all snuggled up. One last cigarette before we go. No matches. No lighter. I go to the stove, remove the saucepan filled with two-month-old chip oil and fire up the last working hot plate. It glows red, we light our cigarettes.

'By the time we were unloading our gear at a mate's place in Bondi, the bottom of the saucepan had burned through, spilling flaming chip oil over the floor of the kitchen. The fire brigade turned up five minutes later and smashed through the front door. Smoke everywhere. Three fireguys rigged out in the latest gear — oxygen helmets, axes and these huge reflective suits, making them look like aliens. They crashed through the house. Carried these girls screaming onto the street.'

'But they weren't screaming because of the fire,' Elroy informed us.

'No,' said Taylor. 'They were screaming because they didn't have time to change. They were all wearing thigh-high bucket boots and nipple clamps.'

'And Janelle had a vibrator stuck in her bottom,' added Elroy.

'But they weren't lesbians. Oh no.'

'Never in a million years.'

They finished their double act. The kitchen was completely still and silent for about three seconds.

Tick.

Tick.

Tick.

Then MacMillan, the senior D.S.S. field investigator, shook his head in astonishment. 'What in God's name has that got to do with anything?' he blurted out, completely exasperated. The other one, a short, pointy-headed sucktooth of a man, never spoke. Just sucked his teeth and bulged his eyes at us. Taylor and Elroy seemed a little dumbfounded and exasperated themselves because the D.S.S. guys couldn't see the point they were making. I shook my head and rubbed my eyelids, hoping I could open them in a few seconds and find myself somewhere else. Anywhere else in fact, other than in the kitchen at York Street with Dumb and Dumber, Leonard, the Decoy and the D.S.S.

Things had accelerated from bad to totally fucked up at the exact moment Taylor and Elroy had returned from a drunken babe-spotting trip to the megamall and blundered into the kitchen inquisition. The Decoy was slumped at the table, his face hidden behind his hands, his ponytail brushing rhythmically against his collar as he shook his head in despair. Leonard leaned up against the fridge, occasionally blowing out his cheeks and making what-the-hell-are-we-gonna-do-now? faces at me when he thought nobody was watching. MacMillan and his nameless partner were still seated at the table but now, in addition to all of the paper they had brought with them, ol' bug eyes was scribbling furiously into a large note pad, or at least he had been until about half-way through Taylor and Elroy's story.

'We just thought you should know,' said Taylor. 'Just in case it became important later. We thought you should know the sort of women our friend here had to deal with. The special circumstances he found himself in.'

'Taylor,' I interrupted, before he could put the Decoy in any deeper. 'They don't need to know. They don't want to know.'

Already numbed by the anti-matter lesbians, the D.S.S. guys agreed. MacMillan pulled a bulging manila folder out of his briefcase. 'If we could return to the audit,' he said. 'I'm afraid I'm having trouble with all this. You say there is not and never has been a Jordan, Gerry or Brandon Chandler living here, and yet we have records of payment to all three brothers at this address . . .'

'No,' I explained. 'I told you. That Jordan guy, he lived here. I think his name was Chandler at that point. Anyhow, he ran away and ripped us off, not you. Well maybe you. But us first.'

'And the brothers?' asked MacMillan.

'What brothers?'

'Gerry and Brandon.'

'There were no brothers,' I said.

MacMillan breathed heavily. 'But we were paying them at this address.'

'What for?' asked Leonard.

MacMillan shuffled through his papers, finding what he wanted after a few seconds. 'Gerry was on a veteran's benefit, and Brandon had a disability pension.'

I snorted, 'What for?'

MacMillan referred to the folder again. But he didn't didn't seem to like what he found there, 'Uhm, born without a tongue.'

We all sniggered at that, a little unwisely I guess.

MacMillan continued darkly, 'So I take it there was Gerry, no Brandon . . .'

'And no tongue,' I smirked.

MacMillan snapped his briefcase shut. 'I'm glad you find this amusing Mr Birmingham. Perhaps you could come back to the office with me and amuse my supervisor with an explanation of how we came to pay thousands of dollars on multiple benefits to what appears to be one person, with or without a tongue, living at this address.'

'Hey, man, he wasn't our responsibility,' protested Leonard.

'Well be that as it may, his case is my responsibility,' replied MacMillan. 'And I'll be frank. I suspect that your flatmate, this Jordan or Gerry character, if he even exists, has been involved in serious fraud. I don't know the extent of knowledge or involvement of anyone else in this house but I soon will.'

'You gonna cut us off?' breathed Leonard.

'I would say that it is a definite possibility. In fact, this is just my initial opinion, but you'll be very lucky if you don't end up being prosecuted, fined or even jailed for defrauding the Commonwealth.'

'Heavy tunes, baby,' murmured Elroy, grabbing for his cigarettes.

'Look,' I said desperately. 'I don't think you understand what's happened here. We're the victims in this case. We're the ones who are five weeks behind in the rent and bills because of this loser. If you cut us off you'll just be making a bad situation worse.'

MacMillan shook his head in wonder. 'I'm afraid you are the one who doesn't understand, Mr Birmingham. Your domestic problems are not our concern. We'll be mailing some questionnaires. I note from your files that most of you have a round of payments due this Friday. I wouldn't hold your breath waiting for them. I don't like the looks of what's going on here. Not at all.'

'But it's not our fault,' protested Leonard.

'But it is your problem,' countered MacMillan. 'Because on present indications I don't see any of those payments going through. Not unless we get some satisfactory answers.'

'But we'll get evicted,' I said. 'We've got to pay rent. We got to find

a thousand bucks or we're out on the street. You can't cut our money off just because of some fucked up flatmate!'

MacMillan stopped cramming his briefcase with files. He looked directly at me.

'It's not your money,' he said. 'It's the taxpayers'. And I really doubt they'd be very impressed if they knew what was going on here.'

'But you don't even know what's going on here.'

'I will, son. Trust me.'

'That's horrible,' said Fingers, shaking his head after I gave him the shareware lite version of the Decoy's imprisonment by the separatists. 'Just horrible.'

'A trail of tears, my friend.'

'You really think we can get 'im?' he asked.

'Got the address in here,' I said, flicking the Decoy's forgotten envelope.

'Right,' muttered Three Fingers, hunching over the wheel and pouring on speed. 'Let's roll.'

The Holden's fat tires bit deeper into the road as it growled, leaned forward and started to chew tarmac. We drove straight through, apart from a few petrol and toilet breaks and one stop at a BP road mart in Coffs Harbour where I bought us a case of Jolt Cola and a handful of speed from some Greek guy hauling five tonnes of frozen chicken up the edge of the continent. Fingers didn't bother with any questions

when I offered him first pick from our small but power-packed selection of contraband pharmaceuticals four hours later. Just made a greedy lunge for them.

'Hey, these ain't fuckin' smarties, you know.'

He turned to face me as we barrelled down the road at about a hundred and sixty. Dark black smudges were starting to emerge under his swollen eyes.

'Sorry man,' he said. 'Bad sleep dep. Lack of REM. It's a killer, you know.'

'Eyes on the road, Fingers.'

'Whoops!' he blurted, jerking the wheel savagely to the right, narrowly avoiding a wandering moo cow.

The new dawn found us twenty miles out of Melbourne. We were in a bad way by then. Unshaven, unwashed. Still wearing our filthy black tie gear. Fucked on junk food, sugar, caffeine and drugs. Fingers was worse of course. He'd carried all of the driving (I don't have a licence) and gobbled the lion's share of the speed. Twitches and tics ran wild over his face and neck and words tumbled out in off-tone staccato riffs of borderline gibberish. Mostly semi-deranged bursts about 'evil bitches' and 'political correctness' and 'ants crawling around under my skin'. Jesus, I thought to myself. Say hello to amphetamine psychosis.

Fingers wound it back a little as we hit the city grid. After a couple of bad moments with the trams we settled into a clean run through to the beach. The morning peak hour was still a way off then and most of the traffic was light commercial, delivery trucks and vans and so on. We slipped around the Grand Prix circuit at Albert Park and down onto Fitzroy Street. Port Phillip Bay lay flat and grey at the end. Half a dozen street people shuffled aimlessly about in front of Leo's pasta bar. 'Down there and a left,' I said as the light changed. 'How you figure we handle this, Fingers?'

'Snatch and grab. Straight in, straight out. No prisoners,' he answered right off.

'"Cept the Decoy.'

'What? Oh! Yeah right, 'cept him.'

Okay. Seemed reasonable. We pulled up in front of the address written down in Decoy's jiffy bag. It looked quiet. The sombre expanse of the Bay was unsettling, an unnatural affront to Queenslanders brought up on booming swells. It didn't smell salty or refreshing. Just kind of thin and oily. Fingers hopped out and started to button up his jacket, bouncing and rolling around on his loafers as his badly damaged nervous system cruised the jagged edge of meltdown. He threw my bow tie and 'bund at me.

'Better suit up, JB. A job worth doing is worth dressing well for.'

A fair enough idea, I thought, betraying my own loose connection to the world of real things. We smoothed our act out, shot our cuffs, spat in our hands, slicked back our hair.

'How you feeling, Fingers?'

'Like the Man! The post-feminist Man, a lean, mean, avenging machine.'

'Wanna do it?'

'And how!'

We charged up the front path to shoulder the door off its hinges but pulled up just before impact. A note was stuck on next to the knob:

> Jackie. Can't do brekky. Gone down Station Pier to the
> warships protest. Meet us all there.

We hammered on the door but no answer came. It was a heavy blow to Three Fingers' precarious sense of balance. He was twitching and shivering and going 'What the ' a lot. But I chilled him out. Said it

was okay. Pointed off down the thin curve of St Kilda Beach to a huge grey mass laid up in the distance.

'Gotta be one of them US nukes visiting. They tie 'em up down at that pier where the Tasmania ferry takes off. Seen it on the news. These dykes musta taken off to protest 'em or something. Probably gonna throw a lot of fake blood over them. It'd be fake blood too you know 'cos these sort of women are always your hard core vegetarians. You can bank on it, my friend.'

His shoulders jerked up violently.

'Damn! That makes *my* blood boil.'

We banged on the door one more time but you know that feeling you get when you're rapping at the door of an empty house? Well, we were way too drug-fucked to get that feeling, but we were firing on eight cylinders each and ready to rock, so we piled back into the big black Holden and made smoke towards the Dykes, the Decoy and a hundred thousand tonnes of nuclear-armed American military might.

The beach whipped by in a blurred ribbon on my side of the car. Fingers' white knuckle wheel grip and crazed, bulging eyes raised the faint but worrying prospect that he might not stop when we reached the pier. Might just plow right into the massed ranks of screaming lefties. But the scene that loomed as we drew closer stopped even him. He jammed the brake pedal and took us into a barely controlled forty metre long skid.

'Sweet mother of God. What madness is this?' whispered Fingers.

'I don't know,' I croaked. 'I think they're possums and, uh, giant koalas?'

'That's right, giant koala bears.'

'Koala's not a bear, Fingers,' I corrected him. 'It's a marsupial.'

'And those things?'

I peered through the bug smeared window screen, shaking my head, 'My guess . . . they'd be giant cockroaches.'

That's right, the Decoy told us later, cockroaches. The anti-nukes had organised a huge demo for the early morning docking of the US battle cruiser. Hundreds of protesters had gathered in secret locations around the bay before dawn, receiving their instructions and equipment as Fingers and I had sped through the last hundred miles of our long journey. The equipment was simple. Animal suits, three types. Koalas, possums and cockroaches. The Wilderness Society had lent the Coalition two dozen furry critter costumes but that wasn't nearly enough to cover the one hundred activists who had volunteered to climb a temporary chain link fence and charge the cruiser in a weird piece of allegorical protest theatre.

'You know,' explained the Decoy. 'The marsupials of Australia don't want your weapons of mass destruction here. That sort of thing?'

Luckily, a sympathetic theatre worker from Sydney had access to a whole bunch of cockroach suits. She had a friend in the Coalition. A long-time companion. Discreet phone calls were made. Certain arrangements entered into.

At seven in the morning thirteen battered Kombies and minibuses had screeched to a stop outside the dock and with a call of 'Possums Ho!' the first wave of demonstrators stormed out of their improvised troop carrier and charged towards a couple of sleepy security guards.

Tactically it was a fine set of moves. The initial attack came from the centre vehicle and each subsequent wave from the next ones out, spreading the field of engagement beyond the small security detail's ability to cope. A couple of International Socialist possums, the shock troops of any well-planned protest, made straight for the guards while their comrades went for the fence. More doors rumbled back to disgorge another squad of determined native fauna. The koalas charged away as fast as their little legs and poorly fitting costumes allowed, which wasn't too well, and quite a few tripped over each other.

Fingers and I climbed out of our car, jaws hanging slack, just staring as the rest of the convoy came to life, with a rallying cry of 'Roaches Away!' Dozens of giant insects swarmed towards the fence which was already shaking and buckling under the weight of fifteen, maybe sixteen possums and koalas who were scaling it and dropping into the arms of the military police on the other side. We started to walk into the melee as the first of the roaches made the fence and sirens began to wail in the distance.

'Sweet jumping Jesus,' muttered Fingers as the tide of roaches hit the fence and stopped dead. A quiet, curiously suspended bubble of time seemed to envelope the whole scene for a second, just before chaos broke out again and the roaches suddenly started running back and forth at the fence, bouncing off each other and the chain link barrier. It was like the unseen hand of God had sprayed them with a giant can of Baygon. You see, nobody had thought to cut arm holes into the costumes and the roaches' own limbs – sewn-on strips of plastic tubing – were useless when it came to scaling obstacles like a six-foot-high barricade. All they could do was to run back and forth, impotently crashing into each other and getting entangled while the first police units arrived to sweep them away.

'Over there, JB,' shouted Three Fingers, grabbing my arm and digging in painfully. A group of roaches which had emerged from a van a hundred metres away was standing around in obvious confusion. One stood a short distance apart from the others with its hood pulled back to reveal a greying ponytail and a preternaturally sour scowl.

'Decoy!' yelled Fingers and set off at full tilt, nearly yanking me off my feet. I ran to catch up. Cockroaches turned to gape at the sight of two dinner-suited lunatics accelerating through the chaos. The Decoy gave a little start when he recognised us and tried to wave. Best he could manage of course was to shake his floppy roach tubing from side to side. A couple of hefty lesbians foolishly tried to block Three

Fingers but mad with sleep deprivation, food poisoning, dirty speed and moral outrage, he simply lowered his shoulders and charged.

Two or three roaches went flying as he crashed in amongst them, grabbed the Decoy in a fireman's lift and came charging back. I turned and headed for the car. Last I saw of the Decoy's failed seaside holiday was a bunch of angry lesbian roaches knocked flat on their arses and struggling to get up again, little hairy brown legs peddling furiously away in the air.

'Jesus, what a disaster,' said Stacey. It was late Tuesday night. Everybody was scattered around the living room, draped over the brown couch or leaning up against the bar. The room seemed very empty and lifeless without Jabba's wide screen lighting it up. One by one the house had come home to discover that our rent and bill crisis had been compounded by the frightening resources of the federal bureaucracy. Nobody seemed to know what to do or even say. Elroy and I were the only ones not sucking on the public tit and although nobody had sunk their fangs in as badly as Jordan, no one in the house would survive a rubber hose and bare light bulbs session in the D.S.S. basement. Taylor and Stacey were the most vulnerable. Their meagre, undeclared incomes from itinerant cab driving and freelance photo-journalism couldn't actually sustain human life but were more than enough – if discovered by the authorities – to see them kicked off the dole and Austudy respectively.

'What'd you call that thing, a terror data?' asked Stacey.

'Close enough,' said Leonard.

'Oh, that little prick is going down,' said Taylor with a vehemence which caught everybody's attention. 'He comes in here, he rips us off, he brings a shit rain of trouble down on our heads. I say we get him. I say we find out where he is now, we kick his fucking teeth out and we throw him through the window down the D.S.S.'

Everyone was taken back a little by his outburst but what Stacey said next surprised us even more.

'I think Taylor's right. I think we do have to find this guy. He owes us big time. And I don't think Jabba should have to bear the loss of his TV alone. We all loved that TV. I'm starting to dread what each day is going to bring with Jordan. I got a feeling he's left little time bombs ticking all over the place and if we don't find them and defuse them they're gonna be going off in our faces for the next six months.'

'But what are we going to do?' asked Leonard. 'If we get cut off we're fucked. We got exams. We don't have time for this.'

'I don't have any exams,' I said. 'I can put some time into tracking him down. Guy like that, lotta people are gonna know him. It's a small town.'

'I can help too,' said the Decoy. 'I want to help.'

'I'll drive you round,' said Taylor, and then everyone wanted to help. We had a mission. Finding Jordan and saving our hides. Missy scuttled away into the kitchen to brew up coffee. Leonard trailed after her to watch. Gay Phil said he'd trawl the Valley, checking all of Jordan's favourite hangouts. Stacey grabbed a note pad from her room and drew up a list of tactical responses to the immediate threat of the D.S.S. She said she'd hit the phones the next day, call the student legal service and whoever else could help slow down the machinery. Elroy volunteered to do any bashing up required. The Thunderbird rolled his shoulders in excitement, flexed his arms and said 'Yeah, right' a lot. Jabba stared mournfully at the lighter rectangle of dust in the corner where his Sony used to live.

Our planning session went on into the wee hours, fuelled in its latter stages by a half done bottle of duty free whisky Gay Phil fished from the depths of his cardboard box. As we broke up around two or three in the morning and the others wandered off to their rooms, to their sleepouts, their foam slabs, brown couches, futons and air mattresses,

I strolled out the back to sit on the steps and clear my head. Tomorrow, as agreed, we would counterattack. We would not be fed quietly into the jaws of the system. We would not let Jordan escape. We would find the money we needed to get out from under this. We would blunt, or turn aside or just avoid the investigations of the *gruppen-haussturmführers*. We would be as water, flowing around the rock.

But as the lights went out behind me and the house settled into weary repose I heard the far away rumble of an early morning freight train and for a moment I feared it was the Sandmen of the Terror Data, already on their way.

GIVE ME NUDE VIDEO-CONFERENCING OR GIVE ME DEATH

On **Wednesday morning** I was a used-car salesman with a Ford dealership. But that was according to Stacey. She knocked and came into my bedroom, pressed and dressed and ready to kick the world's arse. She was carrying her big, battered Filofax and smirking at me.

'Dreamt you were a used car dealer last night,' she said.

'Yeah? I have any clothes on?'

'Oh yes,' she smiled again. 'Brown slip-ons with tassels, a very special shiny grey suit, and one of those eighties shirts, you know, with the thick vertical stripes and the bright white collar. Smooth as.'

'Big moustache?' I frowned.

'Oh no, no no.'

I shook the cobwebs from my head and sat up in bed. 'Well, that's okay, I guess.' She handed me a slip of paper, said it was the call back number we had for Jordan before he moved in. We could probably use it to help track him down now. Of course! A break in the case. At last. I sprang into action. I would get Leonard to hack into the Telecom database. I would buy a trench coat. I would get Missy to draw an identikit sketch. I would have the house dusted for prints and have a handwriting analyst flown in from the F.B.I.'s world-renowned Behavioural Science lab. Yeah. They were the guys to call. They'd know what to do. After all, hadn't they run Hannibal 'The Cannibal' Lecter to ground? Hadn't they . . .

'Yes, you could do all of that,' said Stacey. 'Or you could just call the number and tell them you're trying to find him. He probably ripped them off too.'

'Oh yeah,' I said, slightly deflated.

Stacey said she'd catch me later at cocktails and left to seize her day. I might have slunk back under the covers but the phone started ringing so I rolled out and shuffled into the lounge room. Leonard had cut a hole in his bedroom wall and was sanding off the edges. He was jacked into the Walkman again and I could hear the tinny thrashing of something like Pinhead Gunpowder shredding his ear drums. Jabba was stretched out on his couch with a bowl of Fruit Loops perched on his chest. He seemed not to notice the phone, just kept shovelling spoonfuls of sugary breakfast confection into his face. 'Hey, Jabba,' I said, 'it might feel good, but you're punishing yourself with those things.' He simply sighed, wallowing, as Missy passed by in a small, tattered bath towel and a pair of Snoopy slippers. I plucked the phone out of its cradle and got some deeply creepy sounding guy on the line.

'Hey, Missy,' I cried out. 'Call for you.'

She popped her head around the corner. Leonard pulled out one ear plug and cocked his head towards me.

'What's he sound like?' asked Missy.

'Kinda disturbed. A mouth breather. Possible bed wetter.'

She seemed to know who that was because she wrinkled her nose and shook her head before returning to the bathroom.

'Sorry, she's in a meeting,' I said and hung up. The phone rang again, immediately, and somehow more intensely, but this time I ignored it too. Instead, I considered my breakfast options and noticed that Leonard's underpants were creeping out of his room. Dozens of them, from those generic brand eight-packs I told you about. He

couldn't get enough of the things. He'd wear a new pair for a few days, take them off and chuck them in the pile in the corner of his room. It was like one of those giant sand dunes at the edge of the desert, inching forward, gradually swallowing everything in its path. We had to keep an eye out to make sure it didn't take dominion in the lounge room.

'Hey, Leonard,' I said. 'Your army of the night is on the march again.'

He apologised and stopped sanding the big hole for a second while he kicked and corralled the rogue undies back inside like a bunch of naughty puppies. I meant to ask what was happening with all these wall excavations but a knock at the front door drew me away. If this was D.S.S. again I knew now not to let them in when they came a callin'. Stacey said they were like vampires. They couldn't actually cross your threshold unless you invited them to. But the young smoothie on our front step didn't look like a dole fascist. He was the real thing, with a suit, a tie and luxurious waves of thick, blonde, shampoo-ad hair. Red suspenders peeked out from behind his pin-striped lapels and he took my hand in one of those cool, firm and yet completely icky two-fisted handshakes, you know, where the spare hand grips your forearm like they're a first-time Mayoral candidate or maybe a fat-sucking vampire getting ready to yank you forward and bite right through your collar bone. Nobody like that ever came to our place and at first I thought Missy, or even Gay Phil, might have got lucky, but then the suit gave me his card and it turned out he was a mobile lender for some rapacious mortgage company and he had an appointment to see Jordan about refinancing the house.

'Tick tick tick tick tick . . . kaboom,' said Leonard, who had walked up behind me.

I actually thought about letting the moneylender in. Just a for a second or two. Thought maybe we could raise a quick hundred thou' off him, because these guys they don't give a shit about whether you

can afford to make your payments or not. They borrow fifty million from some South African merchant bank who got their funds on the cheap in Papua New Guinea from a consortium of para-corporate military officers in Jakarta or Taiwan who, in turn, are looking to diversify out of burning down forests and murdering labour organisers into the first world home loan market. Global capital. They give a shit if you don't pay on time? I don't think so. They just repo your house and if you give them any trouble you find out why the application forms you filled in asked where your kids go to school and which roads they walk home along. Tempting as it was to run Jordan's scam back on him, I didn't fancy our chances of getting away with it. So we flicked this smooth operator, told him he must have had a bug in his Newton, there was no Jordan Chandler at this address and we were all renters anyway. Brainthrust Leonard kept shaking his head and looking pityingly at the guy's expensive but basically non-functional PDA which he'd hauled out and fired up when we told him he had the wrong place.

'Piece of crap,' said Leonard. 'Shoulda got yourself a notepad and a biro, man.'

It was a very distressing business for this space cadet who shook his bogus tricorder as though he might have somehow been able to jiggle the electrons free and make sense of this confusion. He was dazed and confused and definitely not in Kansas anymore. His easy commission from some overcommitted yuppie renovator which he had, no doubt, already spent in his head over a *latte* and *baguette* with the other shiny happy people at *La Dolce Vita* that morning . . . well, I'm afraid that little earner had gone the way of safari suits, the Fonz and Bachman Turner Overdrive.

Not that any of us had a wildly productive morning. Operation Payback didn't exactly come tearing out of the blocks like a greyhound with a chilli pepper crammed up its arse. After the mortgage guy I

snatched the Fruit Loops away from Jabba and wandered into the kitchen with hopes of scaring up some unspoiled milk. Missy bustled in and pushed past me to get at the veggie crisper for her breakfast apple. I asked her who the mouth breather on the phone was and she launched into some garbled anecdote about some dude who'd been following her around campus for three or four days until she'd got Elroy and Taylor to jump him and stand on his throat while she extracted a confession. Said he was a secret novelist who'd seen her around, based a character on her, and just wanted to observe her some more. She'd been intrigued. Hadn't even seen the flashing red light when she asked what his book was about.

'Medieval torture princes,' he coughed, choking under the heel of one of Taylor's Blundstones. 'These two guys, the princes? They build a medieval torture castle and . . . uhm . . . they torture lots of guys there.'

'Fuckin' history books,' said Elroy who had pinned down the stalker's arms. 'Only devos read that shit.'

But it was eccentric enough to hold Missy's interest for two or three days, until she sussed that torture boy really was a devo. The stolen box of charity mints he gave her to kick off their first date was a great opener but the finisher came when she rang him the next day only to have some deranged harpie break in on their conversation, shrieking that she was the Queen of the medieval torture castle and nobody was going to steal her crown and if Missy ever fucking came around or ever fucking rang the house, she'd rip her fucking lungs out With Her Bare Fucking Hands. The mouth breather must have tried to take the phone back then, because there was a scuffle on the end of the line. Missy heard pots and pans start to fly, crockery smashing on the ground, and the sound of torture boy running barefoot over the debris, reminding her for one mad moment of Bruce Willis in *Die Hard*. (Ow! Ow! Ow! Ooh! Ooh! Ow!) And then this one huge crash, like nothing she'd ever heard before, the sound of a fridge going over and trapping a man beneath it.

'I am so over men,' she said unconvincingly as she crunched into her apple and spun out the door, almost knocking a bleary-eyed post-milk-run Elroy off his feet.

'You're up early,' I said. He seemed to think about pouring himself a bowl of Fruit Loops but settled instead on eating them straight out of the packet in big, dry fistfuls.

'God a lod of worg oo do,' said Elroy around a mouth full of cereal. He fished a small glossy sachet and a crumpled piece of paper out of his Penthouse pyjamas pocket before swallowing and going on. 'Saw some letterbox droppers putting these out this morning. Got a whole pile of them out in the van.' He pushed the ill-gotten booty across the table with his free hand, the one that wasn't gummed up with sticky, half-chewed Fruit Loop bits. Elroy had made off with seven or eight streets' worth of Pizza Hut Stuffed Crust Two-for-One meal deal flyers and give-away samples of shampoo and conditioner.

'So this is gonna be your contribution to the house budget crisis?' I asked. 'Shaking down letter box retards for a whole suburb of junk mail and promo items?'

'We'll eat like kings with great hair,' he grinned.

'Gee, Elroy,' I said, 'the minute you walked in this joint, I just knew you were a man of distinction . . . a real big spender.'

But in a strange way, Elroy was the big spender of the house. With a regular income and a total inability to see beyond the next five minutes he was the one who could always be counted on to buy three cartons of beer when a six pack would do; who was always topping up the house mull stash because he just liked to know it was there; who'd made stupidity, bad taste and gross moral turpitude his personal leitmotiv. Elroy was the sort of guy who liked to demonstrate his remarkable genital control by getting naked and cradling a bowl of

milk in his lap. He'd drop his dinkus into the milk and drink up every last drop . . . but not with his mouth. Surprisingly few people thought the worse of him for it. He had this raffish charm working for him, you see, and it was basically down to his complete lack of shame. A really weird sort of innocence informed his whole routine. It wasn't so much a psychopathic disconnection from the consequences of his actions as a full-blooded celebration of them.

The first time I'd met Elroy he was being stretchered out the front door after having eaten a whole poison chicken. His lips were green, the onset of some severe form of botulism, I thought – only to be put right by Taylor, who said it was just the remains of a bottle of *Crème de menthe* they'd hopped into before the chicken mishap. Elroy's dream room was pretty much anywhere large enough to hold his sticky fold-up bed, his enormous collection of foreign beer cans and a giant framed photograph of himself, in his jocks, projectile vomiting into the Pacific Ocean. As he already had all of that at York Street I guess life couldn't get any better for him.

Taylor staggered in while I was reading the Pizza Hut flyer. He'd had about three hours' sleep between finishing his shift and the arrival of the mortgage spruiker. That little episode had woken him up, or more accurately, had caused him to stop sleeping. He was crumpled and puffy-faced and quite unsteady on his feet.

'Hey,' said Elroy. 'I'm going to a concert tonight. You in?'

'Uh, yeah,' said Taylor, then, 'Uhm, no. Dunno.' He tottered over to the sink, filled the kettle and got to work on some coffee. We'd run out of beans for the plunger a week ago and Jordan's raid on the kitty had left no money to restock. Taylor muttered an obscenity under his breath. He fetched a big tin of no-name powdered coffee out of the cupboard.

'Mmmmmh,' he said slowly, 'dusty.' He read the ingredients list on the side while the water boiled. 'Anti-foaming agent . . . excellent, just excellent.'

There was a loud bang from somewhere out in the lounge room. Elroy made like 'What the hell was that?' and I shrugged, said it was probably Leonard's doing. He was into some pretty serious structural work out there. Then Missy came hammering up the corridor and went flying into Area 51 in tears. A few seconds later, Leonard stuck his head around the corner into the kitchen. He was carrying an orbital sander and wearing a pair of bug-eyed protective goggles.

'What was that about?' he asked, but none of us knew. Leonard pushed the goggles up on his forehead. 'You right, Missy?' he called out, but there was no answer. I nodded to Taylor, who was pouring himself a mug of instant.

'While you're up mate,' I said.

'Yeah,' said Elroy.

'And me too,' went Leonard.

Taylor sighed deeply and fetched another three mugs. We stood around looking at each other, wondering what to do about Missy while Taylor made the brews.

'Could be . . . uhm, women's issues,' whispered Leonard.

But Elroy shook his head. 'Nah, I got both their periods for the whole year marked on my Playmates calendar,' he said. We all stared at him and he shrugged, 'Just like to make myself scarce, that's all.' And we fell to nodding and agreeing and going, 'Yeah, fair enough.' Taylor plonked the foamy instant coffees down on the table and suggested that maybe there was trouble with the mouth breather, which seemed a reasonable idea and, thankfully, one we were equipped to deal with. We grabbed our mugs and wandered over to Missy's carpet-covered office dividers. Complete silence, but a heavy vibe. We stood around uncomfortably for a few seconds, each nudging and encouraging the other to make the first move. Finally I stuck my head over a divider.

'Hey, babe, what's happening?'

She had retreated under her doona, with just a mop of thick black hair showing.

'Wanna talk or anything?'

The mop shook vigorously.

'Okay. That's cool.'

I turned back to the guys. We were pretty much at a loss after that. We'd shot our whole supportive wad in one go. We sipped our coffee and tried to think of something else to say but nothing came. Leonard eventually broke the silence by murmuring, 'I wish Stacey was here,' and everyone agreed. This was her territory. She was our binder of wounds, our balmer of hurt souls. Leonard poked his head over the divider.

'Like a brew?' he asked.

Missy's mop shook again but this time a small brown arm emerged and she jabbed her finger a couple of times in the direction of the front door.

'Fuck,' said Taylor. 'Maybe he's out there.'

'Let's get him!' said Elroy, suddenly enthused.

We charged up the hallway and into the day, still carrying our coffee mugs. I guess if this was a horror movie and it had been torture boy or Freddy Krueger who'd frightened Missy it would have been the cue for him to sneak in the back way while she was alone. But it wasn't. The street was quiet, if not deserted. A removalist's van had pulled over a few houses down and a couple of guys were unloading a table, supervised by some blonde girl. It didn't look like any sort of trouble. Then Taylor jumped, spilled hot coffee on his hand and yelped. He shook his scalded fingers and said, 'Look up there.'

Our street climbed steeply towards the ridge of Swann Road. High up on that ridge sat a billboard, overlooking a busy intersection. And down from that billboard stared a gigantic pair of cold, pitiless eyes.

 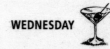

'Shit,' breathed someone. The eyes seemed to bear down and bore right into your skull. The pupils, flat, black and utterly devoid of warmth, would have been one foot across. The poster must have gone up the previous night and the pollution and grime and bleak city grit which hung in the hot air had not yet dimmed its weird, almost otherworldly gloss. A line of thick black text, a question, blared out from a band of white space above the eyes.

Why should real Australians support Pauline Hanson?

And in a smaller band of white below was an invite to a One Nation meeting to 'find out for yourself'. It seemed some over-eager fellow travellers had already dropped by to express their support. A couple of spray-painted swastikas bracketed some wobbly graffiti:

Asians Out

'Heavy tunes,' said Taylor.
   'Yeah,' nodded Elroy.
   'Well, what're we gonna do?' I asked at last.
   'Leave it to us,' said Brainthrust Leonard, who had been conspiring with Elroy a few feet away. Leonard, still toting his orbital sander, hefted it like a big misshapen Magnum .45 and depressed the trigger. The power tool roared into life.
   'Yeah,' said Elroy, 'Pauline's a dead man.'

'Pull over there,' said the Decoy, leaning forward between the seats. 'There's a phone.'
   Taylor spotted the phone booth a hundred metres up the road and angled his cab into the kerb. I fetched the piece of paper with Jordan's old phone number out of Taylor's street directory and passed it back

to the Decoy, saying he should have a go this time. I'd already made a few calls that morning with mixed results. Rang out once, engaged twice.

'Alrighty,' said the Decoy, taking the number and climbing out the back door.

'You think it's wise, letting him make the call?' asked Taylor as he yawned and uncapped his Thermos to pour another cup of black instant.

'Should be,' I said. 'He's very good with women. He sounds very non-threatening . . . hey, looks like we're on.'

The Decoy had got through to someone and seemed to be chatting away amicably enough. I took a swig from the Thermos while we were waiting and noticed that for the first time in a few weeks Taylor wasn't dressed as though he was about to head off to a Bells Beach surf classic. It looked like The Change was about to come over him again. As I might have mentioned, Taylor was infamous around the house for his fickle but fanatical attachment to short-term image make-overs. He was like the Face from The A-Team, or a cut-out character from one of those old kids' books, you know, the ones with a couple of blank, store-dummy-style figures and dozens of pages of pop-out clothes and trappings for you to create your own fully integrated and accessorised 2D person. Because of this I think Taylor's dream room would probably be the holodeck on the next generation Starship Enterprise, rather than the sleepout at the front of York Street. In just the last year we'd seen the Easy Rider phase, when he bought an old Norton motorcycle and walked around the house in his leathers and helmet for hours at a time; the business guy phase, which found him tricked out in these cheap 60s suits, toting a briefcase everywhere and checking his watch, constantly, as though he might be late for a flight, a board meeting or a martini somewhere; and of course the surf Nazi stage inspired by Gay Phil which, apparently, had now run its course.

Nobody ever questioned him about these mildly schizoidal tendencies, figuring it was probably like that deal with sleepwalkers. You weren't supposed to wake them up, nobody could say why exactly, it was just known to be dangerous. Not surprisingly the one person who came close to calling him out on these random identity morphs was Stacey, but that was only once, and under extreme provocation. Taylor had temporarily become a vegetarian fascist by virtue of stumbling into a sexual relationship with some weird vegan chick he'd picked up in the cab and driven to a Triple Zed market day. Still whacked from a couple of breakfast scoobs with Elroy, Taylor had fallen into a bizarre but friendly conversation with this dillberry, who called herself Phraedom and whose mental plugs had obviously come loose from the reality socket and got themselves all tangled up. She must have caught him in an unguarded moment because by the time they made the fair at Musgrave Park he'd decided to ditch the cab and hang out with her instead. They blew off the day smoking dope, listening to bad bands and chewing their way through an acre of alfalfa sprouts. By eight o'clock that night, while everyone else was up at the main stage watching Prik Harness, they were at it like rabbits in the untended bouncy castle. By eight o'clock the next morning Taylor had become Vegan Taylor, perhaps the strangest and most frustrating in his random series of personal paradigm shifts.

Vegan Taylor would open discussion of the weekly grocery list with, 'Well, I suppose I don't mind if somebody absolutely has to have meat . . . ' Vegan Taylor, like Roger the Hippy, could detect the aroma of meat sickness and corruption leaking from your pores three days after that Whopper with Cheese had slid through your plumbing. Vegan Taylor stopped wearing boots and belts. He ate his sandwiches without butter and drank his decaf coffee mixed with this foul, chalky-tasting soy extract. Vegan Taylor left Animal Lib flyers in the toilet magazine rack, hideous things, with all of these battery chickens bent out of

shape and little moo cows imprisoned in fattening pens which could have come straight out of the dungeon of the mouth breather's torture castle. Vegan Taylor was not at all impressed when the house responded by cooking up a big feed of chicken cacciatore and osso bucco for Sunday dinner that week. (*Gentlemen*, said Elroy, placing the first piping hot dish on the table, *the meat has arrived.*)

The saving grace for Vegan Taylor was our certain knowledge that it would not last, and his lengthy retreats to Phraedom's meat-free tofu ranch. It was during one such absence that Stacey unwisely decided we had not seen enough of our flatmate or his girlfriend and it would be nice to have them both around for a meal. Besides, she added, it would do none of us any harm to eat a few vegetables.

'D—o—h,' groaned the house, 'v-e-g-e-t-a-b-l-e-s.'

So Stacey rings Phraedom's place and gets Taylor on the line. 'I'll cook dinner,' she assures him. 'And the boys will behave.'

'Phraedom's got a gluten allergy you know,' he said.

That's okay, replied Stace, she had lots of friends who were picky about their diet. She knows they can't have any flour, any wheat, any dairy products and of course no meat under any circumstances. And Taylor, getting into the role, is like, yeah yeah yeah, so Stace said it was cool, she knew how to prepare all that shit, 'I'll use only organic produce, no processed food, everything will be macro bananas.' She gets the first phone call the next day. It's Phraedom.

'Stace I'm going to bring over our pots and pans if that's all right because when you cook flour in something or pasta in something the gluten will stick there forever, you just can't get it off.'

O-k-a-y, says Stace. That's fine. Gluten atoms are notoriously sticky. But that was not the end. It went on and on, dozens of calls a day. Hyper-finicky questions about every ingredient, every spice, every step of the cooking process. The rest of us were like, 'Ho-Ho-Ho, get yourself out of this one Stacey,' which of course just made her even more

grimly determined to push on and make a success of this preposterous venture.

Sunday night they drift in, a couple of wan apparitions with sunken eyes and that deathly, graveside pallor which creeps up on people who try to live off photosynthesis. Stace had enlisted Missy's help to cook up a feast of Malaysian and Vietnamese stir-fries but Vegan Taylor and Phraedom just sat picking at everything, frowning at their meals as though one of them might suddenly explode and disgorge a sightless, razor-toothed, Alien chestburster. It was not a McHappy meal. Yes, said Stacey, through gritted teeth, only rice flour, cinnamon, organic tofu, and organically grown vegetables went into the pot. Phraedom's pot, that is. The plague-free one. We all sit there grinning at the big purple veins throbbing on Stacey's neck as she starts to flip. We can see her going over, an enormous supertanker of constricted rage, slowly turning and rolling, inching towards the event horizon, the second at which she will split open and spill forth an explosion of destructive fury. Vegan Taylor touches Phraedom on the arm, suddenly aware of the danger. They are approaching the red zone of an explosive Tunguska tanty. They both go very quiet and drop their eyes and shoulders, like animals showing submission.

At that moment Elroy leans over to Stace, slides an arm around and says, 'You got a lot of anger inside, don't you babe.'

Stace and I came home the next day and they were back. Going through the garbage. 'I woke up this morning and I was tight of breath,' whined Phraedom. 'I didn't feel right. I was sick. I just know you used something in that recipe that wasn't right.' So they were rifling through the bin trying to unearth this mystery ingredient, the one that was going to kill her. Stace brainsnapped. She stormed into the house and returned a few seconds later with their pots and pans, started throwing them like missiles. It drove them away temporarily, but later that night Elroy and Leonard came into my room giggling

like a couple of schoolgirls. Come check it out, they said, and, crouched under the window sash in Elroy's room, we passed a joint and bit our lips and listened to the vegan duo vainly attempting to sift silently through the rubbish they'd been unable to search that afternoon.

Eventually of course Vegan Taylor disappeared just like Bikie Taylor, Business Taylor and now, it seemed, Surfing Taylor as well. The malleable yet resilient persona behind this eccentric parade, the inde-structible nerf man whom Brainthrust Leonard sometimes referred to as Core Taylor or Taylor Version 1.0, now opened his door to throw the dregs of his coffee onto the road as the Decoy returned from the phone booth.

'Well, she sounds kinda weird,' he said, climbing into the back seat again. 'But she's okay to see us, keen even.'

'Guess you'd have to be a little elsewhere to have lived with Jordan and want to climb into the sack with him,' I said. The Decoy handed Taylor the slip of paper with Jordan's old number written on it, now matched up to an address.

'She's over in New Farm,' he said.

Stacey returned from her visit to the student welfare office so fully briefed on D.S.S. counter-subterfuge programs that she freaked only mildly upon finding half-a-dozen eighteen-page questionnaires from the Dole Nazis crammed in our mail box. It was another envelope with a repayment book for a $6,000 car loan in Jordan's name – or rather in one of Jordan's *noms-de-fraude* (Steve Bennett for this one) – which really took a piece of her balance, left her vulnerable to the other heavy hits which were streaking in towards impact.

'Hey,' said Brainthrust Leonard, who'd wandered out on the front step when he heard the mail box creak open.

'Hey,' went Stacey in reply, not looking up, just sort of slumping back to lean on the remains of our old wooden fence, turning the loan book over to examine it, flipping through the unmarked pages, shaking her head in amazement.

Leonard was still wearing his overalls but he'd ditched the goggles and orbital sander. He asked Stacey how her trip to the student union had panned out and she came out of her private thoughts, said we'd probably be okay. Even if the cases went to something called 'control, review and recovery' we'd be able to hold them off if we worked the system.

'They're gonna want to burn Jordan,' she said, easing down to sit on the front step. 'But I figure they don't need the grief of chasing us for our pissy rent subsidies or a bit of cash work. If they look like they're going to cause trouble we can each lodge separate appeals, first to the office supervisor, then the area review officer, social security appeals tribunal, admin appeals tribunal, right up the line to the Men In Black if we have to. We just have to make sure the case officer knows we're not worth the hassle. It'd help if we could give them Jordan's severed head on a stick.' She tossed Leonard the car loan repayment book.

'Thing I can't understand is how he keeps pulling these scams off,' she continued. 'I mean, you hear about these finance companies, they'd take the soul of your first born as collateral against a bad loan, but this idiot just seems to wander in, put out his hand and walk off with the fat. I mean, Steve Bennett? He's Singaporean Chinese for Christ's sake!'

'Guess you don't need to hear about how we nearly became home owners this morning then?' grinned Leonard, who had passed through outrage and was now just marvelling the audacity of our former roomie.

'What?' asked Stacey darkly.

'Uhuh,' said Leonard, patting the door frame. 'Welcome to the Bennett residence.'

'Oh my God. He didn't.'

'He tried.'

Stacey closed her eyes, rubbed them, and slowly lay back her head, letting the sun bathe her face. She sat like that, very still and quiet, for a long time. Leonard didn't want to interrupt, but he'd been waiting on the mail too. Eventually it was too much for him.

'Any other post?' he asked.

Stace's eyes fluttered open and she passed everything over, the D.S.S. forms, some junk mail, letters for Gay Phil and Missy and that month's porn pack for Leonard.

'Sorry,' she said. 'Your *Playboy*'s in there. I know you like to keep it close at hand. Think I'm gonna head up to the Kremlin. They'll know what to do about the forms.'

'You reckon?' said Leonard. 'Those losers.'

Stacey shrugged. 'Desperate times, Leonard. Those *losers* been on welfare about three hundred years between them, I guess. Besides, Jhelise isn't too bad. I talk to her on the bus sometimes. They'll probably think of it as their revolutionary duty to help us out. Smash the State and all that. Here, gimme.'

She reached over, plucked a single form out of the thick pile and turned around to walk back up the street, freezing as though struck by an arrow.

'What the hell is that?' she gasped, registering for the first time the abomination on the billboard at the top of the hill.

 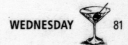

'Don't worry,' said Leonard. 'We've got that situation under control.'

Stacey shook her head, threw a wave back over her shoulder and said she didn't want to know. She stepped out onto the road and started to climb the hill. The street dozed at this time of day, a line of wooden houses asleep in the saddle of a leafy gully. Mango and paw paw trees dangled tyres on ropes. Tennis balls, footballs and bicycles lay abandoned in front yards for the working day. A cat slept on a neighbour's fence. She drank in the serenity, let it ease her mind as she trekked up to the Kremlin.

We called it that because it was full of these Earth First marxist strangeheads. It actually had its own semi-formal name, the York Street Collective or something. All those left-wing houses love to give themselves names like that. The Brunswick Street Co-op or the Petrie Terrace Militant Tendency. I guess it's just another outgrowth of the Left's slightly sad Orwellian fixation on controlling the language which describes things that have proven maddeningly resistant to change. That's why you never find any Michaels or Susans camped out in Left houses, because the name you were born with never really measures up and nobody wants to be Michael or Susan when they could be Connor or Meridian or Jhelise. It's why the occupants of such houses tie themselves into Gordian knots trying to avoid gender or sexuality specific language to describe the person they, or you, may or may not be bonking at that time. Because you wouldn't want to offend someone by assuming they were straight, or gay or bi, or anything. And it's why, when Stacey picked her way through the over-grown front yard around the stacks of mouldering socialist news-papers, and knocked on the door, she was answered by a cadaverous refugee from the University of Edinburgh, in Spanish, mangled by a thick Scottish brogue.

'*Como estas?*'

'What?' she asked, completely thrown.

'*Lo siento,*' he answered in that bizarre pidgin, suggesting to Stacey for one mad moment the impression of a Mediterranean Billy Connolly. '*Hoy es Miercoles. No puedo hablarte en el idioma de los . . . Och! Ah dunnoo . . . oppressadores.*'

A pained expression passed over Stace's features. She peered over the guy's shoulder but he shifted to block her view.

'I just want to see Jhelise,' she protested, waving the dole form at him. 'Jhelise? Comprende, McDoofus?'

Another burst of Spanish, this time from inside the house, drew his attention away. A strange, non-synchronous conversation ensued, with McDoofus floundering and burring his way through his Celtic Spanish while a female voice replied in quicker, more confident bursts of the same language. Stacey thought she recognised the second speaker, a suspicion confirmed when Jhelise appeared at the door and shooed the chastened Scotsman away.

'Sorry,' she said. 'Everyone's learning Spanish because of the South American struggle. On Wednesdays, Nicaragua Day, we're not even supposed to speak English. Whole house ignores you if you do.' She looked around conspiratorially, then confessed, 'It can be kind of a pain.'

Stacey said she wouldn't want to derail the South American struggle or anything but she was wondering if anyone there had any suggestion for fudging a pop quiz by the D.S.S. 'I'm not sure how to handle those forms,' she said. 'They want to know who's sleeping with who, bank accounts, contact details for the landlord, all that shit.'

'Is anyone sleeping with anyone over there?' asked Jhelise.

'Only in their dreams,' smiled Stace.

'Well keep it that way, you'll be right for a while. All share houses, they start looking for busts in terms of de facto relationships. But you have to watch those other questions. Make sure everyone fills in the forms together so nobody's answers conflict. Of course what you really

 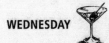

need is a forms committee. We have a forms committee convenes here on Monday morning if you want to come along. We could fill one out in pencil for you and give you the answers they need to hear. That's what you have to remember. Tick the right box and they'll leave you alone.'

Stacey explained that our situation wasn't that simple. With Jordan, we already had a case of massive fraud logged in at our address. A world of hurt was coming down for that, if nothing else. She told Jhelise about the car loan, the attempted mortgage, Jabba's stolen TV, the pot lids and the broken egg whip. 'The problem is going to be keeping them off our backs while we find this guy,' said Stace. 'I'm sure they'll give up and go home on the rest of us, as long as they can close a file on him and . . .'

But Jhelise wasn't listening anymore. It wasn't like she had drifted off or anything. It was an instantaneous transformation. Her eyes suddenly went wide, almost bugged out on their stalks. Her mouth formed a perfect little 'o' for just a second before she mouthed the word 'fuck!' She was staring at a point just over Stacey's shoulder. She moved to one side to get a better look and, just as Stace was about to turn around, she noticed three empty cockroach suits hanging from clothes hooks in the hallway. Her eyes went wide and she quietly said 'fuck!' too.

'I can't believe somebody put that thing up at the end of our street!' squealed Jhelise, before reeling off a mouthful of Spanish which brought the rest of house running and rumbling up the hallway to burst out into the daylight, squinting, pointing and having a giant Left-wing brain haemorrhage at the malevolent visage of Pauline Hanson, glowering down on their world.

'*Sacre caca!*'

'*Madre del diablo!*'

'*Es la bicha fascista grande!*'

Stacey, still processing the implications of the three empty roach suits, caught a flash of red mesh singlet advancing on her. She started backing away towards the gate.

'Well, I think I hear my mother calling. See you later, Jhelise.'

Jordan's old place was a ground-floor, two bedroom flat in a pre-war apartment block over in Llewelyn Street, New Farm. Winespew pink paint boiled off the walls and violent scimitar slashes of gold arced through the chocolate brown carpet. Walking through the door we were assaulted by an overpowering smell – sixty years' worth of previous tenants' foot odour. Still, it was worth the trip. Jordan's ex-flatmate, Sativa, turned out to be this beautiful, really skinny girl of about fifteen. Her background was weird, something like half-Indonesian and half-German. She spoke in this totally tired, monotonous voice as if she was about to fall asleep. Maybe she took a lot of drugs or maybe she was just like that. Soon as we laid eyes on her, a massive blacklight burst of data passed between Taylor and I. It couldn't have been more obvious if we'd sprouted *My Favourite Martian* antennae and started spinning our eyeballs like slot machine icons. There would be trouble over this girl. Deep, deep trouble. No holds barred, blood on the floor, indiscriminate bombing of the civilian population type trouble. Backs straightened, voices dropped and Sativa's small apartment quickly filled up with a warm fog of testosterone; a heady scent, suggestive of old leather and bleach.

She ushered us into her Zen minimalist lounge room. The Decoy was nearly concussed when he got between Taylor and I trying to shoulder charge each other aside. Some milk crate shelving covered with books and odd bits of pottery took up one whole wall. A dying foxtail palm sat in the far corner. Two bar stools next to it. And on the wall behind them, a strip of developing paper with an ominous epigram chemically burned into it: You Are Not Here.

'So my friend Jordan has been playing his little games with you too, yes?' she said, drowsily enunciating each word.

'Looks that way,' said the Decoy, all innocent and ingenuous, in contrast to us two, trawling deep and hard for a suitable approach to this horny under-age weirdo. We must have looked like a couple of Univac processors, circa 1963, with all of our vacuum tubes flashing and needles wobbling back and forth as we riffled through thousands of punch cards per second, each looking to beat the other to the next line. Then:

'He told us he had to move because you tried to pork him!' blurted Taylor.

Everyone stared. The stillness in the room actually seemed to tick through each second. An oily film of sweat broke out on Taylor's high-domed forehead as he fought for a recovery.

'But I said, "That's a lie!"'

I leaned over and muttered, 'Good save, dude.'

'Do you mind if I cook my lunch?' she asked. 'I have to be working soon.'

Sure, we all went, before following her to the kitchen which seemed to be completely empty. There was nothing on any of the benches or shelves. From her pocket Sativa pulled a huge steak wrapped in a plastic bag. She whacked it under the grill and turned it on.

'Jordan was out all hours. Coming and going night and day,' she said soporifically. 'I could hear him but I had no idea where he was going or what he was doing. He had many of these weird situations. He told me he had been married and come out. He told me he was twenty-five but he is not. He is twenty-one. He would say, "People tell me all the time how youthful I look." He was quite vain, yes?'

She flipped the steak which had been under the flame just long enough to lose its bright red colour. She cooked it for maybe a minute

and a half on the other side, mesmerising us as she spoke, and cooking in a sort of trance.

'He said he once had a lover called Damian. They had been very much in love for years. He believed they had chosen each other before they were even born. But Damian's family pressured him about being gay and so Jordan had broken with him and made his way to Brisbane. My clothes disappeared after he moved in here. I had a favourite pair of black vinyl pants. I asked Jordan if he had seen them. He said no and I asked him to look for them. His friends took them I am sure. They were coming around during the day, while I was out.'

'Black vinyl pants, you say?' I asked.

'Yes.'

'Not leather?'

'No.'

'Hmmm. Please continue.'

Sativa pulled a plate out of the cupboard and a knife and fork from a drawer. She devoured this practically raw steak in about ten mouthfuls while we watched in awe. In less than a minute there was nothing left on the plate but a bit of gristle and fat and a puddle of blood. She lifted the plate quite unselfconsciously and drank the blood off the porcelain with a hearty slurp.

'I must have my dessert now,' she said. I nodded. The Decoy gaped openly. I think Taylor may have had an erection. I know I did. Sativa got a bowl and a box of icing sugar from the cupboard. She three-quarters filled the bowl, fetched herself a spoon and ate the sugar straight.

'Excuse me,' mumbled the Decoy before fleeing the room.

'Your friend is all right?' said Sativa, sucking the spoon like a big lolly pop.

'No,' I said. 'But that's not your fault . . . So, Sativa, I'm wondering if Jordan did anything else while he was here. Any scams, that sort of thing?'

 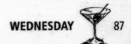

'Oh yes,' she answered and then giggled. 'He was arrested for trying to cash cheques he had written in the disappearing ink. He thought they would turn blank by the time the bank got them. But he was foolish with the amphetamines then. He used cheques pre-printed with his own name and account number on them.'

'That why you threw his bony arse out?' asked Taylor.

'Oh no. There were many reasons. He would dry his underpants on my oven, you see, opening the door and hanging them inside. He would turn out all the lights in the flat because they cost too much and when I would turn them back on he stole the bulbs. He took the handle off his door so I could not burst in on him while he was masturbating. He did that a lot. He would say he wanted to "nut," which is what he called ejaculating. Several times he nutted all over the place. He cracked the toilet bowl once. He said it "just happened" but I believe he got carried away with a very big nutting.'

Taylor and I looked at each other in horror as the Decoy wandered back into the kitchen. He was still wobbly but as long as he didn't have to watch Sativa eat again he'd be okay. Given his delicate condition and that fact that he was now living in Jordan's old room — which I was already thinking of as the nut factory — we considered it best not to bring him up to speed. He waved away Sativa's concern, said he was fine, just needed some air. She pushed open a window over the sink and asked if anyone minded her smoking a clove cigarette. We all shook our heads but Taylor, quicker on his feet than me, lunged at her with a lighter as she brought the smoke to her lips.

'*Danke schön*,' she smiled, taking the lighter and firing up. As she was about to hand it back she arched an eyebrow and held the lighter out to examine it like a small piece of art.

'I didn't realise they still made these . . . with the ladies' boobies which appear and disappear,' she mused.

Taylor was struck dumb for a second and I rushed to exploit this

possibly ruinous *faux pas*. 'Oh yes. They're all the rage with your mad keen nutters. And the thing is, our man Taylor here doesn't even use his with a sense of irony.'

'Hey!' he protested. 'I've got more irony than anyone in our house.'

'Not so my friend. I put it to you that I am the irony king of the house. You merely have an endearing cluelessness which you share with Elroy and the T-Bird.'

'Boys, boys . . .' warned the Decoy, who saw this moving towards an ugly climax of bull-elk-style antler charges and eye gouging.

'Irony, at any rate, is passé,' said Sativa, blowing a thin stream of blue smoke into the air and stopping us dead in our tracks. 'As an individual meta-ethical proposition its time is up because we are all insiders now, all trading on our knowingness and sense of irony when any speaks who claims to speak for anything but naked self-promotion. You see?'

'Uh, yeah,' said Taylor, hastily pocketing his naked boobie lighter.

'Yes,' smiled the Decoy, who was beginning to recover and who – being a hippy – had wasted years of his life thinking about this stuff. 'When you live in a world where murderers cut pay-per-view deals with cable television companies,' the Decoy explained, 'irony becomes a form of deadly sin.'

'Yes,' nodded Sativa, becoming almost animated. 'Trapped between the way things are and the way they ought to be, we are playing the world-weary sophisticate and looking down on anyone without sense to play along. Thus naivety is our doom and innocence an invitation to be pitied. Yeats saw this coming, yes? Things fall apart. The best lack all conviction, while the worst are full of passionate intensity?'

'Look, Sativa,' I butted in, desperate for something to say. 'You wanna come to our cocktail party tonight? We talk like this all the time at cocktails. There'll be lots of other girls there.'

'Perhaps,' she said. 'If you promise not to bore me.'

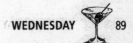

'Oh,' I said. 'Well, maybe you could come anyway.'

'You gotta come,' said Taylor. 'Every cocktail evening needs a guest of honour and everyone is going to want to talk to you about Jordan.'

'We can tell you some of our stories too,' I said. 'And we can cut you in on the action when we find him.'

'Yeah, we're going to take his stuff.'

'Well, in that case,' she mused. 'He owes me three hundred dollars. And he stole all of my furniture.'

'Outstanding!' said Taylor.

We gave her the details of the party and made her promise to turn up. She pushed us out the door then, said she had to go to work at some café, but wouldn't tell us which one. When we hopped into Taylor's cab downstairs I turned to the Decoy, handed him some paper and a pen.

'What's this for?' he asked.

'Just get writing Brainiac. I need at least six conversations like the one you just had and I need them by eight tonight.'

'And put me down for some too,' said Taylor. 'Good ones.'

Ah, the Brisbane formal thing. Such a funny old thing. A lot of places in Brisbane will virtually insist you dress in top hat and tails for breakfast but then won't bat an eyelid when you comb your moustache dandruff into the fruit salad. Maybe it's a colonial hangover, a worthy but hopeless attempt to defy the entropy of subtropical life. Cocktails

were our take on this. Every Wednesday night the house went formal. Ten dollar dinner jackets, patched-up ball gowns, high heels, cummerbunds, everything. We'd been doing it for so long nobody remembered whose idea it had been in the first place. Possibly Taylor's, during one of his phases. Or more likely, now that I think about it, Dirk's.

Not Dirk Fairfax, my perennially paranoid homosexual former flatmate. (Remember him? Wouldn't do the washing up because washing up was something Breeder Supremacists had invented for keeping put-upon gay guys in their place.)

But Dirk 'Some Refuse to Die' Flinthart. Author, adventurer, wine buff, survivalist.

When I'd first met Flinthart he was not such a big celebrity, just some guy making beer money working the fringe press like Stacey and me. Wine reviews were his gig. Cheap wine reviews. Cheap because he got paid ten bucks to write 'em. And cheap because none of the wine he reviewed ever cost more than ten bucks a bottle. (In fact very few even came within cooee of that, mostly tapering off at five or six bucks per four litre flagon.) Flinthart lived over in West End in this calamitous Anarchy House, sort of a fratboy party zone for slightly unbalanced 'activists.' Every Sunday morning he'd crank up the kitchen, cook a mountainous stack of pancakes and hash muffins, and tasters would descend from all over the city to help him rank out these awful fucking wines. I went to a couple of these things but I always seemed to find myself under a table, covered in vomit, with a headache like a meat axe had been smashed into my skull. I dropped out of Flinthart's wine scene after an especially savage tasting of some cleanskin Spumante culminated in the drinking of somebody's urine sample. 'People are always saying this stuff tastes like piss,' roared Flinthart, standing atop a table in his backyard. 'But I say we've had no baseline to measure it against!' So we took a midstream sample – that being sterile according to Barnes, our chemist – and to be fair I've got to say it did go down a lot easier than the Spumante. Which reminds me, off-topic, that Roger the Hippy was into Auto-Urine Therapy for a while. He'd drink a glass of fresh piss every day and take massages with urine which was at least four days old. He insisted the concentration of 'vital bodily essences' was so rich it could cure cancer.

Anyway, those wine breakfasts achieved minor legendary status for a while there – until Flinthart had to flee the city – and I don't know why, but I've got a vague feeling cocktails might have grown out of them. The breakfasts deployed the same faux formal atmosphere and everyone who frequented our cocktail parties could recall at least one encounter with doom at Flinthart's place on a Sunday morning. Whatever. Cocktail Wednesday had developed its own culture and history. There was no study on Cocktail Wednesday. No television. No jeans. No thongs or joggers. Conversation was to be witty, urbane and world weary, although we made an exception for Elroy. Guests, suitably attired, were welcome. And guests were frequent, even numerous. Fingers, for instance, was a regular attendee, although this week of course he was absent at Jupiters preparing for the Pro-Am.

Cocktail Wednesday's ambience was a twisted hybrid of *fin-de-siècle* sophistication and the sort of affectionate in-joke contempt for long dead Cold War cultural totems like fondue sets, disaster movies and airline hijackings which Sativa had dumped on earlier that afternoon. The tone we were searching for was a sort of lost generation Poseidon Adventure. Think of three hundred conventioneering Leyland salesmen and their hookers, all partying in the fabulous Lava Lamp Room of Surfers Paradise's Tiki Resort on the eve of the P-76 launch, all of them circling a brackish, evaporating pool of Kennedy-era super-abundance in ever-tightening rings of desperation, none of them willing to take their noses out of their prawn cocktails and Mai Tais lest the penny drop and they have to face the fact that the fat days are over, things will change, and the Reaper is coming for them and everyone like them

as sure as pestilence and slow death followed the plague rats of Europe.

Cocktail Wednesday was our tea party on the tilting decks of the *Titanic*. In the end the problems unleashed by Jordan were merely the surface eruptions of a deeper calamity. The whole world beneath our feet was treacherous and sliding away. Yes, he'd stiffed us for well over a grand. But between us we already owed forty thousand dollars in tuition fees. And had we drawn a worse ticket in the genetic lottery and been born, say, after punk rock died, that figure would have climbed vertiginously towards the half million dollar mark – in a house where we couldn't afford to restock the coffee beans. But even that wasn't all. It went much deeper. Our stories were fucked. They had no through-line or obvious destination. They were less narratives than atomised mosaics which substituted enticing hot 'n' tasty free food samples during peak hour shopping excursions for character development, interesting subtext or optimism. This collective-option-decay went so far beyond money and job prospects that we had downsized our life expectations to the point where we contemplated each new season's prime time TV line-up with more genuine enthusiasm than we had for our prospects of successful relationships or even biohazard-free sex.

It was a sick joke which nobody had bothered to explain to us, perhaps accounting for the anaemic, uncertain look my friends often turned on the world when it came after them like an investigative Rottweiler from a top-rating current affairs show; smiling doubtfully, not wanting to run or show fear, but not really sure why this hellhound seemed to be charging at them, its flat yellow eyes on fire, long tendrils of hot drool flying everywhere. What had they done? What were their crimes? In another dimension, an alternate Stargate-episode Earth, perhaps, Stacey would go to New York and get a contract with *Vanity Fair*, and maybe Jabba would become a TV critic for *Rolling Stone*, and

Leonard would start his own software company, and Missy would become a sort of multicultural Kate Fischer, and the T-Bird would establish a chain of successful twenty-four-hour gymnasiums, and the Decoy would run a profitable environmental consultancy and Elroy would have a fleet of milk vans with generous quotas provided by all the corrupt politicians he kept in his pocket and . . .

Jesus.

I'm sorry.

Guess I got a bit carried away there.

Let's cut this rant down: our future was not bright, we would not have to wear shades. But dressing up in penguin suits and ball gowns, drinking cocktails and swanning about like Young Rotarians at an outer suburban meet 'n' greet circa 1963 was one way of saying: 'Who gives a fuck.' Our destiny Airbus might have been plummeting to Earth with thick streamers of smoke pouring out of the engines, but by God, at least we had enough style to order a drink, slap the hysterical pansy sitting next to us and say, 'Shut up and die like a man.'

This particular Cocktail Wednesday was surrounded by an even stronger eve-of-destruction aura than usual. Not surprising, given the previous week's events and the approach of exams and assignment deadlines for most of the house. The first sign that it might take a different track from the average run of Cocktail Wednesdays was a preternatural banshee cry from the kitchen. I was sitting out on the back steps with Taylor and Elroy, sharing a beer and waiting on the Decoy who was trying to squeeze into a spare tux, one of two or three mix-and-match outfits we had lying around from previous cocktail evenings and house outings to assorted college balls. The Decoy had just stepped out, Cindy Crawford catwalk style, in a fetching set of long white tails and matching topper when this animal shriek rent the warm, soft afternoon air.

'Jeez,' said the Decoy, a little hurt, 'I didn't think it looked that bad.'

Another shriek, a loud bang and heavy footsteps thumping up the hall, shaking the back steps.

We hurried upstairs and into the kitchen where Gay Phil stood staring at this big, three-pronged barbecue fork he had speared into the wall, fixing there for all to see, an invoice for room, board and services rendered. Phil had opened his mail to discover his ex-boyfriend Jeff had billed him for all those nights spent in Jeffrey's lovin' arms and tastefully renovated two-bedroom apartment. Six hundred bucks on a thirty day account.

'Gee, Phil,' said Elroy. 'Where you gonna get the money for that?'

Phil smiled tightly, said, 'Let's never speak of this again,' and stalked out of the room. It was a little out of character for our gay hipster. But you tear a man's heart out and drop it into a mixmaster right there in front of him, you got to allow at least a small margin for a reaction. And Phil did get it back under control pretty quickly. Said he was gonna go out and make somebody bite the pillow after cocktails.

By seven thirty, half an hour before the official start of proceedings, Stacey had rounded everyone up and corralled us into the lounge. The wall which Leonard had been working on all week was covered in a dirty bed sheet. Sharp, mysterious contours pressed against the covering which he stood beside in his second-hand dinner jacket, nervously shifting from foot to foot. Stace flitted about in an ancient ball gown. When she had us all where she wanted she tapped a tiny *hors d'oeuvres* fork against the side of her champagne glass (which was half-filled with beer rather than champagne because of house budgetary restrictions). The euphonious ding-aling-aling brought us to attention. Stace moved to stand beside Leonard. She was smiling and seemed pleased with herself, happier in fact than any of us had seen her in a while.

'Well, team,' she began, only to be interrupted by a knock at the door. 'Ah, our guest.'

 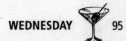

Sativa! both Taylor and I thought at once. We were going to make for the front door but Stacey pointed her miniature fork at us and said, 'I don't think so, gentlemen. Phillip, would you show our visitor in?' Gay Phil nodded and hustled off down the hall. We heard him say hello, then heard Sativa's somnolent tones in reply. We gaped when she appeared in front of Phil, tricked out in an ankle-length electric blue wrap, a flat, bare, brown midriff and a home-made party-bra fashioned into an arresting pair of giant eyes made of shimmering blue-and-gold sequins and designed to wink when triggered by a chunky gold tassel linked to some sort of spring-loaded device.

'*Guten abend*,' she breathed.

Dead silence. Then the entire house broke into restrained applause. It was possibly the best entrance we'd ever seen.

'Welcome to the Chateau,' smiled Stacey, as the ripple died away. 'Phillip? An aperitif for our guest? Quickly now.' She pinged her glass again.

'No, let me,' insisted Taylor, diving behind the bar and reappearing with another stolen champagne flute and a stubbie of Fourex. I leaned over to him and muttered under my breath, 'You cannot win you know, Darth.'

Taylor handed the beer across to Missy, who passed it on to Sativa.

'Love your frock,' said Missy.

'Now then, if we could resume,' said Stacey. 'Sativa, if you would stand over there next to Phillip. In a very roundabout way this concerns you too. For if you had not thrown your flatmate onto the streets he would never have turned up here, Jabba would still have his television and we would not find ourselves, shall we say, in the poo.'

She smiled to indicate she meant no harm by this. She was merely drawing Sativa into the magic circle of our lives.

'Now, Jabba,' Stace continued, turning to our most downcast flat-mate. 'We have all suffered from this recent unpleasantness, but you

have borne the brunt, having lost your Sony widescreen. But the loss will not be yours to bear alone. For who amongst us here had not bathed within the friendly glow of its high definition screen?'

She stood like an earnest contestant in a regional eisteddfod, her flute of cold amber ale raised delicately in one hand, her gaze slowly traversing the room to take us all in. She often worried me with how good she was at this stuff. I wondered whether she might have a lucrative future in day-time television ahead of her. I came back from these brief musings to find she had moved on.

'Mr John Irving,' she said, 'the novelist and wrestler, tells us at the end of *The Hotel New Hampshire*, that a good hotel does not pressure you or tell you how you ought to feel or what you ought to do. It simply provides you with the space and the atmosphere for whatever you really need. A good hotel, he tells us, turns space and atmosphere into something sympathetic and generous. I believe Mr Irving may have been writing allegorically, or with a subtext if you will. That's a hidden meaning, Elroy, one buried below the surface, something like a two dollar scratchie – '

'Thanks Stace!' said Elroy, charging his glass.

' – and Mr Irving's allegory, or perhaps "analogy" is more accurate, was between the idea of the hotel and that of home and family. A good hotel, like a good family and a good home, is always there in a spiritual sense for those who come within its embrace. I would like to think that our home, which shares so many attributes with both a family and a good hotel, shares this with them, that if you come to us, as Mr Irving put it, in broken pieces, when you leave you will be whole again.'

She had us all by then. Elroy, Taylor and I were no longer trying to sneak furtive pervs at Sativa's belly button. Sativa herself was avidly inspecting Leonard's drop sheet, her heavy-lidded eyes alive with a strange light. The T-Bird had stopped flexing his muscles. Gay Phil had

one arm around Missy who was leaning against his solid chest, contemplatively stirring some horrific blue drink she had fixed herself earlier. The Decoy looked like he was going to cry — the big fucking baby — and Jabba actually did wipe his eyes once or twice, but that was only because of the fumes coming off the schooner of hospital-strength brandy he'd been hopping into.

'We all brought our broken bits and pieces here,' said Stacey. 'We all arrived, as the Decoy did most recently, with our sagging boxes and old cardboard suitcases held together by peeling bits of tape and string, our plastic shopping bags bulging with old movie tickets and student cards, with love letters and photographs, with our unwritten books, our vibrating buttplugs, our foreign beer cans, our sins, our secrets, our telltale hearts, all broken up. We try to help each other make them whole again,' she said. 'So remember, Jabba, out of broken pieces something precious comes. Leonard?'

Brainthrust Leonard, who had been caught momentarily off guard, looked at her until he realised what she meant.

'Oh, sure! Right. Uh, Jabba, it ain't the best TV in the world. You'll have to sit up real close actually, but we . . . uhm, we hope it helps.'

He pivoted and whipped the sheet away with a flourish. So much of a flourish that it landed on Jabba's head and it took him a second to get clear. But in that interval we all 'ooohed' and 'aaahed'. When Jabba had freed himself from the sheet he too went 'ooh'.

The wall against which Jabba's TV had once stood now resembled one of those suspicious and impenetrable 'installations' you get down the Art Gallery, bits of old crap and wire and rusty farm machinery all boxed up and hung from a big white wall in clear plastic and plywood cases as though they were some kind of rare Japanese orchid. However, Leonard's presentation wasn't nearly as pretty. For material he'd cannibalised the computer junk in his room, then borrowed, stolen and misappropriated the more critical and expensive components from the

engineering labs at uni. The result now hanging in our lounge room was a gutted, tortured-looking Apple computer with all its insides taken out and fixed to the wall.

'Best of all,' said Leonard, leaning down to flick on the power. 'It's functional.'

There was a reason we called him Brainthrust.

The warm, familiar Apple start-up chime sounded from an eviscerated speaker. The monitor, which he had buried in the wall to hide most of its bulk, came to life.

'I got a faulty A.T.I. card, fixed her up, and rigged her for both PAL and NTSC output,' explained Leonard, pointlessly, because no-one knew what he was talking about. He took the keyboard from where it hung off a large pot plant hook. Keys clacked as his fingers flew in microbursts of lightning-fast typing, the signature tune of a true geek. 'It's got an old Mac TV tuner scavenged from a toasted sixty-one hundred,' he continued, the tip of his tongue poking out as he concentrated. 'And . . . if I haven't . . . fucked this up . . .'

A window appeared on the screen, filled with white noise and static and then, magically, with Helen Hunt's face.

'Bite me,' she said, and the laughter of a studio audience crackled out of the speakers.

'*Mad About You!*' squealed Missy and suddenly the room was alive with cheers and clapping and admiration for our dorky flatmate. We swarmed forward to punch his arms and ruffle his hair, Jabba getting there first, shaking his head in disbelief.

'I didn't realise this was possible,' he said.

'Convergence,' shrugged Leonard. 'The A.T.I.'s got a bitchin' QuickDraw 3D RAVE accelerator. You can watch TV. You can play games. You can hook it up to the Net through my account at uni and you know what that means . . .'

Surprisingly, Elroy did, 'Live nude videoconferencing!'

'Oh, baby,' exclaimed Jabba. 'I'm there!'

We crowded around and jostled for a glimpse of Leonard's marvel, each taking turns to change the channel and inspect the grainy, miraculous images which had sprung into being in the middle of this oddlooking creation. After a few minutes Stacey whispered in his ear and he cut the power. She rang the champagne flute bell again.

'Gentlemen. Your drinks.'

It was eight o'clock. We skolled down whatever beers we had left. Missy popped a lounge music cassette into her boombox. Taylor and I rolled our shoulders, sucked in our guts and quietly traversed the scene like tail gunners, looking for Sativa. Gay Phil, rostered on for serving duty, took up his place behind the bar.

'Tonight's featured cocktail is a time honoured classic,' he announced, fussing about with crushed ice, a dozen glasses and various tinkling bottles while we gathered around to watch. 'I first encountered this little drink on my initial foray to the Orient,' he explained. 'Although as we shall see, it hails from much further away. 'Twas in Taipei. I had decided to throw a soirée for my Chinese friends from the language school.'

'Any chicks at this party, Phil?' asked Elroy. 'Guys in dresses don't count.'

Phil bounced an ice cube off his forehead.

'Yes, as it happens there were a number of young ladies, whose presence, along with their male companions, my drinks cabinet and a single Kylie album, made our gathering illegal. For at the time, Taiwan was under martial law, and one was not supposed to be out after 10.30.'

'Savages!' I cried out.

'Hear, hear!' agreed Taylor.

'Indeed,' said Gay Phil, examining a bottle of tequila. 'I shall assume this worm came with the bottle. Anyway, there were at least forty or

fifty people in attendance, some other foreigners. We were in full swing when there was a loud knock on the door. Someone immediately turned off the stereo and everyone ran to sit down. I answered the door. It was a policeman.'

Gay Phil paused for effect, turning out a tray of ice cubes as he did. They rattled into a blender and he continued.

'Is there something wrong? I asked. He answered in Chinese, saying parties were illegal. I speak a little Chinese, as you may know, but I stared blankly. He looked at me in exasperation then addressed the others, demanding I.D. cards. A Japanese girl stood and chattered away in Japanese. All the Chinese took this as a cue to bow, Japanese-style, murmuring *hai, hai* which means "yes" in Japanese. Common knowledge in Taiwan I can assure you. The policeman began to panic. He couldn't get anyone to admit to being Chinese or speaking the language, and now all the real Japanese in the room were babbling at him in Japanese and we Westerners were contributing a torrent of English and French. Some wag even tried to explain Wagner's Ring Cycle in Dutch.'

A high-pitched rattling screech overwhelmed Missy's lounge music as Phil hit a switch and reduced ice cubes to shavings and mush. When he had the right consistency he began to pour generous measures of alcohol into the artificial snow, finishing his story as he went.

'Beads of sweat had formed on the policeman's forehead. He demanded to use the phone, to get someone who spoke our "devil languages." I forced him to mime "phone" about five different ways before I finally pointed to the floor, and he leapt on the phone. "It's not working!" he cried. He thrust it at me. I could see the cord had been pulled out of the wall by all the subversive dancing. I shrugged in bewilderment and handed it back to the policeman who, swearing and sweating, began to slam the receiver down and pick it up again in an effort to make it work.'

'Haha. Good one, Phil,' laughed Elroy, the natural enemy of authority. 'Stupid coppers.'

'Y-e-s,' nodded Phil. He tasted the cocktail mix and decided it needed a little something. He spoke as he busied himself behind the bar again.

'The officer retreated to the corridor to confer with his men at this point,' said Phil, uncorking a bottle of Cointreau and sniffing it. 'The second he did so, everyone streamed out of the living room, crawling out the windows and shimmying down the drainpipes. When he turned around, just a few foreigners remained, rearranging the furniture. He looked like he was about to burst into tears. I offered him what I am about to offer you, but he shook his head and left. A pity because, although he thought I was inviting him to partake of a snow cone, it was in fact one of the finest cocktails in the western world.'

Phil placed a single glass on the bar as we looked on, keen for closure on the anecdote and commencement on the drinks.

'Based on the *agua miel*, or honey water, of the Mexican agava plant, this cocktail has been famously celebrated in song by Mr Jimmy Buffett,' Phil informed us. 'To make it we rub the rim of our cocktail glass with lime juice and dip it in coarse salt. We add one and a half parts tequila with one of lime juice and a dash of Cointreau – a personal touch – to crushed ice. We strain into our cool salt-rimmed glass, and we serve. Ladies and gentlemen, I present for your drinking pleasure, the one, the only, the fabulous, Margarita.'

A third round of cheers as Phil offered the first cocktail of the evening to Missy, who, with her nightclubbing experience, could drink most of us into the ground. She took a preliminary mouthful, swilled it around for a second and swallowed.

'Excellent as always, Phil,' she declared. And with that, another Cocktail Wednesday roared down the runway and took off.

I swiped a drink from Phil and set off in pursuit of my quarry. Sativa was engrossed in conversation with Stacey and Leonard over by the

new 'installation.' Taylor was fidgeting about at the bar, waiting on his drink and trying to ignore the T-Bird who'd buttonholed him about something, a new recipe for protein shakes, I suppose, or that hilarious story about the time he ate fifty eggs. Seizing my chance, I slid across the room, oozing charm.

'S-a-t-i-v-a. So glad you could make it.'

'Hello,' she nodded. 'I am admiring your flatmate's artwork on the wall here. He has interfused so many elements, yes?'

'Uh . . . yeah,' I answered uncertainly, glancing at Stace, who seemed to find something amusing. Sativa turned to Leonard and placed her fingers lightly on his arm.

'Leonard,' she said, 'are you familiar with French new theory?'

'*Alors, mes enfants, vous êtes un couchon,*' smirked Stace. Leonard merely shrugged and cast about the room as though distracted and bored. His technique with the ladies had not matured much past the level of a fourteen year old. Didn't seem to matter to Sativa though. She obviously mistook his insecure detachment for Zen cool.

'*Gott.* I am finding myself drawn into the relational matrix of this work,' she mused. 'Is it saying that modern technologies such as you have used here, distance collapsing artefacts such as the fax and modem, do they affect regional styles?'

I was smart enough not to dump on something she was obviously very taken with. But I knew I had to shoehorn myself into this ridiculous discussion before Taylor arrived with his topless cigarette lighter. Only one thing for it. Cut to the chase.

'I've always been attracted to women in art galleries,' I said. 'There's something very attractive about them. Perhaps it's because they hold out the prospect of both a good fuck and an intelligent conversation.'

Stacey sniggered but Sativa just stared at me.

'What a pity they have no prospect of the same thing,' she said

before shifting her body to block me out of the conversation. Stace cocked an eyebrow at me.

'Looks like I'll be getting pissed tonight,' I muttered.

Stacey smiled, 'Welcome to a little town I like to call Magaritaville,' clinking her glass against mine as Taylor and Elroy suddenly appeared at her elbow.

'Hey, everyone,' said Taylor. 'Who's for a punch-in-the-guts competition?'

Stacey backhanded him in the bread box.

He gasped. 'Uh, fell at the first hurdle. Damn your jujitsu devilry.'

'So you're into weird art are you, Sativa?' asked Elroy, nakedly checking her out. 'I read about some of that in *People* last week. This art guy in America? He asked a couple of hundred other art guys to send him their poo in glass jars then he puts them on display? But it turned out he was a fraud. Only one guy actually sent the poo so all the other jars were his own work.'

Taylor and I thought that was pretty funny. All of which only encouraged Elroy of course.

'Yeah and this other art guy, well she was an art chick I guess, she locked herself in this plexiglass booth for a month? Said it symbolised the loneliness of menstruating chicks? And each day she's in there she did a new painting by mashing her face into whatever came out of, you know, down there.'

'I guess you'd call that women's issues,' quipped Leonard.

Sativa latched onto his arm. 'Yes, Leonard.' (She pronounced it Lay-o-nid.) 'Exactly. A decomposition, literal and figurative, you see, of the horrality of phallocentric discourse.'

This is not right, I thought. She's going to root Brainthrust Leonard because she's mistaken his nerdy geek genius for some kind of disturbed artist thing. Why couldn't she do that with me? Why not mistake uncouth, unshaven yobbishness for a good-looking-loner-who-

lives-by-his-own-rules thing? Stacey leaned over and whispered in my ear: 'Never mind, baby, she doesn't know what she's missing.'

My heart sort of lurched at that but before I could follow through Stace had turned away and tugged on the tassel of Sativa's winking eye bra.

'My boys tell me you had some interesting times with Jordan,' she said.

Sativa rolled her eyes theatrically, 'Oh yes. I thought I was going to kill him. I stood over him one night with a waffle iron. I was this close to bashing his brains out with it, yes?'

'You hear that Lay-o-nid,' I said. 'A waffle iron.'

Gay Phil arrived from the bar with a tray full of new margaritas. 'Top-ups,' he announced.

'Phil,' said Stacey. 'I was just telling Sativa about our nipple-rubbing undercover man.'

'Good Lord,' said Phil, shaking his head. 'When the going gets weird . . .'

The whole house had gradually gathered around us by then. Tell the story Phil, tell the story, they were all going. Phil distributed the icy cocktails, taking the last one for himself.

'Well let's see,' he said, biting his lip and making a big show of retrieving the details. 'I arose quite late and discovered you were all away for the day. Except for Jabba, of course, and Jordan. JB, you as I recall were gambling away your future with the appalling Mr Fingers. And Decoy, you were being held prisoner by a ruthless cabal of lesbian separatists.'

Missy had sidled up next to me. She seemed to have recovered from the shock of the Hanson billboard but I slipped my arm around her anyway — fraternally, you understand — and whispered, 'How you doin', babe?' She sucked her drink, smiled and leaned into me.

'It was strange because I knew something was up,' continued Phil.

'This particular morning I was enjoying a bowl of Fruit Loops. Fresh from a newly opened pack and deliciously crunchy. Preoccupied with my breakfast treat, it was some time before I became aware of . . . a presence. It was Jordan. He seemed to want to talk, judging by the increased level of nipular stimulation. But, of course, being Jordan he could not come to the point. Hence we went through this elaborate charade of sliding eyes, swivelling hips and pinched nipples before he finally vomited up the horrible fact that he was, quote: "a secret agent", "working in the drug squad", to get "the corrupt cops and the drug barons in the gay community."'

A few of us glanced at Sativa to gauge her reaction. Mild surprise, but not shock. I guess you had to figure she had more time in-country than us.

'Anyway the reason he was telling me this was that he had organ- ised "a big bust" on this very night and "strange things" would be happening; police officers arriving and setting up camp downstairs in his room, squad cars coming and going, tactical radios crackling through the night. I was . . . how to put it delicately? In deep fucking shock. Jordan said don't worry, everything is cool. Because the house is under surveillance for my protection. And it had been under surveil- lance since he'd moved in . . .'

That got a reaction from our exotic visitor. A blast of indecipher- able German. She turned to Brainthrust. 'Leonard. This is true, yes?'

'Oh yeah,' I answered for him. 'Wouldn't worry about it though. It's not like they were very conscientious Big Brothers. They were *Australian* cops after all. Even if they were supposed to be watching your place, most days they were probably away playing golf or snuffling cocaine off some hooker's titties.'

'Following up a line of inquiry,' smiled Leonard.

'Oh, very droll, Leonard,' said Gay Phil. 'But now, if we could have everyone's attention focused back on me . . . I didn't know what to

do. He asked me not to tell Stacey anything, to wait until this deal was over. He was afraid she would freak out.'

'Can't imagine why,' Stace remarked dryly.

'Of course I told everyone. But what was there to do?'

'We coulda shot it out,' protested Elroy.

'Fine words, milkboy,' said Stace. 'Just remind me again though. It was you who tried to keep the cops on side with an endless supply of flavoured milk that night, wasn't it?'

'D'oh!'

'Well, we were all somewhat aggrieved,' said Phil. 'We all hid in our rooms when they turned up. There were three of them, as I recall, although I only saw one through the keyhole. Extremely straight look-ing, acid-wash jeans – so you think "cop" right away. Blonde streaks, a little ponytail. Jordan running about fidgeting the whole time. Of course neither Stace nor I were sleeping. We were pinned to the wall listening for any sound. There was commotion, lots of phone calls. Then this marked patrol car pulled up outside ' Phil paused and took a long hit off his drink.

'Well, that sent the cops into a panic spiral,' he said between drafts. 'They could neither trace this car nor raise the driver for an hour. They were freaking out until they discovered he'd blundered into their scenario because he was servicing some chicky babe across the road, while on duty. It all subsided about three o'clock. Jordan came in and said everything was okay but we said, get the fuck out of here.'

Missy stirred under my arm, interrupting Phil. 'He tried to turn it back on us,' she said. 'Remember that? Like, what have you got to hide now you know I'm an undercover guy.'

'Yes, there were a couple of very hard, difficult days after that,' nodded Phil. 'He said he'd been caught up in the police business because his ex-wife's family was involved with ASIO. He said he hated it all, he was trapped in it. And because of the things he had done he

couldn't go back to Melbourne or Sydney. We said fine, very sad, but you still have to fuck off. It was ugly, all this very broken nothingness happening. Like insects under your skin when you'd see him.'

Everyone nodded and murmured agreement at that. Gay Phil focused back in on Sativa.

'I don't know what it was like at your place, but with us, he never paid rent, ever. He owed bills and bond. There was weird shit going on at all hours. Stuff disappearing. Unmarked cop cars, which are really noticeable. And even the neighbours were asking, "What does he do, what does he do?" He had actually spilled his guts to the people in the corner shop. They'd asked, "Do you work at night or something, because you're always in and out." And he told the shopkeeper straight out that he worked with the drug squad. Then one day we came home and he was gone. Along with our money, the television and the soda siphon.'

A barrage of loud, violent hammering at the front door pulled Gay Phil up short.

'What the hell was that?' he asked.

The pounding, rapid and a little scary, started again.

'Come on out of there, Danny, you little prick! We got a bone to pick with you!'

'Danny?'

'Danny who?'

Angry voices. *Wymyn's* voices.

'Oh my God,' whispered the Decoy.

We all spun to look at him. His eyes bulged in shock and all of the colour had drained from his face, leaving the skin pale and waxy.

'Danny?' inquired Stace.

'That's my name,' he quavered. 'Don't wear it out.'

The attack on the front door began anew. It sounded like somebody was going to smash right through it. The voices, a couple of them

distinguishable now, started up again, calling for 'Danny' to come out and face them, calling him 'a fucking narc' and 'a thief'.

'Oh jeez,' muttered the Decoy.

Uh oh, I thought.

'What's going on?' asked Elroy. 'Is it the cops?'

'Worse,' I said, and the Decoy nodded vigorously. 'It's the dykes.'

BANG. BANG. BANG.

'The lesbians?' went Stace. 'The ones you stayed with?'

The Decoy nodded again. The hammering got louder, as did the demands for him to come out and face them. Gay Phil hurried away to lock the back door.

'What do they want?' asked Stace.

'Lets fight 'em!' cried Elroy.

'Yeah!' cried Taylor.

'No, no, they're karate dykes,' trembled the Decoy.

Something like a club smashed into the door and Stace suddenly got that liver-frying look in her eyes again. She pushed her drink at Leonard.

'Right,' she said.

'Yo! Catfight! Wait for me,' cried Elroy happily as he charged away to his room.

Stacey turned and marched off towards the front of the house, yelling, 'Yeah, coming,' as we fell in behind her, the Decoy right at the back. The hammering stopped as our footsteps pounded up the hallway. Stacey turned on the outside light and flung open the door.

'I hope you're all Christians,' she shouted at the three angry, chunky looking women on our front path. 'Because you touch that fucking door again and I am going to send you to a better place.'

They were startled a little by the vehemence of her attack, by the light coming on, and the sight of a dozen or so people in formal wear wedged into the doorway in front of them. I was standing at Stacey's

 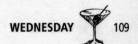

shoulder. Gay Phil and Missy on the other side. Taylor behind me. The Decoy surrounded by everyone else.

'That's him,' shouted the biggest of the women, the one with a purple bandanna tied around her noggin, pirate style. 'You fucking narc!'

A terrified peep escaped from the Decoy.

'Just give us our money! You fucking spy!'

'And our costume!'

'Enough!' snapped Stacey. 'You will speak politely to my friend. Or I will have my brother unleash the hounds.'

'You stay out of this, Barbie,' the woman growled. 'Your friend sold us out and ripped us off . . . And you! You're the other one!' the pirate said, pointing at me. 'I recognise that fucking penguin suit.'

'Yeah . . . but who you gonna call?' I grinned.

'John, what's going on?' sighed Stace.

'These are the guys we told you about,' I said keeping my eyes on the angry pirate dyke. 'You know. At that demo in Melbourne? The big insects and things? I think they think we had something to do with fucking it up.'

'Oh and the rest of it!' protested the woman.

I shrugged. One of the other women, a bit smaller but just as intense, pointed a long black object with a small link of chain at me. 'You've got our costume.'

'A nunchuk?' said Stace sceptically. 'What are you, Hong Kong Phooey?'

'Your friend stayed at our place, accepted our hospitality . . .'

'Your what?' exclaimed the Decoy, roused to resistance at last.

'. . . and made off with our kitty and our cockroach suit after selling our demo out to the cops,' she finished.

'Oh, I did not, Brie!' shouted the Decoy from in back. I remembered then. He'd told us about Brie, the one who'd found him on the floor

of the co-op. She was a nasty one all right. Andrea Dworkin on elephant steroids. I seem to recall Fingers had swerved especially to crash into her at the demo. ('Cut off the head and the body will die,' he'd explained somewhat cryptically a bit later.)

'Well, there you go then,' said Stacey. 'The Decoy says he didn't do anything. Case closed.'

'I don't think so,' said Brie.

Stace stepped away from the rest of us, took two paces and stood with her nose just a few inches away from her. 'Well I do,' she said quietly, staring into the woman's eyes. 'Now, we are in the middle of cocktails, a private function, and you are not dressed appropriately.'

'Isn't this great?' whispered Leonard to Sativa.

Elroy, carrying a cricket bat, pushed through the crush and strode down to stand next to Stacey. 'Aaaarr,' he went like a deranged old sea dog. Gay Phil stepped down and stood on the other side of his sister. Then Taylor, then me, then everyone else. The Decoy picked his way hesitantly through the centre of our scrum to face his accusers. They were obviously surprised to find him in white tails and a topper.

'I didn't take your money,' he said. 'Or do anything else . . . and your hospitality sucks. I had a terrible time.'

'Well my heart pumps piss for you,' said Brie, recovering a piece of her equilibrium.

'I really think you'd better leave,' said Stacey. 'We've all been drinking tequila. Things could get out of hand.'

It was a perverse stand off. Stacey in her ball gown which looked like it might have done service at regimental dining-in nights as far back as the Indian Mutiny, toe to toe with this psychotic bull dyke in motorcycle leathers and a great line in murderous glares. The other two dykes shifting about restlessly like a couple of thugs off-the-rack from 'Goons R Us.' The rest of us, slightly pissed, swaying and trying to look as threatening as Stace, or at least as dangerously unpredictable as Elroy. I had no idea how it would end. For one second I thought maybe Stace and Brie might just haul off and start beating seven kinds of hell out of each other. But then Brie just smiled.

'We'll be back,' she said to the Decoy, ignoring Stacey altogether.

'We'll be here, cheese girl,' said Stace. 'All of us.'

First Brie, then the other two turned their backs on us and walked out the gate to mount their big Japanese motorcycles.

'Nice bike, camembert,' called Elroy.

Brie gave him the finger and kicked her Honda to life. All three peeled out, roaring away like rolling thunder. We stood there in silence for a few seconds. Stacey finally broke the spell.

'What the hell was that?'

'I guess science would call it a woman,' I said.

She looked at me. 'John, the Decoy didn't take their kitty money did he.'

It was more of a statement than a question.

'No, Stacey. He didn't.'

'You and Fingers took it and gave it to some blackjack dealers didn't you.'

'Uhm, not all of it,' I said.

'Oh God no,' pleaded the Decoy to me. 'Say it ain't so.'

'John,' sighed Stace, shaking her head, 'I think you owe us a drink. The Decoy especially.'

So we filed back into the house. Elroy and I bringing up the rear. The Decoy stood on the step staring up the road where the bikes had gone. He'd pushed his top hat back and was shaking his head despondently. 'Don't sweat it big guy,' I said, punching him lightly on the shoulder. 'Come and have a margarita.'

'I'm a dead man,' he moaned. 'The vengeance dykes are coming to get me. That's what they do. That's all they do. You can't reason with them, you can't bargain with them. They will not stop!'

I put my arm around him and led him back inside.

'Oh there's no need for thanks, Decoy,' I said. 'You know me. Bringing people together. That's what I'm all about.'

Late Wednesday night, or maybe early Thursday morning. All quiet on the western front. The Decoy snoring softly on a foam slab by the bar in the lounge room, having refused to stay in the bedroom downstairs for fear the lesbians would come back to get him. Jabba perched on a bar stool, his face about six inches from the glow of the computer screen, a set of ear phones jacked into the wall. Dinner jackets, cocktail glasses, empty Pizza Hut boxes and cut-up 2-for-1 Meal Deal vouchers everywhere. Elroy missing, rumoured to be at a concert in town. The T-Bird in his room studying, or maybe sleeping by now. Gay Phil, down the Valley again checking out a nightclub, the name supplied by Sativa, which Jordan 'worked' at for a while. Whatever the hell that means.

And Sativa and Leonard?

Well, what can I say? It was like watching a puma stalk down a furry little forest friend. I tell you. He was out of his depth. He should have let me or even Taylor take care of things. A woman like that, she'd probably have sex then kill him and inject the eggs of her young into the husk. *Are you frightened of me, Lay-o-nid*, she'd asked after backing him into a corner sometime around midnight. *You are familiar with Ishiguro, perhaps?* 'As with a wound on one's body it is possible to become intimate with the most disturbing of things.'

He almost fainted then. Desperate for something to say, he babbled that his personal philosophy was frisbeetarianism, the belief that when you die your soul flies up on the roof and gets stuck there. She led him out the front door and that was the last we saw of him.

Don't worry, Stacey had said. She doesn't know what she's missing.

I shake my head drunkenly. Where had that come from? I'm sitting on the floor, propped up against the wall in my bedroom. Six margaritas, three or four pre-cocktail beers, and now a couple of hits off the bucket bong have done for me. I'm fucked. But so are the others. Missy sitting on an old beach towel on the floor, and leaned up against me. Stacey in Dame Edna sunnies sprawled over my bed, sucking the margarita dregs out of Phil's blender with a straw. Taylor plunging his head into the bucket, taking down a huge cloud of dope smoke, holding it, releasing it and falling back to bang his head against my desk. Doesn't even notice. Just goes back to crapping on.

'I'm telling you, man,' he croaks, completely whacked. 'Had motherfuckers diss me and I had motherfuckers doubt but when I put my plan together gonna be no doubting dissing motherfuckers any more, just gonna be one long line of kneelin' down dick suckin' motherfuckers waitin' for me to come along and give them a taste. Oh yeah.'

Missy, pushing forward to pack another cone, 'You got a name for it yet?'

'Oh yeah. Gonna call it the Woomera.'

Stacey snorts and giggles uncontrollably.

'No, serious man . . .' says Taylor and he is. Serious in the way that only somebody as trashed as he is could be. 'All of our money problems. All gone. Just think about it . . . Go further, go longer, with the Woomera.'

Stacey lets the blender roll to the floor with a bang. 'But how you

gonna get the designs on, Taylor?' she asks. 'I don't see how you're gonna do that. Like if it was so easy someone would have thought of it for sure.'

'That's just details,' he slurs. 'They got guys for that sort of stuff. It ain't details which make the money. It's the idea. Any moron can work out details, but coming up with the idea, that's something else. You just gotta think about it. Guys gonna be beating a path to my fuckin' door to buy condoms with aboriginal tribal paintings on them. I mean those lines and dots they got? Ridges and bumps for added sensitivity! Fuckin' guys get these things on, they'll think they're fuckin' Tarzan.'

Missy has a coughing spasm. She leans back against me and takes a long mouthful of my beer. Taylor's mood shifts in an instant of stoned flakiness.

'Course, I can't get workin' on the design till after semester. I got assignments coming out of my arse.'

Stacey stares at him deadpan. 'Semester's been finished for eight weeks, Taylor,' she lies.

'Oh,' he says. 'Shit.'

And we all laugh because he's so wasted he doesn't even know what year it is.

It's quiet for a few seconds while we catch our breath and Taylor tries to figure out what we're laughing about. Then Missy speaks.

'How d'you think Leonard's going?'

'Missy,' I grimaced. 'They won't even find a body.'

The phone rings.

'Jeez,' goes Stace. 'What's the time?'

'Late,' says Taylor to himself. 'S'really late.'

Stace rolls off the bed and staggers out to take the call. When she comes back she is shaking her head kind of ruefully, as though she regrets getting up.

'What's wrong?' asks Missy.

'Oh, well, I'm not sure anything's wrong . . . yet. We're just going to have to find room for another guest.'

Who! we all wanted to know.

'Flinthart,' she said. 'He's coming to party.'

WE ARE THE BORG.
RESISTANCE IS FUTILE

I hadn't been in to the clipping service for a week or so and figured with all this money trouble around it wouldn't do to have to turn up, hands out, at the unemployment shack again. So even though I knew I'd be suffering post-cocktails, I set aside the first part of Thursday to go rack up a few hours.

I woke up in Stacey's bed but you don't want to go getting excited over that. She'd simply passed out on my bed after all those high octane cones and drinks so I crashed in her room, praying that Gay Phil wouldn't come home with a skin full and make me bite the pillow by mistake. He didn't come home at all as it turned out so I got about four hours sleep to clear the toxins from my system before I had to get up, go out and start reading the papers. I had a filthy hangover. Felt like I'd been force fed a drum of cod liver oil, sewn up in a huge pig's bladder and beaten with broom handles by a couple of Christian Brothers. Swallowing and breathing slowly to control my queasy stomach I shuffled out to the kitchen. Jabba was asleep on his couch, the Decoy on his mattress. Thunderbird Ron's door was ajar. As I moved into the kitchen I heard him down in the back yard working through his daily pyramid; twenty-five sit-ups and twenty-five push-ups, then fifty, then seventy-five, then a hundred. Every day, even in the rain, even in the middle of winter. I tell you. He was an odd guy that T-Bird.

He didn't talk much. Wasn't real comfortable with conversation. Picking up heavy furniture with his teeth was more his thing. But we all liked him, I guess. He always seemed to be around, hovering on the edge of things, arms akimbo, head swivelling from side to side to follow a discussion he'd probably never contribute to.

His dream room was any city gymnasium at three in the morning; all of that shiny, unattended Nautilus equipment just waiting for him. His room at York Street more of a walk-in closet, Soviet gulag style, with an exposed light bulb, a hammock and an old wooden desk. His turn-ons were . . .

Well, I don't even want to think about that.

I put the kettle on and scooped three teaspoons of foamy instant coffee into a mug. Then, thinking the T-Bird might want some I repeated the exercise. I was swaying on my feet I was so tired. I plopped down in a chair and waited for the water to boil. I must have dozed off momentarily because the whistle brought me awake with a start. I made the brews and wandered out onto the back stairs. The T-Bird was pacing around really agitated and I got the impression he was talking himself into something before he noticed me on the patio.

'Hey,' he mumbled.

'Hey,' I went. 'Brew?'

He nodded and I carefully negotiated the steps down to the grass. I was always amazed at how different the day seemed before six o'clock in the morning, before anyone had had a chance to take it out of the wrapping and fuck it up. It was a different world. An empty one, I sometimes thought. All of those offices and shops, all vacant and unclaimed, as though you could actually ride out into the crisp pre dawn air and plant your flag in them and go 'Three cheers for me' and everyone else would wake up just that little bit late and eat their Weet-bix and stumble bleary-eyed into the world to find that you'd beaten them there and it was all yours now.

But of course that's not how it worked. Most days by the time I walked out the front door hordes of greedy, sugar-mad boomer kinder had swarmed over the hypermart of existence and stripped the shelves of everything except tinned beetroot and pipe cleaners.

'Can I ask you something?' mumbled the T-Bird, interrupting my daydream.

'Uh, yeah,' I said groggily. 'Sure.'

The T-Bird sipped at his coffee and flexed and chewed his lower lip and mumbled some more. Took another sip. Grunted. Walked away. Came back . . .

'Thunderbird,' I yawned. 'What's your problem? Just give it up, man.'

He glanced up furtively, as if he thought somebody might have been listening at the top of the back steps. At first when he spoke, he spoke so softly that I missed a lot of what he said.

'. . . they . . . um . . . well, you know . . . a lot of sex.'

I cocked an eyebrow and sipped on my coffee. I didn't say anything. After a few seconds he tumbled on.

'I hear that . . . I hear they have a lot of sex and . . . um . . . it's just . . .'

I became aware of birdsong in the trees for the first time, and the sound of traffic a way off in the distance.

'Yes?' I said. 'It's just that?'

'Homosexuals!' he blurted out, immediately worrying he may have been overheard.

'Yes,' I said again. 'Homosexuals.'

'They have a lot of sex.'

'That's what I hear, T-Bird.'

'In nightclubs,' he nodded.

'Mmmmh . . . And this is important because?'

'AIDS,' he said apprehensively. 'AIDS in the nightclubs . . . the women . . . and um . . . homosexuals. Do you think they might . . . uh . . .'

I threw the cold remains of my coffee away, rubbed at the heavy stubble on my face and tried to decode this madness. But a bone deep weariness had stolen over me again, dampening my thought processes. I was going to need a big nap this afternoon.

'I was thinking . . .' said the T-Bird.

'You keep doing that,' I yawned.

He looked puzzled but carried on.

'I was going . . . if you think . . . do you think we could . . . um, you know the guys . . . we could go to . . . the coast . . . for schoolies.'

'What? You want to procure some school children?' I asked, confused.

'No no. I just want to go to . . . um . . . to Schoolies Week. At the Coast.'

'That's a fine idea T-Bird. I'm always up for an orgy with a bunch of naive school girls. But we got a few things on our plate at the moment. You know? Rent, bills, dole fascists, vengeance dykes? I don't think Stacey would be very impressed, do you?'

'I know, it's just that . . . with the AIDS.'

'Oh my God, again with the AIDS!'

But he wouldn't be stopped. 'The girls at the coast . . . they'd be school girls,' he said. 'Young and, um . . . you know, they would have . . . they'd be, you know, virgins so they'd be . . .'

He looked at me desperately. A man with a big hurting. And I suddenly knew what he was getting at. He wanted to go to the Gold Coast and have sex with school girls because they'd be virgins and so would not have slept with any homosexuals and caught AIDS.

Oh man, I really had to get some more sleep.

'Look, T-Bird,' I said. He craned forward like a big old Labrador hoping for a chocolate from the dinner table. 'You haven't . . . well, been with a lot of ladies before. Have you?'

He grinned a weak apologetic little smile.

'It's not unusual for a lot of guys to go to pieces around the women folk,' I said. 'Even guys who should know better.'

He looked at me, waiting for more. I chewed my lip and tried to think of somewhere I could take this. After a few moments consideration I continued, not really knowing what I was doing, but aware that I had to do something.

'I had this friend, right? An old school friend, Grant, who was always going to be a surgeon. He was handsome and smart and he stood to inherit a million bucks from some obscure uncle somewhere. He got great marks in all his courses. He could run a hundred metres slightly faster than you. He could play cricket slightly better than you.'

The T-Bird looked perturbed by this.

'When I say "you" I don't mean you. I'm speaking generically,' I explained. 'I just mean that he was a winner, a guy who'd never hit a hurdle in his life. But having seen *Lambada – The Forbidden Dance*, he decided he was going to throw it all away and become a ballet dancer.'

The T-Bird furrowed his brow and nodded, 'A ballet dancer.'

'That's right. Now he didn't come right out and admit this, but he'd been behaving weirdly since that film and one night I tailed him into the city. Followed him all the way into Arthur Murray's dance studio and confronted him. I said, "So are you going to be a ballet dancer or something?" And he 'fessed up about the whole scheme. And, man, I thought he had it sussed. While the rest of us were studying or working crappy jobs he was doing ballet, hanging out with nude sixteen-year-old girls. I know this because I went visiting backstage after a show and there they were. Young. And nude. An inexhaustible supply of nude teenage girls. But no. Grant just wanted to dance. These girls were furniture to him. As soon as a real girl came near him, he'd go to water. He got to the age of twenty-five before he even went out on a date. And that was only because a ballet dancer tricked him into it.'

I let the T-Bird try to absorb the import of this parable. He nodded some more and furrowed his brow again, but I don't know if he was just pretending.

'The body building,' I said. 'I figure that's a chick thing, right? You haven't had a lot of luck on the babe front – and we all been there, believe me – so you got pumped. Figured you'd bulk up and get some. Right?'

'Sure,' he said, not really embarrassed. He was proud of his body.

'Well, I don't know,' I said. 'With the schoolies? I'm not so sure there. Maybe you don't want to get your hopes up. Most of them down there, they travel in packs and they stay with their own. You know, they keep to the friends they had at school. Very private school. Very cliquey.'

I could see he was disappointed so I hurried on.

'Not to worry. I have a cunning plan. What we do is this, right? We get all this other stuff sorted out first. Then we get together with the guys, we see about lining you up. The concentration of evil geniuses we got in this house, I don't see how you can go wrong. We'll have a party. Maybe get you a blonde girly along. Give her a few drinky poos. Maybe some drugs, you know, hallucinogens. I don't think we want to place too heavy a burden on reality for this caper. And then we get Missy to tell her you're hung like a baby's arm with an apple in its fist.'

'That'll work?' he asked.

'If she's a normal red-blooded sort of gal it cannot fail. I guarantee you. One hunnert percent.'

'You think?'

'For sure,' I nodded.

But I was wrong. Who'd have thought?

Taylor was coming in as I was going out. He had a copy of the paper,

a take-away coffee and a chicken schnitzel sandwich from the Windmill. He looked like shit but I knew he couldn't have pulled a shift in the cab, the state he was in. Must have just been following his biorhythms. Sun comes up and his system demands a caffeine and grease hit.

'Hey there,' he croaked.

'Fuckin' right,' I said lethargically.

Taylor muttered a tired obscenity and levered himself down on the front step. The street was empty but you could feel it coming to life around you, people clanking about in kitchens, taking showers, trying not to think about the office. I asked Taylor what sort of coffee he'd bought.

'NATO standard,' he answered. (White and one. A hangover from his 'military' period. Missed by nobody, believe me.)

'You give me that coffee I could save a man's life with it,' I said.

He passed it up and I took a sip as he unwrapped the sandwich.

'Thanks, man,' I said as that beautiful caffeine rush burned through my circuits. I asked if he was supposed to have Austudy or dole or whatever coming through today. He shrugged.

'Who fuckin' knows, mate.'

I leaned against the door frame while he finished his breakfast. I've always been very easily distracted. Chances were I would have stood there all morning, probably dozed off, except Elroy's milk van pulled up and disgorged Leonard's remains onto the footpath.

'Jeez,' said Taylor. 'Look at that.'

Leonard, who normally sported a deathly pallor – on account of all the time he spent hunkered down in computer labs and video game parlours – looked even more anaemic than usual. As though someone had opened his jugular and drained off all but a few litres of his blood. Livid bite marks stood out on his neck, like hickies left by giant sci-fi sucker worms. He seemed a little disoriented but Elroy, who hopped out behind him, was full of energy.

'Man you shoulda heard these guys last night,' he crowed. Leonard just raised a shaky hand, staggered past us and disappeared into the house. Taylor and I stared in bewilderment.

'What were you doing with them?' I asked, not really wanting to know.

'Brainthrust and I had some chores,' said Elroy, indicating something back over his shoulder with a toss of his hand. I walked out on to the footpath as he continued, 'I said I'd give them a lift to Sativa's place if she'd let me crash on the floor after my concert. Didn't want to risk driving all the way back here with the cops out.'

I yawned and looked around for whatever he'd meant by 'chores'.

'Check out Pauline,' he said.

I glanced up to the billboard at the end of the street. The demonic eyes still glowered down on me but now I could see that late last night Elroy and Leonard had spray-painted an answer to the question of why Australians should support her.

BECAUSE SHE'S A GODDAMN
COCK-SUCKING WORSHIPPER, THAT'S WHY!

'Was Sativa with you guys when you did that?' I said.

'Oh yeah.'

'And Leonard did the graffiti?'

'Yup.'

I sighed. 'And I'll bet she thought that was too cool for words.'

'Man,' he shook his head. 'I thought she was going to climb up there and fuck him before he could even shake up the can.'

Taylor hopped up and moved out onto the street for a better view. 'Jeez. What happened then?' he asked

'She offered her honour, he honoured her offer and all night long it was on her and off her,' laughed Elroy. 'The beast with two backs. It was pounding and bumping around that apartment all night. I could

hear it all without even having to put my ear to the door. Kind of odd though. She'd stop screeching every now and then. Give him instructions, you know, like, "Don't put it there, put it here, like this," and then pow! Brainthrust, he must take orders well 'cos she'd always go off again. Never heard anything like it. 'Cept maybe those epileptic chicks I went out with. Oh boy, remember them? Wow! Once you been down that road . . .'

Taylor finished his schnitzel sandwich and belched enormously, cutting him off. 'Well, she was a weird chick anyway,' he said. 'All that stuff she went on with.'

'Yeah,' I scoffed.

'I don't even like art chicks,' said Taylor.

'No,' I agreed. 'I went out with an art chick once. Man, what a Valley of Darkness that was. About a million poetry nights and gallery openings, all full of these tossers wearing black polo neck sweaters in the middle of summer and using made-up words like "horrality" and "interfuse" and "discourse". Fifteen minutes into one of those things all I'd want to do is run a key along the sides of their Renaults, poke holes in the wine bladders and send all of their stupid torn jeans out to be repaired.'

'Yeah,' said Taylor. 'We don't need that.'

'No,' said Elroy. 'That's why you chased Leonard's babe around with your fly down and your pud in your hand all night.'

Taylor bounced his wadded-up sandwich wrapper off Elroy's head and said he wanted a cone to get the day underway. They meandered off into the house to see if they could scrape up the fixings from last night's mull bowl leftovers. I pushed off into the morning and tried to convince myself that I was better off not having done the wild thing all night with a spooky underage sexual vampire. Trudging up the hill to the train station I told myself I agreed with Taylor. I didn't like artistic types much. Matter of fact, I told myself, I hated them. Hated them from the tops of their hilarious black berets to the tips of their absurdly pointy boots. The ancient Greeks had the right idea. They were known for putting street mimes to the sword and slipping hemlock into the cheese dip at bad poetry festivals. The ancient Greeks also invented a primitive form of napalm and conquered lots of people. I think the ancient Greeks really had their shit together.

Mulling this over, I hopped a packed commuter train from Taringa to Toowong. Just one stop. After alighting I lurked within a pod of worker drones and squeezed through the exit gate without having to show a ticket, which I didn't actually have. Traffic was already snarled and angry in the knot of intersecting streets outside Toowong Village, this giant retail and office centre which sits atop the train station and which I always think looks a lot more like a neo-brutalist sculpture of Nazi gun emplacements on the coast of Fortress Europe than a shopping village.

I hurried past all the cafés which had sprouted so mysteriously the last few years, all these overpriced yuppie coffee troughs, all charging around three bucks for a milky flat white (which only dumb non-discerning yuppies would be rich enough or, you know, dumb enough to pay). The clipping service provided coffee and donuts. So I hustled on, keen to get in for a big hit of sugar and stim but also because the office was the best place I knew to suss out a few things on the Jordan front.

We operated out of an older asbestos-era office block just down the street from the Village. It wasn't nearly as much fun there since the Decoy had split. Getting two anarchist bosses in a row would have been a bit of an ask. But at least Tony, the old journo who took his place, was a terrible boozer, which was almost as good. As long as you went to the Royal Exchange and got plastered with him every couple of weeks he could be almost as cool as the Decoy. We even had an informal roster of sorts, divvying up Royal escort duties among

126 **THURSDAY**

the office proles. My last session with Tony, a fortnight earlier, I'd broken the thirty scotch barrier and vomited into my backpack, a performance which guaranteed me a berth in his good books for the duration.

'Morning Johnno!' he bellowed as I entered the office. 'Heard you were dead.'

'That was some other guy,' I said. 'Got any donuts?'

'Donuts we have, and coffee, and a pile of old fish wrap for your prompt attention.'

'Outstanding,' I grunted, heading through to the kitchen. One good thing about Tony, after thirty years of drinking powdered crap out of plastic newsroom cups he didn't stint on the coffee budget. I think our well-stocked kitchen was what he had instead of superannuation. Enough fresh coffee, hi-tar cigarettes, donuts and schooners of Mt Binger Riesling and he wouldn't have to worry about providing for his old age.

I grabbed my breakfast and settled in at one of the big reading room tables to work through a stack of *Sydney Morning Herald*s, just myself and some bitter Eng Lit post-grad there at that time of the day. 'Hey, Marty,' I said, 'what's going down.'

'Just my self esteem,' he replied quietly and that was pretty much it for office banter with Marty. Fine by me. I wanted to clear my backlog and get onto my own research. I flew through the paper mountain, marking off the usual catalogue of lies and disasters, thankful that I wasn't responsible for cutting, scanning and filing this dreck. I remember the Decoy once telling me a story about some guy the cops picked up and beat to death with the Yellow Pages. They threw him into a dumpster and told the coroner he was just some old derro who'd crawled in there and been 'overcome by poisonous newsprint fumes' after a ton of Courier Mails were dumped in on top of him. I'd laughed, but sometimes I could almost believe it. As I sat there flagging hundreds of stories, my fingers turning black and my head pounding,

I could easy believe there was something malignant seeping up from the pages. Something I was drawing inside me with each breath, rubbing into the folds of my skin as I massaged the back of my neck. A sort of psychic Agent Orange. What did it mean to be immersed in this every day? I read somewhere that you're as responsible for everything you see as for everything you do, the problem being that often you don't know what you're seeing until years later, and even then a lot of it never penetrates, it's just frozen in your eyeballs.

That's why I liked to slip in a random, confounding fragment of data every now and then. Let the computers deal with a different sort of virus, a rogue meme in the system to act as a defence against the horrors grand and banal which our scanners sucked up and saved to laser disk every single day. After two hours of reading about economic cretinism, racial backlash, toxic waste spills, poison meat, serial killers, pedophiles, corruption and Super League I figured it was time for a circuit breaker. I thought about giving my little red tick of relevance to some pointless celebrity puff piece, or perhaps to the wild flatulence of a right wing shockmeister. (Reading the column in front of me I noted with a barren smile of satisfaction that some champion of the overdog had taken up his cudgels on behalf of Japanese whaling interests again.) But after fetching another coffee and a Scotch finger biscuit I settled on an AAP wire piece out of Frankfurt, where Ernst Gerber, a dog trainer from Wuppertal, had told reporters he would not be having Lucky the guide dog put down, even though he had been directly implicated in the deaths of all four previous owners. I dunked my biscuit with relish while reading about Gerber telling a press conference that Lucky was basically 'a damn good guide dog' who just needed to brush-up on some basic skills. He admitted that Lucky had led his first owner in front of a bus, and the second off the end of a pier. He pushed number three off a railway platform and under the wheels of the Cologne–Frankfurt express. He walked number four into

heavy traffic before abandoning him and running away to safety. 'But, apart from epileptic fits, he has a lovely temperament,' said Ernst. They asked him if he intended to tell the next owner about Lucky's history but Gerber demurred, saying, 'No. It would make them nervous, and would make Lucky nervous. And when Lucky gets nervous he's liable to do something silly.'

Oh yeah. Lucky was the one, I decided. They could cross reference him with transport systems and services for the disabled. I wondered what sort of dog he was. The report didn't say. A Labrador I hoped. A big black lab with wet happy eyes, a vacant grin and absolutely no sense of responsibility. He'd fit right in at York Street. The T-Bird could take him on road runs, as long as he was careful. He could eat our leftovers, ride around in Elroy's milk van, fetch the ball in corridor cricket and act as a chick magnet. I've noticed that chicks will talk to guys with a good-looking dog.

I entertained myself with these idle thoughts for a few minutes until Bill the geek came in. Bill was another reader, a young conservative with a fondness for powder blue body shirts and listening to Beatles cassettes while he worked. He and Marty the resentful post-grad had said about four words to each other in six months. Something like 'Fuck off and die' as best I recall.

'Hey, Bill,' I said, sliding past him on my way to the computer room. He nodded vaguely, but whether at me or in time to 'Eleanor Rigby' I couldn't say. My hangover was clearing and I didn't want to stay around while Bill and Marty did their cold war thing. Besides I still had a mission.

'Just running a file trace,' I said to Tony as I passed his office. Engrossed in the sports pages he grunted in reply. In the data library I folded myself into one of those ugly, uncomfortable ergonomic chairs you kneel in to hurt your back, and used a pen to remove a tea towel from the keyboard. There were tea towels everywhere in this room.

They were an industrial obscurity, some gain hard won by the Union even though nobody knew why. In the days before ergonomic chairs they'd been draped over our backrests. Now they seemed to fuck like tribbles and had increased their numbers to plague level. I'd once thought them useful for wiping down the computer screens but during last winter's flu epidemic I'd noticed Tony using them as conveniently disposable hankies and after that I never touched another one again.

We used a Netscape interface to handle the story files. There were hundreds of thousands of articles in the system and the company hit its clients up for five bucks each time one popped out in a search. There was also a fifty dollar service fee to be paid before we'd even click on a mouse. If I'd had to pay for my session that Thursday it would have eaten up most of my next pay cheque. I keyed in all of Jordan's names and aliases that I knew of, but feeding stuff like 'Chandler' and 'Bennett' into a database like ours just brought up thousands of garbage links. I sat back and thought about refining the search. In between sucking down gobbets of raw meat Sativa had mentioned something about Jordan getting busted for passing bad cheques. I tried a couple of variations of his names with 'fraud squad' as a matched search term but without luck. I tried matching him to 'cheque,' 'bank' and 'fraud' on their own. Once again no result. However, when I linked Bennett to 'Magistrates Court' . . . bingo! In among the tabloid fodder of dozens of crime reports I found two accounts of a Stephen Bennett. Spelt 'ph' not 'v.' First up an appearance for 'obtaining a benefit by deception', and second, a week later, for car theft and drug possession. The D.P.P. had declined to pursue either case, entering something called a *nolle prosequi*. I wasn't sure what that meant, we hadn't covered it in the three weeks of Law lectures I'd endured, but it sounded kind of sneaky. I made a note and headed back down the corridor to Tony's room.

'Hey, Tone, what's a n-o-l-l-e p-r-o-s-e-q-u-i,' I asked, reading off my note.

He looked up from his desk and rubbed his bloodshot eyes. 'It's where the cops or the state decide they're not going to pursue a legal action,' he said.

'Why would they do that?'

'Well, it depends,' he mused, leaning back from his desk for a big stretch. 'If the defendant's a property developer in Sydney it's probably because they brown-bagged the right minister. Up here it's more likely that they're performing a bit of state-sponsored larceny for Johnny Hopper.'

'Sorry?' I said, a bit lost.

'All sorts of villains grabbed nollies and indemnities a while back,' he explained, his cold, cynical soul warming to the topic. 'It was supposed to be a big operation to break a car stealing ring but in the end it was just a big fuckin' mess. All these jokers stealing cars, fuckin' hundreds of them, from Joe Six-pack and Wendy Homemaker, and it's supposed to be this Sherlock Holmes mastermind scenario, you know, working back up the line to Mr Big, but it pans out in the end that the crims were nicking the motors and selling them on, trousering the dough and laughing all the way to the bank because there was no Mr Big behind it all, just the dopey buggers at police HQ.'

'Jeez,' I said. 'Guess I should read the papers more.'

Tony had a bit of a chuckle, a low rumbling sound which turned into an explosive series of coughs after a bit of badly abused lung tissue broke free and started rattling around. When he'd settled down and sucked in some fresh cigarette smoke he asked why I wanted to know. I quickly filled him in on the Jordan story. He lapped it up like a big plate of cream. Or bourbon. Tony loved any story which confirmed his theories of the darkness of the human heart.

'Coppers in your house, eh?' he said when I'd finished. 'That's no fuckin' good.'

'Well I wasn't there, but no, you don't want people of that ilk around.'

'Sounds to me like this fudge packer's sold them a story. I'll bet they've pinged him on something, drugs probably, and he's given 'em all blowies and a fairytale about plugging them into his supplier. I always say, Johnno, the best minds of a generation do not go into the Force.'

'What can we do about it?' I asked.

Tony gave it a few seconds thought before asking, 'What's this bloke's name. The botty bandit. Jordan?'

'Yeah, Jordan, sometimes Gerry, or Steve,' I said. 'Last name Chandler, or Brandon or Bennett.'

He jotted a few notes down on a pad. 'I still know a few blokes on the job who'll have a drink with me,' he said. 'I'll ask around. See if anyone knows about your mate.'

'If they do, tell them to stop calling around. He don't live with us no more.'

'No wuckin' furries,' he said. 'But you'll owe me a six pack.'

'Tony, you help us with this idiot you'll be the guest of honour at Cocktail Wednesdays for a year.'

I thanked him, promised to drop in for a couple of cleansing ales at the R.E. on Friday night and started to the computer room. I never made it. Hilda, our receptionist, interrupted me on the way. Said I had a call from an 'anxious-sounding chap'. I took it in the foyer. It was the Decoy with a garbled message from Stacey to get back A.S.A.P. I told him I'd be right over, hung up, grabbed my bag from the reading room and stuck my head into Tony's office again.

'Hey, Tone. Sorry, I gotta go. Trouble at the homestead.'

'Coppers?' he asked.

'No. Bulldozers.'

Before I saw the bulldozers I saw the red Mustang. Turning the corner into York Street a painful star burst of white light stabbed into my eyes, the sun's reflection caught on a brightly polished chrome fender. It was a big car. In the second that I stopped and squeezed my eyes shut against the tiny supernova, the car seemed to stretch for half the length of the street. I stood, blind, slightly dazed and dizzy, fearing a migraine from the intense flare which had just cooked my retina. But nothing happened, which was lucky, because I was due for one, what with all the stress and lack of sleep and artificial stimulants I'd been loading onto my system.

I breathed out, relieved. Opened my eyes and took in the scene I'd only barely caught before. A cluster of people on the footpath in front of the vacant house next door to our place. I immediately recognised Stacey, the Decoy and Missy. As I slowly walked towards the scene two other figures resolved themselves. That girl Jhelise from the Kremlin and . . .

(Oh no.)

Red Mesh Singlet Guy.

I paused momentarily. He must have blended in with the finish of the Mustang when I first saw him. But there was no mistaking him now. An awkward figure, all jutting angles and wild straw blond hair.

Hands going everywhere. Incoherent rage rendering his speech meaningless.

Three strangers flinched away from his assault. The people from the Mustang, I gathered. Two men and one woman, all of them dressed in frightening suits, their eyes hidden behind sunglasses. I had started to walk again, down the hill towards the animated gathering, when another two men joined it from the yard of the empty place. They weren't wearing suits. They were real workers, in King Gees, blue singlets, footy socks and battered boots. I noticed the 'bulldozer' then. Not a bulldozer but a crane of some sort beside the house, a futuristic thing on caterpillar tracks with a black bubble cabin and a long mechanical arm. The workmen emerged from behind it, ambled over to the little group and lightly pushed Red Mesh Singlet Guy in the chest. He staggered back a few inches and seemed about ready to explode but one of the men levelled a finger at him and everything went very still and quiet for a second, until the Singlet visibly deflated. I was only a few metres away by then, but nobody had noticed my approach, so tense was the stand-off.

'What's going on?' I asked, and everyone's heads jerked around in surprise.

'They want to knock our house down!' said Stace.

'But we live there,' I said, more to the suits than in reply to Stacey.

'Well, I'll file that under U for Useful,' said the woman sarcastically. She was a looker, in an evil superbitch sort of way; long, expensively styled jet black hair, strong features, a distractingly short skirt, and shoulder pads you could land a helicopter on. Fingers would have been a sticky mess around her.

'You on the lease next-door?' asked one of her partners, a maximum yuppie in a navy blue Zegna suit which seemed to come with its own air conditioning. It must have been over thirty degrees in the sun but he hadn't raised a single bead of sweat. Examining him closely

before I answered, I suddenly realised it was because he was wearing make-up. It threw me completely and I stumbled over my reply.

'Uh . . . yeah . . . I. Me and Stacey. We're on the lease.'

'Well maybe you should go home and read your lease,' said the woman. 'You're already four weeks behind on the rent and about to go to six.'

I felt everyone looking at me.

'Look, we're working on that,' I said. 'We had some trouble with a previous flatmate and I know that's not your problem or anything, but . . .'

She held up one hand, like a traffic cop. She spoke slowly and clearly, 'I don't care. Social Security contacted us. They say you've all been overclaiming and you will be cut off. There's no way you can get the money you owe us on time and frankly I don't care. We've been sitting on this property for three years waiting for the right time and that time has come.' She swept one arm in a short arc, taking in our house, next door and the place beyond that. 'We've just bought number three, we already own number five, and when you break your lease on Monday I'm afraid you'll have to go because we have plans approved to consolidate all three properties for a townhouse complex.'

'But our lease has months to run!' I objected.

'I just explained to you, you will be in breach of your lease when you fail to pay all the rent you owe come Monday. In fact I suspect you're already in breach because of the number of people you've sublet to. I'm sure if we did an inspection we'd find a whole college dorm in there. That was certainly the impression I got from Social Security.'

'You have to inform us in writing at least two weeks before any inspection,' said Stace quickly.

'And you have to do repairs,' said Missy. 'Which you never do. I fell through the bathroom floor last Christmas and you guys did nothing about it. We had to repair it ourselves.'

'Look, you don't seem to understand,' said the woman who was becoming quite heated. 'You've had a very good run in this place. We could have evicted you months ago but we let the lease run its course. But if you are so irresponsible that you cannot even pay the rent I don't see why we should have to put up with it. We are not a welfare agency, you know. We have our own responsibilities to meet.'

'Oh yeah, like destroying low-income housing stock,' said Jhelise.

'And your responsibilities to the World Bank fascists,' added Red Mesh Singlet Guy aggressively.

'Shut up, shithead,' warned one of the builders.

'Don't you threaten us,' spat Jhelise.

'People, people . . . please, let's all calm down,' said the third man, the one who had not spoken until then. He had a soft but strong voice, curly hair going a little grey, dry lips and a hint of stubble around his chin. When he removed his sunnies to rub his eyes I was startled by the brightness of his green-grey pupils. He smiled thinly, an expression which creased a small net of wrinkles at the corner of those striking eyes. 'I'm sure we can work this out without resort to ugliness,' he said. 'We don't want ugliness. Nobody does.'

'And who are you?' asked Stace defiantly.

'Icarus Investments,' he said, handing her a business card. 'We're putting up the capital for the project.'

Stacey passed the card to me, a small rectangle of rich creamy cardboard, a brilliant yellow sun with a tiny winged figure in a business suit flying across it.

'That's a cool card, Mr Icarus,' I said. 'And you're right. Nobody wants ugliness. But parking your wrecking ball there . . . well, it kind of nudges right up against ugly, don't you think?'

He showed me his open, honest palms. 'You have to understand,' he said mildly. 'My clients here, they own this land, it is theirs . . .'

'It is not! It's stolen land,' declared the Singlet.

136   THURSDAY

'What?' asked Icarus, briefly disoriented. 'Oh . . . Right. The aboriginal thing,' he said, catching on quickly. 'Well, for our purposes let's just say they have legal title. That means they can do what they want with it. And all they want to do is provide many more people with an opportunity to enjoy this very pleasant neighbourhood. Don't you see? It's a matter of quality. *In Sola Vista* will be a development of unparalleled quality. Serviced apartments. Cutting edge design. A gym and pool complex. Only the finest materials and craftsmanship. It will be less a building than a work of art. Almost a suburban cathedral if you will.'

'*In Sola Vista*?' I went, sceptically.

'I guess they're in sympathy with the South American struggle too,' Stace remarked dryly.

'That's fine for the people who can afford to live there, but what about us?' asked Missy. 'Where do we go?'

Mr Icarus made another soothing gesture with his hands. 'I've spoken to Brian and Debbie,' he said. 'They are willing to forgo the rent you owe them. Refund your bond in full and provide good references for your next landlords.'

From the look Brian and Debbie shot him I got the impression they'd spoken about nothing of the sort. But he continued in his urbane, polished way. 'I personally know of a number of exceptional two-bedroom units which are coming on line in the New Farm area,' he said. 'I'm sure you'd be much happier there. And in return for helping us expedite this development we'd be only too willing to help you get a look in. Think of the vibrancy of that environment. It's really going ahead. Cafés, book shops, nightclubs. So much more dynamic than here, you'd have to agree?'

'No we wouldn't,' said Stace. 'If we wanted to live in some fucking lumpen beau monde toy town we'd all move down to Balmain.'

'All right!' snapped Debbie. 'I've had enough of this. Monday

morning I will be on your doorstep with an eviction notice. I suggest you be packed and ready to go because I will have security guards with me and they are under no legal obligation to go lightly if they find trespassers on my property.'

'We'll see about that,' said Jhelise fiercely.

'You don't even live there, you stupid bint,' sputtered Brian, the make-up boy, in a fit of pique.

'Oh but I know how it is with you people,' she said. 'If you get your way, twelve months from now this whole street will be nothing but boxy apartments full of graphic designers and bulimic models.'

'You got that right, honey,' muttered Debbie through thin white lips. 'Come on, Icarus, Brian. We've wasted enough time with these losers.'

'Middle-class toxic swill!' cried Red Mesh Singlet Guy as they climbed into the Mustang. Brian gave us the finger and Debbie buried herself in some papers. We weren't even there for her anymore. Icarus looked pained as he keyed the ignition and pulled away. He shook his head at us reproachfully.

'Ha! Class warfare,' said the Singlet triumphantly. 'It always come down to this in the end.'

'What would you know about it, needle dick?' laughed one of the building workers.

'Fucking pooftahs,' said his mate, and they turned their backs on us too, sauntering back to their work site without another glance. The two lefties watched them sadly.

'False consciousness is a terrible thing,' said Jhelise.

'So when'd this happen,' I asked Stace.

'About an hour and a half back,' she said. 'They weren't even going to tell us. Just turn up with the bouncers on Monday. But the Decoy went out and fronted them.'

The Decoy shrugged.

'What a bitch,' said Missy, shaking her head. 'And that outfit. So try-hard first-season Melrose.'

'What are we going to do?' I asked, hot waves of lassitude abruptly breaking over me.

'I don't know,' said Stacey with genuine anguish.

'I do,' said Jhelise, staring narrowly at the empty house. 'Direct action.'

'Oh. Wacko,' said the Decoy, quietly, because he knew what she meant.

Early evening, but there was still some daylight outside. Most of the house were sitting around burping and licking stolen chicken bones clean. Our cash reserves were right down but Elroy and Taylor could always provide a feast by cruising a couple of KFC joints and simply filling a plastic bag with the paying customers' leftovers. Family tables were best, according to Elroy. Those kiddies always had eyes too big for their tummies and as long as he stuck to recovering fully intact chicken pieces it wasn't too gross. An early adolescent introduction to shoplifting had prepared him for the challenge of successful junk food scavenging but even so, to get enough to feed everyone he and Taylor had to hit at least four different outlets.

'This is a great selection tonight, Elroy,' I said as I plucked another breast from the pile. 'You've excelled yourself.'

'Just lucky,' he mumbled around a mouthful of wing. 'Got two tables of teenage girls. They never finish what they order and they always order up big time.'

'Yeah, we coulda snapped up a whole bunch of desserts from the same place,' added Taylor. 'But people were beginning to stare.'

'Then a manager came over.'

'What'd you do?' asked the Decoy, eyes wide.

'We told him we were building a Frankenchicken,' said Taylor.

Stacey snorted and wiped her hands on her jeans. 'Oh man, we really gotta get our shit together,' she said. 'It's bad enough having to eat this stuff when you actually pay for it.'

'Yeah,' said Missy. 'Why can't you steal something healthy next time. My face is gonna look like a pizza if I don't get some fruit and veggies soon.'

'Don't know what your problem is,' said Taylor. 'We got three of the four main food groups here. Wings, breasts, legs and nuggets.'

'Well it'll all be irrelevant by next week if we don't come up with some money,' sighed Stacey.

A few other sighs and resigned nods confirmed the sad truth of that statement. Quiet enveloped us for a few seconds, a couple of chicken wings being sucked skinless and a small gurgle from Taylor the only sounds. Everybody but Leonard and Gay Phil was there; Jabba and Elroy on the brown couch, the rest of us scattered about on bar stools or sitting with our backs against the walls. Brainthrust was home but still asleep, recovering from Sativa's onslaught. Gay Phil was missing in action. It was kind of a sad moment. Nobody wanted our house pulled down and replaced by a poxy apartment block with no warmth or comfort save that provided by electric heating and Swedish furniture.

'Fucking yuppies,' said Missy, breaking the reverie.

'Hate those yuppies,' I nodded.

'Yeah,' said the T-Bird somewhat redundantly.

'I thought they were all gone,' the Decoy pondered aloud.

'You don't get out enough,' I said. 'There are thousands of them out there. Go down to Riverside or the Heritage on a Friday night. Just don't put your fingers near their mouths while they're networking. You got swarms of them down there, management consultants, legal partners, forex traders. Acres of Armani and Hunt Club. Porsches and SAABs in the underground car park. Rolexes and twin sets everywhere, business cards flying around like ninja throwing stars.'

'You can hear the noise a mile off,' said Stacey. 'It's like ten thousand carnivore ebola chimps broke loose in the hold of a Panamanian tramp steamer and they're all frantically masturbating and shrieking and spitting, biting each other on the arse, clawing and climbing over each other.'

'What're we going to do?' asked Missy.

'Go to the meeting for starters, I guess,' said Stacey.

Elroy threw his last piece of chicken onto the rubbish pile and said he had plenty of ideas if only we'd vote on them. Stacey shook her head sternly. 'We are not setting up a phone sex line, or a dial-a-stripper agency, or ripping off Church poor boxes or searching through bins out the back of restaurants for credit card slips. You hear me? Never.'

'What about you, Jabba?' I ventured. 'Surely there must be an analogous sitcom predicament we could draw inspiration from. What about when Richie and Ralph Malph lost all their money to card sharks. What happened then. How did they get out of it?'

'I think the Fonz went a-a-a-a-a-a-y-y-y-y-y,' shrugged Jabba.

A knock at the front door, Jhelise and the Kremlin guys, brought these gloomy proceedings to an end.

'Time to go,' said Stacey, pushing herself up off the floor. Everyone followed, wiping themselves off on jeans and tee shirts, the T-Bird picking up the KFC scraps and taking them out to the kitchen.

Our numbers combined with the lefties added at least fifteen or sixteen to the group milling about on the corner about sixty metres down the slope from our front door. Half the street seemed to be there, all clutching the flyers we had run up on the printer in Leonard's room earlier that day. (He'd just buried his head further under a pile of old clothes when we told him we had to use his computer.) They seemed to be waiting for us to arrive, which was reasonable given that it was our flyer which had called this street meeting to discuss 'the giant construction development' due to commence on Monday. We really bore down on these people's hip pocket nerves. They were very much your decent, rate-paying Mainstream Australia types (or 'middle class toxic swill' as the Singlet would have it) and they were horrified by the prospect of their charming little renovated workers cottages being devalued by a monstrous, inappropriate horror like *In Sola Vista*. (In reality we had no idea what final shape the development would take but we couldn't allow that sort of detail to get in the way of a good scare campaign. The presence of the 'bulldozer' probably helped too, giving verifiable form to their fears of uncontrolled property devaluation.)

'Thank God for NIMBYs,' Stacey muttered to me as we drew up to the corner, smiling and being right neighbourly about everything. There were a few minutes of restrained befuddlement as thirty or forty people who would normally have had little to do with each beyond a nod or a wave on the way to the shops were forced into close contact. Stacey was chatting with some lonely school teacher I vaguely recognised when I saw Red Mesh Singlet Guy produce a megaphone from a satchel. I hastily elbowed her and nodded at the Singlet. She made a little panic face, looked at me and suddenly shouted, 'If I could have everybody's attention . . . can everyone hear me?' They could, they all replied.

'Hang on,' I said loudly. 'Pass that megaphone over.'

I grabbed the thing and twisted it politely but firmly out of the Singlet's grasp. He glowered at me but to little avail and I passed the loud-hailer to Stace. It coughed white noise and static when she thumbed a switch and Jhelise had to show her how to use it. She tried again and this time her voice crackled out with much greater power. 'Hello . . . Oh cool,' she said at about a hundred decibels, drawing laughter from the crowd, which had undoubtedly been her intent.

'Thanks so much for coming on such short notice,' she said. 'I'm

sorry we couldn't put too much detail in the flyer you got under your doors today but we only found out about this development a few hours ago ourselves. My name is Stace Robinson and I rent number seven, that place just over there, the one you've probably all been wishing for years would be pulled down so those terrible boys would be out of the neighbourhood at last . . .'

More laughter.

' Well, sadly, it looks like we might be going but I don't think anyone is going to like what comes after us '

'No!' cried a couple of the lefties, well versed in street meeting theatrics.

'We had a meeting with the developers today,' Stace continued. 'And they put their case – pretty menacingly, I must say – for just smashing down the three old Queenslanders over there and replacing them with a gated, four story, virtual hotel . . .'

A ripple of murmurs and worried chatter broke out at that. Stace let it run for a second before keying the speaker again.

'They are talking about jamming a lot of extra residents into this street, a lot extra traffic and noise. They want to build a sports annex with tennis courts and a pool for exclusive use by their own residents and guests. I haven't seen any plans but I don't think we need have illusions about the sort of architecture we're talking about here. This will not be a sensitive, low density development. It will not pay heed to the existing streetscape or to the work that so many of you have done in restoring your houses and gardens to their original states. It will be a giant brick and concrete monstrosity with palm trees and flood-lights and one of those obnoxious garbage bin corrals you can smell from across the street . . .'

More troubled murmurs.

'. . . of course it's in my interests to oppose this development. I like living in this street and I don't want to leave just yet. But if we do

have to leave and these developers get their way the beauty of this neighbourhood, its quiet, green environment, will be destroyed. They will ruin the very thing they're trying to cash in on. And it won't stop here,' she warned, working herself into a rhythm, starting to punch her words out like a boxer who knows he's on top in the ninth, putting more and more into each successive blow. 'You've all seen the sorts of developments which are chewing up the ridge line along Swann Road,' she said.

'Yeah!' bellowed Elroy.

'Right on, sister!' shouted Taylor.

'You've seen dozens of old homes demolished and replaced by pink concrete villages. You've woken up to find things known for generations just didn't exist anymore. Unthought at the stroke of a pen on a cheque. You've seen the land itself changed. Hills, bluffs, gullies, little remnant forests all disappeared and the landscape bludgeoned into submission. Well, the machines have arrived on your doorstep now. They're going to tear down that beautiful old house at number five, then our place at number seven, and the little cottage at number three, and the question you have to ask yourselves is when will it end. Where will they stop? At your front gate? You really believe that? Ask yourselves. Do you feel that lucky?'

'Hell no!' cried the Decoy, his thick Canadian accent startling a few people in the twilight.

'No way,' shouted the teacher Stace had been talking to a few minutes earlier. He'd been watching her, rapt, the whole time she'd been speaking.

'Do you want to speak Jerry?' asked Stace. He declined at first, shaking his head and waving away the loud-hailer but Stacey pressed it on him. He coughed nervously into the mouthpiece.

'I . . . uh, I think Stace is right,' he said. Everybody from our house and all of the Kremlin guys gave him a big cheer and the applause

spread through the group. 'I think we should set up some sort of group, a resident's action group to oppose this development.'

The applause was spontaneous then, and not just confined to our little fifth column of trouble makers. Things moved quickly. Jerry spoke for a minute, followed by some old guy who looked like a living fossil from some TV gardening program but whose rhetoric turned out to be the most inflammatory of all. Old dude was a genuine firebrand, fought for the International Brigade in the Spanish Civil War or something. He really whipped the other pensioners up and got the lefties all hot and bothered, clenching their fists and punching the air and all that.

'Hot damn,' I whispered to the Decoy. 'Looks like we got us a convoy!'

'Or a wrinklie riot.'

The meeting devolved into swirling pools and eddies of conversation, most of them circling around Stace, Jerry and Civil War guy. A vote was taken to organise an emergency street festival for Saturday, stalls, barbecues and outdoor music to protest the rapacious encroachment of *In Sola Vista*. Neighbours of ten years standing met for the first time. I spoke to maybe eight or nine people. Sowing the seeds as I went.

'Yeah, these guys, these developers are infamous,' I told them. 'I'm an investigative reporter you know. I've dealt with them before . . . In Coffs Harbour. They built a humungous multi-storey resort down there. Never opened its doors . . . They built their condos in the middle of a fairway . . . yeah, those Japanese they're just golf crazy, but the condos are empty. I mean who wants to live in the flight path of a thousand little white missiles, right? . . . And a species of killer ant has taken over the greens too. You drive through there, you'd mistake their anthills for thousands of little doggy turds.'

'Japanese you say?'

'Oh yeah. And you know what that means . . . Yakuza money. White slavery. That sort of thing. But you didn't hear it from me.'

'Fast work on that megaphone,' said the Decoy an hour later, as we walked the short distance home in the darkness and warmth of the early summer's evening.

'Man, I could see where that was going,' I mouthed quietly, checking nobody from the Kremlin had insinuated themselves into our group. 'I've seen it a million times. Your poor old punters get some citizens' group together to protest a sewerage plant or an airport and before you know it they got five rival communist factions punching it out in their living room for control of The Struggle.'

Taylor asked if anybody wanted a brew. Beer would have been better but we were tapped for funds. I said yes. So did Stacey, the Decoy and Elroy. Missy phoned some boy and asked him to take her out for dinner and drinks.

'Not that mouth-breathing motherfucker I hope,' said Stacey.

'As if.'

I put my arm around Stace as she sat down next to me on the front step. 'What you have to ask yourself is, Do I feel lucky?' I said through gritted teeth, Dirty Harry style. 'Well do you? Punk?'

'Just giving the punters what they want,' she smiled.

'And just in time,' said the Decoy. 'That guy always looks like he's about to get very weird. And he was very intense this afternoon, with those yuppies.'

'That's Red Mesh Singlet Guy,' I said. 'Intense is his natural state of being.'

'Oh my God!' went Stace abruptly. 'Decoy! Up at their place the other day . . . when I went up to see Jhelise about our forms, they had three of those big cockroach suits just like you had . . . from the Melbourne protest.'

The Decoy became very still, like a little forest animal who's just heard the first dread footfall of the hunter outside their lair. 'Oh,' he said.

'Do you think that's how the dykes found out about you living here?' she asked.

We watched him turn the possibility over, Stacey and I from the step, Elroy from where he was leaned up against the fence and the T-Bird from under the lemon tree outside Stace's bedroom window, which he was using to do some kind of painful looking pull-up exercise.

'I didn't think about it at the time,' he said. 'Maybe. But I doubt it. I think they would have said something otherwise. The Left are never shy or backwards about going somebody they think has sold them out. I don't know. I thought Jesse, the girl I went down with . . . I just figured she told them, but you're right. She doesn't know I'm here. She only knows my address down the coast.' He gave it some more thought before concluding the karate dykes must have called in first at the tree house. 'Maybe I should give them a call,' he mused. Maybe, we agreed. Poor old Naked Tree Guy and Roger the Hippy were no match for a posse of angry, hog-riding vengeance bitches with nunchucks and a thirst for violence.

The Left really does tend to attract more than its fair share of lunatics, I thought, as the Decoy went to make a phone call. Hard core mad keen teen believers with surrogate Sixties nostalgia who hadn't even been born when Elvis kicked off, class warrior poets with corduroy jackets and axes in their eyes, academic guerrilla wannabes and unrealised missionaries for mass homicide. (*Sorry, JB,* one said to me, *nothing personal, but come the revolution, you're going up against the fucking wall.*) Like the Decoy, I had a bit of history with the Brisbane Left. You just couldn't avoid them if you were going to live in the city and have any sort of a life beyond work, television and blind, unthinking consumption. Like the goths, they would not die.

But they had fractured into a multitude of pathologically meaningless splinter sects. It could become very difficult following who was splitting or amalgamating with whom, although actually telling who was whom was relatively easy once you knew the signs. The International Socialists for instance, the lumbering brontosaurus of revolutionary politics, they preferred to get around in really dreary English working-class dress of work boots, grey pants and white shirts, whilst Resistance were generally tricked out like New Age goths, swampies or grungers. There was also Black Flag, this violent anarchist group of two or three people who had this great little flag with a cannon on it. You never saw them too much because they'd invariably turn up at a demo, throw the switch to vaudeville and charge headlong into the police lines, getting themselves arrested and beaten half to death before anyone else had even had time to unfurl their banners. ('A glorious day, comrade!') There was the Socialist Labour League and Socialist Action, whose flag had an angry-looking cat shooting some sort of cannon, as I recall, but I can't remember whether they hated each other because they had split or were trying to get into bed and amalgamate.

Another half dozen or more micro movements probably made up the full list but you get the point. A lot of very extreme people into some very muscular politics. Not surprising then that a lot of fruit loops came out when you shook up the pack. Dudes like Red Mesh Singlet Guy. I'd met him a long time before he even became The Singlet. I had this friend, Pete, who lived in a Resistance house in Brunswick Street for a while. Every time I'd visit him there'd be these melodramatically dissolute youths draped over the furniture worrying about the world. It'd be 'the fuckin' system this' and 'the fuckin' system that' and 'I wish the fucking system would hurry up with my rent subsidy.' But this one guy in particular stood out. Had a combat fetish. Used to wear army camouflage all the time, never a good sign. He mostly kept to himself which was okay because he was always sharpening his machete

under the house. Or sitting out the front rattling his collection of shopping bags at passers-by. He was a very natural example of how conspiracy theories, the bread and butter of extreme politics, spill over into individual madness. Because whenever a rental ute would pass the house, Plastic Bag Man, as we knew him, would run out and throw stones at it. Rental utes were part of the Conspiracy, something involving government agents and the Ford motor company. But of course being a Left house, nobody would ever front this guy and go, 'Knock it off, you fucking nutter.' So he just got weirder and weirder, until the red mesh singlets came out and he was no longer Plastic Bag Man, but Red Mesh Singlet Guy, our eventual neighbour and unwanted ally in the fight against *In Sola Vista.*

There was a fairly well-worn path you see, through those inner city suburbs, through a raft of green/left/aware/enlightened/radical share houses which passed their members on to one another like an underground railway in the Second World War. That's why the Decoy had freaked a little at news of Stacey's cockroach suit discovery. Because word gets around. If the fat karate dykes really did blame him for their warship protest peeling off the freeway in a big orange ball of flame, or even for putting his stickies into the cookie jar then word could boomerang back up north pretty quickly. Even faster if a couple of the true believers in the Kremlin had road tripped it down south for the warship protest – which now seemed not only possible but probable.

The Decoy's face, when he emerged from the house behind Taylor, seemed to indicate something along those lines might have happened. I took a mug of tea off the tray Taylor offered around, took a sip and said to the Decoy, 'So what's the story?' Everybody waited on his reply.

'Well,' he said, a little bit elsewhere. 'They have been to my place down the coast and Roger . . . well, he told them where I was . . . but only after they roughed him up a bit. He pulled one of his knives on them. I told you about them . . . he keeps them under his pillow? I think all the auto-urine therapy might have done him some good after all though. Apparently they didn't want to beat on him too much . . . because it'd mean actually touching him . . . and I guess, you know, when he rubs that four-day-old piss all over himself I can understand their not wanting to get all up close and personal.'

'Well don't you worry,' Stacey assured him. 'You're here with us now. No karate dyke's gonna lay a finger on you and you won't have to have a pee-pee bath to be sure either.'

'Thanks,' he said. 'I guess.'

Jabba appeared at the door, a perplexed look on his face.

'Anyone seen the toaster?' he asked. 'I can't find it.'

'You want to make some toast?' asked the T-Bird, in a rare conversational sortie.

Jabba stared at him for a second, 'No. Why would you think that, Ron?'

'You check in the cupboards?' asked Stace.

He said he had. And under the sink and out on the back patio. The toaster was *el disapparro*. It was a mystery. More importantly, it was all we had to entertain ourselves with at that point so everybody got involved in the search, checking behind the bar, under the sofa, in the bathroom, all the obvious places. After a few minutes Taylor came out of the kitchen with an even more bewildered look than Jabba's.

'The clock's gone,' he informed us.

'The what?' went Stacey.

'The clock, you know, Felix the Cat, his eyes go tick tock . . .' Taylor made the oscillatory movement with his own eyes, using his index fingers for emphasis.

'Yeah, I know,' said Stacey, comprehension dawning on her first of all. She dashed into her room and about three seconds later, after the sound of a perfunctory search, she cursed once, loudly. It seemed to

hit everyone then. Nobody had to say anything, it was as though we beamed each other the knowledge.

Jordan.

'He got my cameras,' Stace ground out through clenched teeth as she rejoined us. 'I can't believe he came back and took my cameras.'

Nobody knew what to say. Stacey's cameras were holy objects. They were her ticket to New York, her talisman, the proof that she wasn't just dicking about like the rest of us. She'd paid for those cameras with hundreds of hours of braindead service sector employment; punching check-outs, waitressing, and running a one hour photo booth in the Village. Jordan sneaking in and taking them while we were just down the street, was close to the final outrage. We didn't know how she'd react.

Jabba crab-scuttled sideways along the couch as Stace plopped down, shaking her head and letting her face fall into her hands. We stood about, shifting nervously on our feet, folding and unfolding our arms. Missy chewed her lip and placed a hand on Stacey's shoulder.

'We'll get them back, Stace,' I said.

She shook her head, just a small movement.

'Jeez,' said Elroy quietly, 'It's like deja vu all over again.'

I was about to wake up Leonard, ask him if he'd noticed anything, when Gay Phil's heavy tread sounded in the hallway.

'What's up?' he asked as he came around the corner and took in his sister's distress.

'Jordan came back,' said Elroy. 'Took Stacey's cameras and our Felix the Cat clock.'

'And the toaster,' added Jabba.

'Oh really,' said Phil. 'Well, let's go get them back.'

We all stared at him and he smiled without any warmth.

'I know where he lives now.'

Five minutes later we were in the car, chewing up bitumen. Besides Jordan's address, Gay Phil had a new five dollar haircut and a tattoo, a battleship on a bicep with the words 'In the Navy' standing out boldly underneath.

'So, a big night, Phil?' I ventured.

'Well, let's just say I know some sailor boys who'll be eating their dinners off the mantelpiece for a while,' he said.

Taylor threw the cab into a sharp corner, sending Phil and Stacey sprawling over the back seat and causing me to knock my head on the window.

'Sorry about that,' he said.

'Don't worry about it,' said Stacey, who'd been very quiet up to that point.

I craned around to peer through the rear window in time to see Elroy's milk van take the same corner at the same speed with a squeal of distressed tires. I wondered how T-Bird was faring in the back. I could just make out the Decoy's silhouette in the passenger seat. seemed to be gripping the roof for support. It was only twenty minutes since Jabba had gone looking for the toaster. Despite Stacey's bleak demeanour I thought we might be in with a chance to cap this fucker off.

Phil had come across more than the pride of the Fleet last night. He'd gone to some bender joint which Sativa said Jordan sometimes worked at; a pitch black hole at the bottom of a precipitous staircase. A pit, literally. A sunken dance floor dropped at least three metres

through a series of terraces with a U.V. strip around the bar as the only light source so you couldn't make out any familiar faces, just impressions of a huge, pulsing crowd and the screams of stoned gay people occasionally falling into the dance pit to be trampled to death. A very flash joint according to Phil, everyone who was someone in the little goldfish bowl of Brisbane grooverdom turned up there for free drinks. He quickly got to talking with some of the guys behind the bar. I don't know what it is with those guys, they all seem to know each other, like they went to the same boarding school or something. Anyway, Missy says Phil's always very popular in these places. Stands out as a bit of rough trade. So before too long he's knocking back the free Stollies and hearing all about the weird little bi-guy who worked the bar for a few weeks. Always rubbing his nips and short-changing the customers. Used to hang out after his shift with the lead singer from some awful death metal band. Thick as thieves they were, an appropriate analogy as it turned out. The singer went down for breaking into someone's home, stoned off his nut, insisting that he was to meet 'Billy' there, demanding a drink and the directions to the bathroom. The frightened suburbanite had complied with the request then phoned the cops from another room. When they arrived to intervene they had no trouble picking the guy up because he'd passed out on the bathroom floor with a spike in his arm and a big ring of milk around his mouth.

It had to be the guy from the Dream Fuckers, said Phil. The one who'd given Missy so much trouble. That's right, the boys at the bar said. The Dream Fuckers. A thoroughly vile person. Jordan, who seemed to have called himself Brendan at the bar, eventually went down with his friend, trying to evade a drug bust in an underground car park. They might have gotten away too had they not been slowed down by trying to roll a spare tyre containing about three kilos of marijuana along with them. Jordan disappeared from the bar for a while after that, the boys said. After cross checking our data, Phil and I decided this had to be in the period just before he bailed on Sativa and darkened our doorstep – about the time Tony figured he would have been cutting a deal with the cops, if that's in fact what he had done.

Who could tell anymore with this guy?

Taylor climbed onto Enoggera Terrace at Red Hill and put the pedal to the metal. 'Almost there,' he said as we sped along under a dark canopy of trees. Elroy's headlights flashed a few times, warning Taylor, if he didn't already know, that a sharp corner was coming up. We slowed marginally and he handbrake-turned into Arthur Terrace. The wide, quiet road sloped down and curved off into the darkness a few hundred metres ahead.

'Got the number, Phil?' asked Taylor.

'No, but it doesn't matter. They said it was just near the first big bend and you couldn't miss it. A block of flats without a second storey.'

'What? You mean a one-storey block of flats?'

No, explained Phil. The fagbar boys had been quite emphatic about it. Jordan was staying in these weird units that had only been half-finished. The top floor apartments had no roof. Just walls with empty spaces for door and windows. Been like that for years they said. And they were right, I realised, as soon as I saw them. You simply couldn't miss the eerie way in which the stars winked through the windows. As we pulled over, the milk van came charging up behind us, Wagner thundering into the night as the doors rumbled back to disgorge Elroy, the Decoy and the T-Bird.

'What are you doing?' Stace shouted over the din, climbing out and trotting back to meet them.

'Ride of the Valeries,' said Elroy. 'You know, to strike fear into our enemies and scatter them before us.'

She leaned into the cabin and killed the tape. Night sounds suddenly closed in around us, dogs barking across the valley, the screech of

fruitbats, a slight breeze and television. Stace shook her head, 'We could have just phoned ahead and told him we were on our way.'

'Why would we do that?' Elroy mused to himself.

'Okay,' said Stacey as we gathered around her. 'Let's try get him out without alarming the other neighbours. Elroy, no biffing unless I say it's cool, okay?'

'All right,' he agreed, a little disappointed.

'Okay. Wait here.'

Stace, the least suspicious-looking, pushed through the front gate and disappeared for a few minutes. We loitered on the footpath and tried not to look too much like a bunch of short-tempered North Korean frogmen washed up in the wrong place and looking for trouble.

'I was in North Korea once,' said the Decoy when I voiced this observation.

Get outta here, goes Gay Phil, who's been just about everywhere but P'yongyang. No, says the Decoy, it's true and he tells us about this tour he went on for progressive students and unionists about fifteen years earlier. It was organised by the Stalinist Party of Australia a hard left splinter from the old C.P.A.

'They were just straight-out yobbos,' said the Decoy, leaning against the milk van. 'They'd decided the way to win the hearts of the workers was to be the most disgusting yobbos they could be. They were really fucking crazy. They were the ones I went to North Korea with. By mistake.'

He hadn't actually intended to go North Korea, he told us. Their left wing travel agent had promised them a heavily subsidised trip to Cuba to check out Comrade Fidel's Caribbean paradise. Decoy didn't give a shit about that. He'd just figured to get a cheap trip, buy up a few crates of genuine Cuban cigars and sell them at vastly inflated prices through a network of friends in the US where they were a prohibited import. He paid his money and laid his plans on this basis. Turning up at the airport, however, linking up with this motley crew of student peace activists and S.P.A. nutters, he was horrified to discover their itinerary had changed two days earlier. Cuba was out. North Korea and the International Workers Festival was in. He was trapped. The S.P.A. guys, building union yahoos mostly, just sat around their disintegrating ferro-concrete hotel sucking Sapporo Dry all the time.

Every country in the old-world order had a delegation there and being a festival there was a very heavy, serious cultural component. 'That was the only saving grace,' said the Decoy as we waited for Stace to return. 'All the delegations were called on to give these cultural performances. You'd get this fantastic reggae music from the Caribbean delegates. The Koreans put on this excellent theatre, the Europeans too. All outstanding gear. But then the Australian delegation was called upon, in front of these thousands of delegates, to give their cultural contribution, and no kidding, this happened, a lot of shitfaced drunken S.P.A. yobs staggered on to the stage and sang, 'Singin' in the Rain'. You could see the North Koreans had no fucking idea. They thought it might possibly be a comedy act . . .'

Stace came back to find the six of us sprawled all over the footpath, doubled over with laughter. Her own mood had lifted during her brief absence but not as much as ours. She said she'd found the place and we might want to settle down and start acting our age. Suitably told off we followed her back, single file, Elroy sniggering all the way. 'Singin' in the rain . . . heh heh heh.' Phil asked if she'd had any trouble locating Jordan's place. Stace said no, we'd see why soon.

We did. Forming up outside the door of the last unit in the block we could see through a crack in the curtains. Inside, the kitchen was lit up and every surface which wasn't covered in electrical goods, most still in their store wrapping, was covered by teddy bears. The clincher though, was our Felix the Cat clock, his eyes still tick-tock-ticking away, propped up on the fridge. Bingo, said Elroy. Jordan must have

been here recently. Stace had already tried knocking and ringing the bell. No answer. For good measure she'd hammered on the neighbour's door too. Nobody there either.

'What now?' asked Taylor.

'I could . . . you know, probably kick it down,' offered the T-Bird.

'No need,' said Elroy, fishing a pair of thin rubber gloves from his pocket. He slipped them on and began to work on the sliding window, pushing it in and up, trying to manoeuvre the simple hook device which secured the window off its latch.

'Hmmm,' went Gay Phil. 'I'm guessing this isn't your first time in Boys' Town is it, little Jim Bob?'

'Not the first, no,' grunted Elroy as the window slid to one side. It seemed like a very loud noise. 'Give us a boost,' he whispered. The T-Bird bent down to lift Elroy through the opening.

He scrambled through, dropped into the darkness. The T-Bird turned around and said in his natural deadpan, 'Elroy has entered the building.'

A few seconds later the front door opened.

'Keep your hands in your pockets unless you're touching something we're going to take with us,' advised Elroy. 'It's really important.'

'Not a problem,' said Stace. 'Since we're probably taking every-thing.'

'And if anyone asks anything, try to think of yourself as a repo man rather than a burglar,' Elroy added.

'And again,' said Stacey. 'Lets go.'

We fanned out through the hot, stuffy two-bedroom unit, a peculiar sight with our hands all jammed into our jeans. Like wary tourists who'd stumbled into Aladdin's Cave, assuming Aladdin had been a nipple-rubbing amphetamine abuser with a passion for girls' clothing, credit card fraud and accumulating completely random collections of electrical goods and homewares. Boxes of plain white Ikea crockery were stacked up next to piles of throw rugs and shrink-wrapped compact discs. Three different types of stereo system fought for floor space with half a dozen novelty telephones. And wrapping everywhere; cardboard, bubble wrap, clear plastic and coloured paper. Traces of our pilfered belongings gradually began to emerge from the clutter and jumble. Missy's black vinyl pants. My micro-cassette recorder, which I hadn't even realised was missing. The egg whip and our long-lost soda shooter — we decided he could keep them. I was sorting through a pile of waffle irons and Sunbeam juicers when Taylor called us through to one of the bedrooms.

'Is that Jabba's teev?' the Decoy asked as I squeezed into the room. It was a home entertainment goods showcase to put a small department store to shame. Televisions, stereos, faxes, all sorts of things I didn't even recognise.

Taylor whistled. 'Nah, that's a Bang and Olufsen. Same size screen but really expensive; that car loan he scammed might just have paid for it . . . if Steve Bennett knows how to drive a hard bargain.'

'It'll do,' said Stace with a hard edge to her voice. She still hadn't found her camera bag. 'Taylor. Elroy. You clear a path through the lounge room. Phil? T-Bird? You think you can lift this thing? It looks like it weighs a ton.'

The T-Bird laughed, a short flat exhalation of breath, 'Ha!' He positioned himself in front of the massive TV, bent his knees, spread his arms wide, kept his back straight, took a deep breath, and lifted the thing as easily as if it was made of balsa wood and chewing gum.

'I'll get the remote,' said Phil.

Taylor and Elroy preceded them, clearing a path by simply kicking aside anything that got in their way. The T-Bird wrestled our new teev down the pathway into the back of Elroy's van. Then the procession began. Over the next thirty minutes we cleaned the place out. When there was no more room in the van Elroy and the T-Bird climbed in

and belted up. We said we'd follow in a few minutes. Elroy, surfing a crime-inspired natural high, was laughing like a loon as he fired the motor and started shouting a pre-flight check list at the T-Bird.

'Fuel!' roars Elroy.

'Huh,' goes the T-Bird.

'Fuel!'

'Excuse me?'

'You're supposed to say "check", dumb arse!'

'What?'

'Check! You say "check" when I say fuel.'

'Oh . . . right. Check.'

'Flaps!'

'Huh?'

Wagner's *Ride of the Valeries* was pounding from the milk van before it had lumbered more than fifty metres back up the hill. Taylor and Phil packed a few more things into the boot of the taxi; a Nintendo power glove with total immersion heads-up display, a six pack of Bundy 'n' Coke from the fridge, Felix the Clock. And all of Jordan's toilet paper. We actually had plenty at home but Taylor was just being spiteful. That was another thing about Jordan, you'd buy a jumbo family pack of Sorbent but after he came out of the bathroom there'd only be one and a half rolls left. We never did figure out what the little prick did with all that paper.

Stace and I went back to the flat for one last look around. I took it all in, searching for anything really worth having. There were plenty of unopened boxes lying around amongst the drifts of bubble wrap and packing paper. And over in the far corner, a testament to the bower bird mentality of a true speed freak, a couple of industrial-sized gas tanks, like giant nitrous bulbs, on a trolley.

'You want the laughing gas?' I asked.

Stacey peered at the tanks. 'Nah. It's just compressed air,' she said.

'Elroy was playing with it before. He thought it was helium, wanted to fill the place with it and give us all cartoon voices.' We hadn't laid eyes on her camera bag and as we stood in the kitchen surrounded by Jordan's extended family of stuffed animals she sighed and said, 'He's probably pawned 'em and shot the lot up his arm already.'

'We'll get those cameras back, Stace,' I promised. 'Even if we have to break his fingers. Hell, even if we do get them back we'll still break his fingers.'

'It's okay,' she smiled wearily, pushing one hand through her hair. 'It's not like they have a lot of sentimental value. The videos we got will pay for a new body and all of the lenses I need. Probably some I don't need too.'

'And you figure you can move a bunch of red hot gear like that, do you?'

'Well, I'm thinking Elroy might be able to help out there.' She opened the fridge, had a poke around and pulled out a bottle of Evian. She examined it dubiously, took the cap off and sniffed. 'Guess it's safe.' She took a pull on the bottle and passed it over, 'It's just that, you know . . . I worked so fucking hard . . .'

'I know.'

I took another swig before passing the bottle back to Stacey. She suddenly remembered Elroy's warning about fingerprints and wiped the fridge down with her tee shirt. I was dog tired by then, almost nauseous with it. My eyes felt like somebody had ground big grains of salt and pepper into them. We stood in silence for a a few seconds, wondering whether there might be anything else to do. Wondering what the consequences of what we'd already done might be. I glanced over at Stace. She looked ready for a long hot bath and a glass of milk, lost in her own thoughts, until she became aware of my gaze. We stared at each other in the raw light of the exposed bulb which hung

over Jordan's kitchen table. I didn't know what to say or if she was even waiting for me to say anything. Finally, I spoke.

'We could wait here for him. Phil and me. Some of the guys. They'd be up for it.'

Stace continued to look at me, a level questioning study. But then her gaze softened and eventually she smiled and shook her head, but at what I'm not sure.

'I love you guys,' she said. 'All of you.'

Late night. Thursday. The living room is crowded. Everyone bathed in the soft phosphorescence of a giant TV screen, our new Bang and Olufsen. Nothing on really, nothing worth watching at that time of night, just telemarketing shows, the noxious weeds of insomniac TV. They're evil, these shows. Like those fork-tongued space aliens from Invasion of the Body snatchers. They take the outward form of normality, but underneath? Giant carnivorous space lizards.

Leonard is awake at last. He is the most alert of us, given the fifteen hours of daylight sack time he has racked up today. We have given him a very hard time about Sativa. Jabba is happy. A man reborn. He drove everyone crazy demonstrating his new TV's split screen function. *Homicide* on the huge, principal cinema scope screen, *Duckman* in a smaller box up in the left hand corner. Obsessively and compulsively flipping between them until Stacey goes 'Enough!' and takes the remote off him. He is still happy though. We have agreed the Bang and Olufsen is morally his, to replace the Sony which Jordan stole.

Elroy is shaking the empty cans of Bundy 'n' Coke, looking for one last drink. Taylor poured them into a huge jug with a tray full of ice cubes so that everyone could have at least one tumbler. Taylor himself is sitting in the most ridiculous chair I have ever seen. An opaque orange inflatable P.V.C. lounge chair. We didn't even know we'd taken it until we unpacked the milk van. It took Taylor forty minutes to pump it up properly and now he will not leave it for fear that Elroy or Leonard will jump in and take his place and refuse to budge until the heat death of the universe.

The Danny Bonaduce Show comes on. It puts itself about as the 'hottest talk show on TV', hosted by 'our favourite member of the Partridge Family'. 'He's the one who made a small name for himself coming out of rehab a few years back,' Jabba informs us. 'Vomiting the details of his slide into the celebrity abyss all over real talkback shows.'

'It's like David Letterman of the Living Dead,' says Missy. After all the excitement she piked on her date. Volunteered to hang at the house with Leonard in case we got ripped off again while we were out ripping off Jordan. She is right about The Danny Bonaduce Show. All of the talk show elements are there, it's just they're shambling about with bits of rotting flesh hanging off them. The live audience – an evolutionary step down from the showbiz offal and fad diet victims bussed in for Sally Jesse – they fill a little less than a quarter of the available seats and the camera guys have to be careful not to linger on the fringes too long lest eagle-eyed viewers such as us notice the hundreds of empty chairs climbing away into darkness. Bonaduce's house band, The Critics, are a bunch of no-talent, overweight air guitar specialists. The set looks like it has been stolen from a second-hand furniture barn on the outskirts of Tijuana and everybody's favourite Partridge presents like a red-headed pit bull terrier with a small amount of brain damage. We all think this is great, our definition of must-see-teev, and we sit there viciously ranking it out, Beavis-and-Butthead-style, for the next thirty minutes.

Gay Phil appears with popcorn. So much popcorn it's like a bean bag full of the stuff has split open and spewed its hot contents all over the kitchen. There had been three new popcorn makers at Jordan's flat. This is no longer the case. The T-Bird has made milkshakes so we

drink milkshakes, eat fistfuls of salty, buttered popcorn and watch television until the wee hours. I drift off once or twice, always waking to another telemarketing pitch. If they could only see us at Telemall headquarters, I think drowsily. We are not really an identifiable demographic. Just a cheaply accessed lumpen market of shift workers, nightclubbers, students and the sloughed-off, broken bits of audience drifting down from prime time. Half of us don't know if there will be any money in our bank accounts when we check tomorrow.

I fall asleep on the brown couch and someone, Stacey or Missy I think, drapes a blanket over me.

ACHY BREAKY STACEY

The money did not turn up. Taylor was the first to find out. Up early for a schnitzel and coffee he pulled over to an autobank but sadly all the cash machine had for him was four cruel words: Insufficient funds for withdrawal. And with that he knew, we all knew, the hammer was down, the deal was done. At that very moment half a dozen Sandmen were shuffling towards us through the darkness at the edge of town. If we were going to hold back the yuppies, the Sandmen and *In Sola Vista*, if we were going to survive being caught in the threshing machine of Jordan's chaotic, drug-addled villainy, we would have to come up with a cunning plan, very quickly. And probably something better than sticking our thumbs in our arses and going '*A-a-a-a-a-y-y-y-y-y.*' But even Elroy and I, the putative wage earners of the house, were of little immediate use. Neither of us would be paid for a week.

Breakfast, which became a formal house meeting, was attended by all and conducted with the strained atmosphere of a first strike briefing for B-52 pilots during the Cuban missile crisis. Everyone had gathered at the kitchen table, in the middle of which sat three large, wooden salad bowls piled high with stale popcorn. Stacey, Taylor, Missy, Jabba and Elroy were sitting at the table, occasionally dipping into the bowls. Leonard and I perched on bar stools carried through from the living room. Gay Phil and the T-Bird leaned up against the wall, arms folded, a pair of circus strongmen who'd lost their way. The Decoy was on powdered coffee duty. Stacey had a block of foolscap in front of her on which she'd written a list of our newly acquired assets which could be sold quickly through Elroy's underworld network of shady milk van guys. After taking out Jabba's new television, and the stuff Stacey would need to recoup her losses, Elroy figured on a maximum fire sale return of roughly twelve hundred dollars. About two hundred short of what we needed. And of course, all dependent on his being able to move the stuff in time.

Even then, as Stace pointed out, our position wasn't that simple. Say we raised enough money to pay the rent and bills on Monday, the yuppies would be back again and again. And if the house had been consigned to welfare Siberia we'd soon find ourselves turfed out anyway, unless we wanted to go into stolen goods warehousing on a permanent basis. Stacey passed around the D.S.S. forms, placing two completed examples on the table.

'Jhelise did them with generic answers designed to ruffle as few feathers as possible,' she informed everyone. 'Study them closely. Get them done this morning. Jhelise and I will check them. We have to make sure we don't contradict each other or set any alarm bells ringing. I'll take them in today, try to find out why we've been cut off. Chances are they're going to claim overpayment on something.'

'What about Jordan?' asked Leonard, giving voice to our collective hopelessness. 'He's the one caused all this fuckin' trouble. He's the one who's been ripping them off . . . mostly. Even if we get a hundred percent on this,' he said holding up the form, 'what difference is it gonna make with all the scams he's run out of here?'

Stacey smiled but without much warmth. 'His turn'll come,' she said.

The Decoy placed a tray crammed with coffee mugs down on the table. We had no sugar left, but he'd found half a jar of fossilised honey somewhere. I leaned through the tangle of arms to grab my trusty black Life's a Bitch – Then You Die cup. I couldn't come at the idea of any more fucking popcorn though, and I was seriously tossing up a call to the office to ask Tony to set aside a donut for me. When everybody had settled back with their coffee Stacey continued.

'Even getting ourselves clear with the D.S.S. we're still going to come up short of some rent and bill money,' she said. 'Everyone's going to have to get out there today and hustle. I don't care where you get it from – No, Elroy, that is not a licence to go pull a heist on a church poor box – but we're going to need at least another three hundred, four to be safe. About fifty bucks each.'

'What, me too?' asked Elroy.

Stacey shook her head. 'No, you're going to have enough on your plate selling that fucking blow-up armchair.'

'Hey!' goes Taylor.

'Sorry, Taylor,' said Stacey, taking a sip of her coffee. 'But these are the dark fucking days of our lives. At least you didn't have too long to get attached to it.'

'But what if I pull a double shift in the cab, chip in some extra?' he pleaded. 'Can I keep the chair then?'

Stacey pushed her lips out, considering the offer. 'It'll cost you an extra fifty,' she said.

'Done deal!'

Elroy leaned over to him, 'Yeah, you really screwed her on that one buddy,' he said, as we fell into a long, unstructured discussion of how we might go about raising our contributions. This was largely a frantic exercise in compiling lists of people we might be able to hit up for loans; Fingers in my case, assuming he hadn't already bombed at Jupiters; family for most everyone else, except for Missy who didn't get on with her loony Muslim oldies, Gay Phil who didn't get on with his loony Christian ones, and the Decoy who'd had no idea of his oldies' exact location since they went into hiding at the start of the first

Reagan presidency. Nobody felt they had enough time to go out and find work, because of the exams which were looming, which of course nobody but the T-Bird and Stacey had done any work for.

I linked up with Stacey about four hours later in the food court at the Village. We'd agreed to meet for lunch after her recon mission to the D.S.S. Tony had lent me a redback and I'd used it to buy a foot-long hot dog and a Coke. I'd also left an urgent message at Jupiters Casino for Fingers to call me before he lost all his money. Like Taylor, I planned on pulling a double shift which meant I wouldn't get home until late in the evening. I was already tired and a bit depressed and not looking forward to spending another ten hours marking off newspapers. It was odd when I got in these moods. I'd seek out the worst possible food; processed lumps of starch and animal by-products, artificially flavoured, nuked to death in the microwave, and devoid of any taste except that provided by the magic of industrial chemistry. Pushing that garbage inside me was a curiously comforting experience, a balancing of my internal and external worlds. Stacey was different. Under stress, she tended to revert to a nuts and berries diet. I didn't notice her arrive because of the lunch time food court rush but when a big tumbler of apple and celery juice and some wholesome-looking salad roll thing plonked down on my table I didn't have to look up to know it was her.

'Wanna bite?' she said, holding out her roll.

'What is it . . . a felafel? Hmmm, maybe not.'

'Staying loyal to your tube of reconstituted cows lips on a bun, eh?'

'That's my plan.'

She folded herself into the cramped space defined by the fixed base and swivelling seat of the food court's moulded metal furniture. She looked like she was dressed for a job interview, a skirt and blouse, a light touch of lipstick. She had photocopies of everyone's interrogation forms in an imitation leather satchel which she kept close at hand. The originals were now in the System.

'So how'd we go with the Gestapo?' I asked. 'Think you can get my boys out of this mess, Colonel Hogan?'

Stacey made a throwaway gesture. A Zen movement. I have met defeat and accepted it. 'They said they understood that we weren't responsible for Jordan's bullshit,' she said. 'It'll take a while to straighten out exactly what he was responsible for. But I dropped a stack of paper on them this morning. All the loan repayment books that turned up at our place, a contact number for that mortgage guy who turned up, and the lease papers from his Red Hill place.'

'Where'd you get them?' I asked, a little surprised.

'They were in the kitchen drawer, third one down, same place everyone puts their lease papers. It should be enough for their fraud guys to go on with.'

'Busy morning.'

She smiled a frayed, jaded smile.

'I also rang the Church of Scientology. I said I'd loved reading Dianetics and it'd really helped me out but I needed more help because my brother had a huge win at the casino and he was spending it all on drugs. I begged them to help him, demanded they intervene, then I gave them Jordan's address. Pleaded with them to get over there and get on his case because he had a lot of money to spend and he was very vulnerable.'

'Bet that gave them a woody.'

'Made me feel like a natural woman.'

'So . . . problemo?'

She took a nibble of her felafel roll before speaking. 'D.S.S. say we've been overpaid two and a half grand in rent assistance. Their data cross-matching thingy with Austudy showed everybody in the house claiming the maximum rate, which turns out to be four times more than our actual rent. We're cut off until they get it back and if we don't pay they'll prosecute.'

'Can't you appeal?'

'Yeah, but there's not much point. They're right. We owe them.'

We sat quietly for a minute, as the lunchtime crowd surged around us. Stacey looked about, taking in the teeming parade, the fast food stands, the cafés and shoppers, the roving packs of school kids high on late November freedom, other uni students trapped in assessment panic, the lines of their faces drawn too long and hard, consumers and commuters pushing the envelope of their fifty minutes of freedom, pushing themselves to get everything done before they had to yoke themselves to the machine again. I experienced a familiar weird inverted feeling, like I'd been turned inside out, exposed to the world but the world either didn't see or didn't care. Faces rushed past, morphed together, became one metafeature, without age, sex or race, a disembodied face you'd feel floating towards you on the street but you'd know that whoever had been there was gone and this was only hollow space moving around in their shape. I often felt like this in shopping malls. By contrast, Stacey sitting so close, chewing on a plastic straw, seemed hyper-real and contemplative. I forgot myself, staring at a few soft strands of hair which fell across her face. She caught me looking.

'Don't you get tired of this?' she asked.

'The food court? I guess so. But I can't stay away. I'm a weak man, Stacey. A weak and worthless man.'

She didn't smile as I expected. Just gave me this keen, appraising look which left me unprotected and deeply uncomfortable, as though she'd scanned me, cracked my codes and read all my deepest, pass-protected files between drawing one breath and the next.

'That's not what I'm talking about,' she said. 'I mean, never knowing where your next dollar is coming from, whether there's even going to be a next dollar . . . I mean, you've been hanging out on campus for seven years now, but you haven't even been enrolled for the last three. You haven't written anything in ages except for that dumb review of the Donut King two months ago. You're going to get old one day, John. You're going to wake up old in a house full of dumb kids, living on fish fingers and home brew and social security.'

She said her piece, waited and watched. She knew she'd taken my balance. But her own footing wasn't too certain either. I examined her, peered clandestinely past the lipstick and power babe facade, and noticed for the first time a line in the shoulders, an aspect of the eye, something not seen before. It was not Stace as I knew her; the confident, two-fisted Stace; the Stace of battles past and inward greatness; Stace who wrenched the arrow from our slain fridge and in turn slew the rotating, spitted pig; Stace who faced down a pack of angry vengeance dykes; John Irving's Stace, generous and sympathetic, always there, putting our broken pieces back together; Shakespeare's Stace, stiffening the sinews, summoning up the blood, disguising fair nature with hard-favoured rage.

I glanced at the satchel full of government forms, wondered whether her moment of clarity was in there. That moment you suddenly wonder why you're standing there in your underwear and torn tee shirt, the unattended TV set blaring Bonaduce all over you, eight bucks to your name in the whole world. Why you're not in New York yet, working for *Vanity Fair*, flying business class and eating out in restaurants where they never ask if you want fries with that.

'Well I don't know, Stace,' I answered carefully. 'I mean, it can be a drag, but we all chose to be here.'

'Oh God, John,' she groaned. 'Don't try it on with me. How long have we been friends? How many years now? So don't. Save the existentialist voodoo for Sativa. I'm sure she'd swallow it without gagging. We chose to be here. Can't you see that makes it worse?'

For some reason, unrelated to my foot-long hot dog, my heart started to pound, slow and heavy. 'I'm sorry,' I said. 'I don't know where you want to take this.'

She took a long drink of fruit juice, staring at the condensation rings left on the table top. The food court was really packed by then, the crowd's roar bouncing off hard tile and glass, forcing me to lean in to hear her.

'Look, I don't know how long I'm going to be hanging around,' she confided quietly. 'I don't know how committed I am to running a dormitory for indigent frat boys and wandering gay surfers, family or not.'

'You're gonna move out?' I said, suddenly scared.

'I don't know yet. I don't know what I'm going to do. About anything.'

'What about your degree? You gotta hang around to finish that.'

'I don't know if there's much point,' she shrugged. 'I'm going thousands of dollars deeper into the hole with every semester. I don't want to have to take baby photos or shoot fucking weddings for five years just to pay off an Arts degree. I mean, Jesus! Get real. I want to take news photos. And I'm beginning to think I don't actually need a double major in journalism for that. I might be better off just getting a new rig and shooting the hell out of things. I think I'm good enough. All I have to do is go places nobody else will go and get the shots nobody else can get. That has to be worth something. I'm sure your bingeing boss Tony would say the same.'

'I'm sure he would,' I reluctantly agreed. 'And you're right. You are

good enough. Coupla years you'll be able to walk in anywhere, you won't need a degree, you'll have the shots.'

'You don't seem very happy about it,' she said gently. 'Would you prefer that I hang around looking after you boys until you've grown up enough to leave the nest under your own power?'

'Well . . . if not you, who? I mean, don't you worry about them? Don't you worry about Elroy? He doesn't think. He doesn't plan ahead. Jeez, he broke his nose once because he tripped over and didn't want to spill his beer by putting his hands out to break his fall. Or the T-Bird? Sure he can bench press a washing machine but he still doesn't know how to have sex yet. Or the Decoy . . .'

'Or you?' she smiled.

'Hey, babe, I know how to have sex. Believe you me. I know a lot of . . . great sex stuff.'

'You told me the last time you had sex you used veterinary anaesthetic instead of lubricating gel. You said you put your dick to sleep for three days.'

'It was dark.'

A couple of women in black took the other chairs at our table, lit up cigarettes and began to bitch about their morning. There were no free tables anywhere now. At least a dozen schoolgirls were piled all over each other on the four seater next to us. I was starting to feel uncomfortable, trapped. Stacey could be intensely forensic when the mood took her.

'John,' she asked, oblivious to the smoking women and giggling schoolies, 'Why don't you have a girlfriend?'

I almost stopped breathing, but managed to get out, 'What, are you canvassing for Phil or something?'

She fixed me with her X-ray vision again. I was sure those women had their radar on full power too. They had stopped running down their morning in retail hell and I could feel their sensors locking on me.

'You can't tell me you're still mourning that girl. Sarah?' said Stace. 'That stripper?'

'She was an exotic dancer, my censorious friend.'

'God,' she marvelled. 'She was a pin-eyed loser. But you guys . . . you just will not let them go will you? It's like the ones who hurt you go under this beautiful crystal dome and you put them out on exhibit for the whole world to walk past and have a look. The Girl Who Broke My Heart.'

'Well what d'you expect?' I protested. 'She did me wrong that girl, put a real hurting on me.'

The women in black were almost openly eavesdropping now. I expected one of them to butt in with her unique perspective at any moment.

'Look,' I said. 'This isn't the place. And I got to get back to work. Do you want to have a drink later?'

I got another long, evaluative look.

'I've got to do some study,' she said at last. 'I've got to dig up fifty bucks from somewhere and put my head in at a meeting for the street fair, make sure the lefties don't hijack it and try to take the whole street to Libya or something. If I can get it all done by six I'll give you a call at the office.'

'Okay.'

She finished her drink, wrapped the remains of her roll, smiled a little sadly, and left. I finished my cold foot-long hot dog and flat Coke. As I was getting up to leave one of the women in black, the younger one, shook her head at me.

'You weren't supposed to let her go like that,' she said.

I stared at her for a second.

'I don't know what you're talking about,' I said.

*

You have to understand. I did not think of Stacey and myself as having this tortured, unrequited will-they-won't-they thing going. By now you probably think I had it real bad for her. Well pat yourself on the back, Professor, but last I heard, they don't hand out Nobel prizes for the tragically fucking obvious. It didn't matter for shit anyway. You see, if you pressed in on her, Stacey could be just like Juliana Hatfield's sister; she had a wall around her nobody could climb. Sometimes, like the night before at Jordan's flat, that distance she kept between herself and the world might collapse down to three microns of warm space, but the gap was still there and even her best friend wouldn't be game to reach across it.

Stace was aware of it too. She'd use it against you if you crossed her or anyone she cared about. I'm sure if those vengeance dykes had actually raised a finger against the Decoy she'd have been all over them like a cheap suit with her fucking jujitsu and secret ninja stuff. Wouldn't have held back at all. That distance, that basic lack of a connection would have let her do it. I don't know why she was that way, whether it was something in her history, her family perhaps. I knew she had a fairly disastrous relationship record, as bad as any of us, even Missy. But whether that was a cause or a symptom of this deep emotional autonomy I don't know.

I do know that Stacey had been good to me after I broke up with Sarah. Man, that was a real Medusa scenario. You know, head full of snakes? When I'd met Sarah I thought she was Irish. She had these green eyes. And piles of dark, wine coloured hair. She wore cheese-cloth and hung rubber bats from her bedroom ceiling. Kept a skull with a candle melted on top by her bed. We first kissed under a dinner table while Guns 'n' Roses screamed out of a really old, cheap Sanyo and two of our friends tried to sleep off three helpings of her awesome lasagne. She was beautiful. After we went to bed for the first time we had cheese and pepper on crackers for breakfast. She taught me how

to drink tequila slammers and move safely through a room where everyone has recently risen from the Dead. I cooked chicken curries, used her toothbrush and made a bucket bong from which we pulled a thousand cones.

It finished badly, on a Christmas Eve, with her curled at the foot of a rumpled bed. It was explosively hot in that dark little bedroom and she lay just in front of me, close enough to reach out and touch had I felt like it – which I didn't. She had drawn herself up into a tight foetal ball and I stood back with my hands in my pockets, regarding her long, shuddering sobs and cries with a sort of wry, empowered detachment. I loved her desperately, you understand, and it felt good to see her this way. At that moment I was enjoying the fiction of breaking up with her. Really, quietly, getting off on it even though she'd actually put a bullet into our relationship a long time beforehand. A weak little thing, it had twitched and thrashed about on the floor and neither of us had had the sense to finish it off until now. I had intended to say my piece and escape with some dignity after a few minutes. But as she curled into a bundle of woe at the foot of the bed something weird happened. I started to feel good. I was behaving badly and really enjoying it. I felt stronger than I had in weeks. Such a change from the timid spectre I had presented to the world. Such a pity nobody was there to see it and applaud.

I've forgotten exactly what I said to affect her so badly. It was probably just a lot of bitter bullshit anyway. Hardly worth repeating. I do remember being taken with the sound of the word 'dog' though. I've got a really vivid, digital standard memory of lashing her with the phrase 'you treated me like a dog' maybe six or seven times over the course of an hour. Really whipped into her with it. And she cringed and curled up, just like a mutt on the end a chain. It's really kind of shameful to think about it now.

Anyway, the sense of power which filled my bones at the foot of the

bed turned cold and sour about fifteen minutes after I pimp-rolled out the front door. Although I'd been the one to lash out and end the horror of our entanglement it didn't make me the power player of the relationship. I never had been. I'd only walked about five blocks before the chain mail fist of God closed around my insides, ripped everything out, and dropped it in a big steaming pile by the side of the road.

'Uh oh,' I thought. 'This don't look good.'

It was Stacey, and to a lesser extent Missy, who tied me up and stopped me crawling back to Sarah over my own trail of glistening, decanted entrails. They insisted on taking me out to the Sheraton for Christmas drinks. Refused to back up their sister at all. Said she was an emotional cannibal, a succubus. I didn't need the likes of her. I had my friends and my house.

'The thing I like about our house,' said Missy between picking at a bowl of nuts and sipping her vodka martini, 'is that it's kind of a sanctuary from the dating world. I remembering coming around for the interview and it was amazing, you boys were all playing this computer game. Leonard had built it. He had all these terminals set up in the living room and you were all playing on them, all the way through the interview. God what a bunch of nerds! It was freaky, you know these twenty-three year olds, twenty-five year olds, like kids tapping away, and getting really angry when they lost. Throwing tantrums and storming out of the house. That was really, really funny. But the thing that got me, that made me want to live there, was that the only question you asked me was whether I liked Star Trek and did I mind if you sat up playing videos all night. It was the first place I went where nobody made a deal about my being "Asian."'

She made the little inverted comma sign with her fingers. 'Not one question. It was like nobody even noticed. Sometimes you need that. A place you can hang without worrying about stuff. Just kick back with

a packet of Tim Tams and a bottle of vodka and lick your wounds. They will heal, JB. They always do.'

I played disconsolately with my swizzle stick. 'Care to strip your sleeves and show your scars?' A half smile, half shrug. 'I'll bet mine are bigger.'

'Doubt it,' said Stace.

'Yeah, you're drinking with the bust-up queens here,' Missy smiled.

'My first bad break-up,' said Stace, 'my first ever break-up in fact, I thought I was going to die. I curled into a mewling ball of heartache in the corner of my bedroom and wouldn't come out for three days.'

'Yeah,' I went, a flicker of interest. 'How'd that turn out?'

'I survived,' she smiled. 'And now of course I can see that no way was he ever worth three days of mewling time.'

'Floppy boy?' asked Missy.

'The floppiest.'

I shook my head uncertainly, 'You're speaking in babe code again.'

'For a long time,' explained Stacey, 'a time now known as The Great Confusion, "boys" were back in prominence. Not your hardy, cricket-playing, Turkish trench attacking lads of yesteryear. More your foppish, pigeon-toed refugees from the Romantic novels of the early nineteenth century.'

'Floppy boys,' nodded Missy. 'Every thinking girl's first boyfriend. Depressive introspection, Morrisey and holding hands.'

'I knew so many strange boys who just didn't make any sense that I sometimes felt like a beacon for the bemused and deranged, or maybe like a queen bee whose little workers have flipped out on some freak-ish electrical storm tangent,' said Stace. 'Painfully shy, sensitive, shoe-gazing floppy-haired boys, boys so far into undergrad feminism they'd actually read The Beauty Myth and were all ashamed to have a cock. My first boyfriend was very much in this tradition. The smallest tiffs were thrown into surrealist relief by making up rituals in which he dumped enormous amounts of chocolate/flowers/love poems on my bed while I was at school. Well, I didn't want him snooping in my teen angst theme room. I hadn't actually realised we were fighting and I was deeply disoriented. I ate the chocolate but it all got a little tetchy, there were tears before bed time and I turfed him out, only to have him return with a New Look.

'He appeared at my door festooned with an interesting assortment of punkish clothes – you know, a tentative rip here and there, a zip or two, a disappointing lack of muscle, chest hair or clear skin. The whole outfit rendered even more ridiculous by the fact that all the clothes were brand new from K-Mart. His hair was a daunting shade of comatose black and was short. So short that both of us finally realised what a peculiar looking guy he really was. A tendency to lower his face and hide behind all that now-missing hair had made observation difficult before. I had an oestrogen epiphany. I could not go out with him anymore. It was the right thing. But breaking up didn't make me feel any better. Far fucking from it. I felt desolate and abandoned, like I'd been split open and had my soul wrenched out for me to behold; but when I opened my eyes all I could see was one of those small, desiccated heaps of bones and teeth and scraps of mammoth pelt they found in that super dry valley in Antarctica, you know, that place where it hasn't rained for about ten thousand years – and it's biologically pure, there's nothing living there, not even a single bacterium because every rock and grain of sand has been nuked clean by radiation pouring in through the ozone hole. I'm looking at this and I think this is me, my soul, all I am and all I'll ever be.' Stace raised her glass. 'So it was good evening ladies and gentlemen and welcome to the corner of my bedroom.'

We clinked glasses, Stacey's champagne cocktail, my Scotch and Missy's martini.

'To madness, desolation and despair,' we toasted.

An orbiting hotel goon seemed to take note of the subversive ambience surrounding our gathering. You could tell he wasn't sure about us. We didn't fit in with the small knots of suits and shoulder pads, although we'd all worn shoes and I'd dug a shirt with a collar out of my laundry bag for this foray uptown. We still gave off an incongruous vibe, a definite tonal shift down from the jet-setting trader trash who grazed on the complimentary peanuts, zapped digital business cards at each other's P.D.A.s and worked their jaw bones like atomic-powered wind-up novelty chattering teeth. Missy, so much more at home in this setting than either Stacey or myself, picked up on the bar manager's bad attitude, cocked an eyebrow at him, crossed her brown, finely muscled legs and brought him to heel.

'We need refills on all of these,' she said, smiling, leaning forward and setting her phasers to stun. He nodded and scuttled away to do her bidding.

'Men,' she scoffed. 'You know after my first boyfriend, Thomas, I was the biggest man hater in the world. I was sure I'd never have another boyfriend as long as I lived.'

Stacey laughed and I smiled at this piece of sophistry.

'True,' she said. 'Everyone thought he was sweet and gentle but he lost his temper and beat on me all the time.'

'Missy, that's terrible,' gasped Stace.

'You know where he lives now?' I said. 'You want we should get the boys together?'

She shrugged. 'Don't worry about it. No point. You'll see. After he hit me he'd come over all sorry and guilty and promise never to do it again and I stupidly believed him. I was sort of cut off from reality. Really living in my own private Idaho. Thomas was also seeing this fat little bush pig called Angie. Didn't even try to hide it. I went to work every day. He'd be asleep when I left and this Angie would come around while I was gone. She'd spend the day with my boyfriend, in my bed, and if he wasn't home she'd leave these notes on the door. Dear Thomas, came to visit but you weren't in, love Angie-poo. She used to draw little hearts and piggies on them.' She shook her head, still incredulous after four years. 'What the fuck those little piggies meant I'll never know. But I'd come home and find those oinkers pinned to the front door. I'd flip. Thomas wouldn't be there. I'd make dinner, maybe do a bit of painting, maybe get bent. I'd finally go to bed and he might roll home an hour or so later. I could go for days without actually seeing him. But I stayed with him through all that. I don't know why I didn't dump him. He had a pretty good line in mind games. Had me believing that no other man would want me except him. I must have been soft in the head.'

Our drinks came and she flipped a fifty onto the tray without acknowledging the lounge goon.

'Anyway he got busted pretty badly and I was so glad. He had two pounds of pot, two hundred trips, five grams of coke and speed and a handful of eccy tabs, the whole chemistry set, plus eight thousand in cash and a pager that went off twenty-seven times while he was in police custody. The cops couldn't believe their luck. They were levitating when they realised. They sat this nice young constable down and had him jot out all the messages as they scrolled across the screen.

'I had to tell Thomas's parents because his friends were all too scared. I had to go around and say, "Look your son's in jail, he's been arrested for drugs, he needs about twenty-five thousand dollars for bail." It was his fourth bust, he'd dropped out of school, never had a job, all he aspired to was being a drug dealer. Anyway he went down and I split from him. He's dead now. A cat fight in the prison showers. My next boyfriend helped himself to my money and my clothes. He didn't know the first thing about laundry so he was always leaving my pants nice and crusty. Even though I broke up with him years ago I

still see him walking around in my clothes and he still hasn't been to the fucking Laundromat. Then I found a speedfreak who couldn't have sex because it depleted his resources.'

I rattled and swirled the ice cubes around in my whisky glass. 'The point of this being?'

'Gotta get back on the hog, JB!' beamed Missy, punching me on the arm.

'Right. And how about you, Mrs Robinson?' I asked Stacey. 'Been a long time since we've seen you cruising the freeway of lerv.'

Stacey grinned. A lopsided, indulgent smile. 'Well I've got my reasons,' she said. 'For now anyway.'

And she was right. We all knew about Stacey's horror stretch with the brothers. We'd heard the stories over the years, over coffee late at night, after movies, between hits off the bong. Primarily, she'd blown off four years with some loser called Dave. A real mismatch. But he was the first fully-grown (if not grown up) man she went out with. He got to her before any one else and she had nobody to compare him with besides the floppy boy. Of the four years they went out together they spent maybe eighteen months apart. With Stacey in Sydney, shooting rock stars for the street press and remaining faithful while Dave was in Perth trying to find his 'true calling' – mostly a matter of him racking up huge Mastercard bills at the local Liquorland and crashing a series of stolen cars into telephone poles, animal-shaped hedges and take-away chicken stores.

Stacey eventually drove across the Nullabor to save him. You do these things when you're in these doomed transcontinental love-torn scenarios and it was even romantic in a made-for-TV movie kind of way. She turned up in Perth and they went out on a bender, a night of drinking and raging and gobbling down fistfuls of high octane drugs. The next morning, lying on a filthy mattress in someone's sticky flat, with Neil Young yowling at full volume from the next room, Dave

chose to tell Stacey that he'd been cheating on her for two years.

There were break-ups, as you'd imagine. Pretty regular in fact. Sometimes they'd go for weeks without talking, which made it difficult to order home delivery. Other times they'd be screeching and clawing at each other over breakfast and having jungle sex by lunch time. Sometimes making up could lead to breaking up. They once spent a week apart, torturing themselves with these emotionally mutilated never-ending, mostly silent phone calls. Friday night was eventually set aside for dinner and a cease-fire. Stacey was living with her parents at this stage. She'd fled back to the nest after some previous temporary break-up. The oldies looked on unconvinced as their vestal virgin prepared herself for the sacrifice. Hours in a bath with oils and shampoos. Hours more at the mirror with perfumes and make-up. A ninety dollar hairdo. A two hundred dollar dress. Her parents tried to be supportive and hip about it all even though they hated Dave and wanted to cut off his head, put salt in the mouth and bury the body at a crossroads at midnight.

At seven o'clock she was ready.

Seven thirty, still ready.

Eight o'clock, she changed her eye shadow.

Eight thirty, she's getting fidgety.

Nine. Getting really fidgety.

Nine thirty and that's it. She knew exactly where to find him. Stormed out to her V.W. in all her finery. Drove out to the Rooty Hill hotel, marched into the public bar and there he was.

'Hi Sweetie, what's . . .'

Stacey flipped a drink into his face and punched him off his bar stool. The whole bar gave her a big cheer as she flounced out the door again.

But they didn't permanently split. Not even then. Not the next week either, when Dave pawned her beloved childhood collection of Pookie

the Rabbit books – although that was a close one. (Well jeez, Stacey! You said you'd read them all!)

Their splits were more in the nature of diplomatic incidents. Sabres were rattled. Ambassadors recalled. Threats were often issued and sometimes troops were even massed along the border. But these were just the ritual manoeuvres. The Big Red Button was always in the background, infusing every confrontation with the possibility of mutually assured emotional destruction. The ever-present menace of The Button checked and neutralised disputes which would have blown other relationships to atoms.

'Strangely the cause of the final break, when it came, was less dramatic,' she'd told me late one night in the kitchen. 'We'd been going out a long time by then. Long enough for Dave to crash eleven or twelve cars, most of them stolen. We're sitting up in bed one morning and I'm taken by the sudden urge to write a five year plan. My list was this lengthy, complex document with all sorts of attachments and addendum. I had to bully Dave into playing along and even then he only wrote two lines, one of which was "get a new car". And that was it. Game over. No Time Left. Do Not Insert Coins to Continue. I'd run out of small change and patience.'

Stacey pressed The Button. Cold white fire filled the room and scientists around the world ran excitedly to earthquake-measuring machines. She moved her stuff into a girlfriend's place that afternoon.

Thing was, though, after going out with somebody like Dave for so long, it wasn't all that simple. She found herself breaking up with guys for completely boring reasons. One chewed gum all the time, which gave him dry lips, so he got the flick. Another never wore any underpants. The next guy seemed okay for a whole month, but then it turned out he was a secret Human League fan and it was *Hasta la vista* baby. Her disconnection from the masculine universe seemed to pick up speed. She started work with a photographic lab only to have both her new boss and the intense Henry Rollins style weirdo from the dark recesses of the storeroom come over all creepy and peculiar on her. Two days into this job and these guys were following her around like dogs on heat. She didn't know which was worse; the boss with his slobbering, over-friendly root-your-leg enthusiasm or Henry, the growling psychotic with no ears and a pair of flat, yellow eyes which tracked you like a heat-seeking missile. Every time Stacey sensed him behind her she got the heebie-jeebies and a flapping spool of audio spun around in her mind *I'm dead I'm dead I'm dead I'm dead I'm dead.*

The photo lab job was only part time. She also had a freelance gig, actual photography, and she had to shoot a motorcycle Grand Prix for a P.R. company. Not the race itself though. Just a couple of corporate boxes with about two dozen drunken horror pigs in business suits and mirror shades, scarfing up the free food and knocking down the crates of Chivas and Heineken like cold jugs of orange cordial.

She spends thirteen hours with these guys, watching them try to impress the roving lycra babes by pissing into champagne bottles from a distance. Thirteen hours where it's about forty degrees in the shade and the ripping thunder of the big bikes is like a chainsaw in her head. Thirteen hours when they're all trying to push their business cards down the front of her shirt and telling her she'll just have to come out and party with them. And the boss-cock-drunken-monster of them all, the reason she is there, the guy who signs the cheques on her employer's multi-million dollar contract, can't stop following her round, touching her arm and grabbing her pants and turning his wet imploring eyes on her, pleading with her to work for him and only him.

Then, on a trip to the pits to take a stress break from the savagery of the corporate box enclosure she was fronted by some grinning idiot who bumped into her and shouted, 'Stacey!' She was hiding behind a huge floppy hat and sunglasses and she didn't know this guy to piss on if his heart caught fire. But he said, 'It's Stacey, isn't it?' And she

was like, 'Y-e-s,' very suspicious, adding that she thinks he got lucky with the name, ''Cos I really don't know you.'

He insisted however and they got to talking and he did seem vaguely familiar. Still, Stacey the photographer didn't normally forget faces. This guy asked if he could give her a call. She reluctantly said okay. He didn't look like a serial killer or anything, but when she got home that night he'd already phoned. He phoned the next day too, tracked her down at the photo lab and asked her out for a coffee. Stacey flogged herself for such an undergraduate mistake. She should have given him a different number, that's what her girlfriends always did. She was a lot harder now, demanding to know where he knew her from. And he was like, 'Oh, it's just in the back of my mind, just on the tip of my tongue, I'm not sure where, but I do know you from somewhere.' She made some excuse and hung up with the hackles on the back of her neck starting to rise. She was tossing up whether to point Henry from the storeroom in this guy's direction.

When she got home that night she found he had called seven times.

He turned up at the lab the next day, making out that it was pure coincidence. Said he was a salesman for a greeting card outfit and this was his new beat. Now, how about that coffee? She knew then she had some kind of freak to deal with but at least she had the fire power for the job and the guy bounced at least one foot off the pavement and gave Henry something to grin about for the rest of the week.

Fast forward to the Sheraton, on Christmas Eve.

Missy was sitting in a cavernous cocktail lounge chair with her legs tucked away underneath her. I was leaned back with one foot propped on a glass-topped table. The bowl of nut scraps resting on my belly. Stacey was sucking contemplatively on another champagne cocktail. She wasn't sad. Just reflective, even a little amused at the twisted chicane her luck had run through.

'I was ready to crawl under a rock by then,' she remembered. 'But

I had one last roll of the dice. A date with this guy I'd been seeing a bit. He seemed safe in a monotone, socialist kind of way. I was looking forward to a night of uncomplicated boozing and screwing followed by a recovery weekend of solitary cones and videos. Trouble was this guy had a full-on new age sensitive routine, which took a very odd turn when I unloaded on him about my week from Testosterone Hell. This guy took real offence. Said maybe I shouldn't condemn and judge men for their behaviour, that maybe I should try and understand what it's like to have this terrible hormone raging through your system all the time. He said it's probably like having your period every day. And I'm sitting there thinking you've got to be fucking joking, pal.

'But he went on, insisted it's exactly like when a woman is ovulating, and he'd know, he said, because he knew more about women's bodies than most women do. I was wondering if maybe he's going to spring a pop quiz later,' she laughed. 'I decided to cut to the chase, started throwing down the red wine and crawling all over him. I was looking to bonk myself senseless whether he liked it or not. But this guy, he just couldn't give it up. In the middle of foreplay he grabs hold of my breast and starts a semantic deconstruction. Like, this is a breast, consisting of nipple and aureole. And that, at last was it. The moment was dead. I threw him out of bed, called him the Passion Killer and decided I was over men. But they weren't over me.'

Same time as this spooky shit's going down, this guy Adam, with whom Stacey had been good friends for nearly seven years, started to wig out. Started to behave really oddly with her. So she's going to sit down and have coffee with him, find out what's the problem. She figures she can at least sort out her old buddy Adam's troubles even if she can't deal with her own. But she's wrong. Between the coffee and the carrot cake Adam lays it on her. He's sorry but he's desperately in love with her. He must have her. He will die without her. And she thinks, Oh Jesus spare me.

'I was pretty hard with poor old Adam,' she said. 'He's down on his knees in this outrageous performance of Unrequited Love, praying for deliverance, begging me to give him a just a little chance.'

But she emptied a full clip into him anyway. Said she couldn't see him while he was wigging out like this, tells him to grow up and get his shit together, says being around him is like having the lamest sort of boyfriend without actually having one.

'I hate it when guys do that,' said Missy.

'Yeah,' I said. 'Me too.'

Stacey called the office late in the afternoon. I snatched the hand piece out of its cradle when Hilda called through, told me it was her.

'Hi, roomie.'

'Hi, John. Look, I'm sorry,' she said quickly. 'I was a monster this morning. That meeting with the D.S.S. freaked me out a bit. They were threatening to prosecute us. Lock us up.'

'That's okay,' I said. 'They can go fuck 'emselves. How you doin'? You feeling okay now?'

'Better,' she said. 'Taylor baked a cake. And Elroy's in his element. He's been wandering round the house misquoting that Smashing Pumpkins' song all day. You know. This day is the greatest day of them all . . .' she sang.

'Yeah, I know it. How'd he go with his garage sale?'

'Scary. Most of it's already gone. We've had suspicious-looking milk vans turning up here all day carting stuff away. He's raised about six or seven hundred bucks so far. But he's obsessing about this church poor box issue. Insists we are the poor it's meant to go to. Wants to cut out the middle man.'

'You keep an eye on him, Stace,' I warned. 'You know how he gets.'

'I know,' she said mock ruefully. 'I remember the first time I realised this house was different. You remember that? The first time I encountered Elroy's coupon fetish? That used car guy ran that ad, that cut-out coupon for $250 off your next car.'

I did remember but Stacey was reminiscing and I didn't want to interrupt her.

'God, I'd only been there a week when I came home from uni one day and found you boys trying to raise bail money for Elroy. He'd assaulted some car salesman who wouldn't give him a new car even though he'd bought about a hundred copies of the newspaper and clipped the coupon from each of them.'

I smiled. She seemed a lot more together than this morning. I leaned back from the reading table. I'd had a grim day, crouched under the office fluoros, but listening to Stace's voice lifted my spirits.

'You wanna get that drink later?' I asked. 'I need to take a dinner break at some stage.'

'You're having beer for dinner again?'

'There's a steak in every stubbie, babe.'

'Okay,' she said. 'May as well. I still don't know that we're going to raise the money we need. You want to meet at the Exchange? The boys will want to come too. They've put a big day in. But first I got to put some flyers up for the street fair tomorrow.'

'Right. How's that going? Those lefties behaving themselves?'

She let go a short, flat laugh.

'They're in their element too. They already set up a dozen different committees and sub-committees to coordinate things. It's not a street fair anymore, by the way. It's an action.'

'Outstanding,' I grinned. I'd seen that pathological committee compulsion before. It's a sickness with those guys. Even the most mundane domestic responsibility has to be chopped up and fed through their version of participatory democracy. The washing up committee. The vacuuming committee. The biscuit purchases committee and the cheese buying sub-committee. All overseen by the weekly shopping working party. People can be very serious young insects about it. They oscillate between getting nothing done because house work is a bourgeois facade, and people getting incredibly fanatical about it, spending hours running fish bowl discussions on the procedure for administering the garbage recycling effort.

'I can meet you about seven or so at the pub,' I said. 'I'll bring Tony, if you like. You can ask him about finding some press work.'

'Oh that'd be good,' Stace remarked dryly. 'I think I've only heard the story of his trip to *Khe Sanh* with Sean Flynn about three hundred times.'

'Well then you got a lot of catching up to do, lady,' I said. 'I'll see you about seven.'

She rang off and I went back to reading the papers with a little more enthusiasm. As the day darkened outside I buzzed Tony on the internal line, told him I was putting in a late one and asked if he was up for a few cleansing dinner ales. Well of course, the Pope is a Catholic, the Kennedys are a tad gun shy, and bears have been known to make potty in the woods. Tony called an early mark and we cut out for the beer garden at six thirty, picking up a couple of kebabs to wolf down on the way.

'You still got a home to go to?' he asked as we dodged through the commuter traffic which streamed past the pub and out to the burbs.

'For now. Don't know about next week.'

We made the safety of the footpath and pushed into the crowded beer garden. An eclectic crowd of students, urban fringe dwellers and workers both blue and white collar rubbed up hard against each other. I saw Stacey, Missy, Elroy, Taylor and the Thunderbird at a table down the back, an impressive collection of empty schooners and stubbies of Coopers already amassed in front of them.

'What're you having, you poor bastard?' shouted Tony over the din of the crowd.

'Something in a jug,' I shouted back, pointing towards the rear of the beer garden. 'I'll just see if the others need re-sup.'

Tony nodded and turned away to thread himself expertly into the crush at the bar.

The crowd was tight packed and rowdy. The place reeked of beer, sweat and cigarette smoke and by the time I'd negotiated a path to my flatmates I did too. Stace saw me first, smiling and lifting a beer. We exchanged greetings all round and I asked if they needed anything from the bar.

'Peanuts,' said Elroy.

'Corn chips,' said Taylor.

'Yeah, corn chips,' agreed Elroy, 'and peanuts.'

They were obviously already eight or nine beers into the wind. Elroy must have had some luck on the underground retail scene. Right, I said, and hurried back to help Tony with the beer. He'd bought three jugs when I found him. I grabbed a few salty treats and we wrestled the lot back to the table.

'Evenin' all,' boomed Tony. The jugs made him a very popular arrival, especially with Elroy and Taylor. Stace had confiscated Elroy's ill-gotten gains before he had a chance to blow them. Ever mindful of the big picture, she was doling the funds out way too slowly for them. Left to their own devices the trickle of funds leaking from our stolen goods

FRIDAY

bonanza would have quickly become a gusher of Alaskan pipeline proportions.

We'd come upon them in a slightly elegiac mood. At first I put it down to Stacey's tight control of the purse strings, but after settling down and pouring the beers I realised they were having something of a last supper, reliving memories of the house. Even the T-Bird contributed and conversation normally had to be prised from him by the jaws of life. Indeed, we'd intruded on one of his rare moments of discourse by arriving with the beers. Stacey prompted him into motion again.

'Go on, T-Bird,' she nudged. 'You were telling us about things that go grunt in the night.'

He blushed and took a swig of beer, the schooner dwarfed by his enormous paws.

'My last flatmate made . . . uh, sex noises,' he said. Elroy snorted beer through his nostrils and Stacey smacked him in the ear.

'Shush, Elroy.'

'They uh . . . they went through the night,' said the T-Bird. 'I don't know what he was doing . . . But they were definitely sex noises. I had just moved into this place. This guy was strange. He was a skinhead . . . A frightening guy from the north of England. He used, uh . . . he'd wear a dress on Sundays. A green strapless dress. Always the same dress. And he had these dragon tattoos from Thailand. You'd see him wearing this backless ball gown on Sunday showing off his dragon tatts. I'd have friends over, guys from the gym, and they'd nudge me. He's wearing a dress. Yes, I'd say. But I didn't want to make too big a deal out of it. This guy was scary, you see, so I'd never mention it.'

The T-Bird took another long pull off his beer. He didn't drink much and was quite tipsy after two schooners. It wasn't a bad thing however. It loosened him up, made him a little more confident. As soon as he placed his empty glass on the table, Taylor swooped and refilled it.

The T-Bird explained that the skinhead wore a full set of pyjamas on his first night in the flat but after that he progressively shed his bed wear. Then he was naked. That's actually when the noises started.

'I'd go to sleep and . . . uh . . . wake up to this noise in the middle of the night. Full on sex noise . . . oh oh oh yes yes oh oh . . . But there was nobody in bed with him. And I was in this room just across the hall. I'd hear him get up out of the bed and the noises would stop. Then he'd go back to bed and the noises would start again. It went for hours. I was frightened of staying in my bed. I thought he was all around me. There was no light at all. Then one night he came home on a Wednesday and climbed into the green dress. Then he goes . . . uh . . . he goes into the kitchen, opens the fridge, takes everything out of it . . . all the shelves . . . all the food. Stacks it neatly on the table and climbs inside the fridge. I went to make myself a protein shake. I opened the fridge and he was in there, repeating over and over again, I've been a very bad boy. I've been a very bad boy. That's when I ran away and you let me move into York Street.'

We all knew how the T-Bird had come amongst us of course, just as we all knew how Missy had fled the house of eco-terrorists. We knew she wasn't allowed to flush the toilet, or get rid of the bath water. Or use toilet paper. Because it was full of C.F.C.s and you couldn't recycle it. We knew her former flatmates had been around the neighbourhood nicking old telephone books. But we all smiled and nodded in recognition of something anyway when they told these stories again.

'You'd go into the bathroom, which was a filthy disgusting pigsty and the bathtub would be full,' said Missy. 'They'd pour one bath in the morning then the same bath water had to be used by everyone, saved and used to flush the toilet through the day. We had a bucket system. These dirty hippies would actually stand in each other's bath water even if it had been in there all day. And they'd scoop it up with

FRIDAY

a bucket to flush the toilet. I just couldn't tolerate that. I used to let out all the water in secret.'

Eco-terrorism wasn't just a bathroom thing of course. She wasn't allowed to buy anything in packaging. And they'd eat food which was rotten because they didn't believe in wastage. You'd have an avocado, open it up and it would be completely brown but you'd still have to eat it, because they didn't believe in leaving any waste at all.

'A lot of food went off in the fridge,' she said as Taylor topped up her glass. 'Because the fridge was environmentally sound, powered by methane or chicken shit or something. Very sound but not very cold. They purposely kept it warm so it was always in a permanent state of brown. Brown, smelly and lukewarm. It was really repulsive.'

'I remember,' said Stacey drawing the attention of the circle to her. 'I remember the boys were in pretty poor shape cooking-wise when I moved in. I remember Taylor seemed to be the designated cook. But I remember he liked experimenting with tried-and-true recipes so you'd get curried lasagne. Or liver and bacon, except with minced offal and Spam. He was also a very temperamental chef . . .'

Taylor lit a cigarette, squinted against the smoke and grinned. Stacey addressed herself to Tony, who was the only one who had not heard this story six or seven times.

'I remember they set up a big dinner to welcome me,' she said. 'And they bought these three free-range chickens. They were trying so hard. But after five hours in the kitchen, and a lot of beery, boisterous shouting, these black, smoking chickens suddenly came flying out like missiles. One. Two. Three. Thudding into the lounge room wall and sliding to the ground. I remember looking at John and he was like, All righty then! Hungry Jacks it is!'

I guess these were our war stories and legends. If our lives could not be channelled into a flow of meaningful narrative, we could at least illuminate the passing moments. The reasons for our lack of a reassuring future or even a comforting present arose like a hundred Phoenixes from stories of anti-matter lesbians, a skinhead in a green dress, or the Legendary Lost Tab of Acid. As myths, our stories didn't need to be justified or rendered plausible. They simply presented themselves as the Truth, no matter how far removed they might seem at first from ordinary experience or the laws of physics.

In that way they were a little like the news stories I marked for scanning to disk at work. Not the ones I was supposed to mark, but the other ones, about chest clairvoyance and pizza cheese landslides. If millions of words about politics, money and war, about the will to power gone mad, if that was, in the end, so complex, so shattered in effect as to be absurd on an individual level, perhaps Lucky the killer guide dog could lead us to meaning, if not safety. His story was ours. We were always wandering into life's heavy traffic, in front of the speeding trains of circumstance, off the end of a pier. And yet somehow we seemed to muddle through, like a drunk through a minefield, with a dopey *Who, me?* grin. We were our stories and they were us. Fantastic tales without proof, because they did not need it. They were sufficient of themselves, needing only to be spoken to impart their deeper message.

And so we sat in the pub telling our stories. The hour came and went at which I was supposed to return to work. But Tony marked its passing with another three jugs of beer, so it was not sorely missed. Leonard joined us eventually, and the Decoy much later in the evening, when our table had been cleared of empty glasses many times over. I watched Stace throughout. I had to make sure I didn't find myself staring at the soft bow of her mouth while she spoke, or dwelling on a mote of light reflected in her green eyes, lest the black fear well up inside my chest, the fear of eventually, inevitably, losing her. But it seemed that whatever had stalked her in the morning, in the bright lit shopping mall, had disappeared or been banished by the night.

Friday night. Much, much later. I am in bed. Drunk. So drunk that when I shut my eyes I'm taking helicopter rides inside my head, swirling around up there, looping the loop, popping barrel rolls which would make Gay Phil green with envy but which leave me green with nausea. It must be three or four in the morning. Saturday morning. The front door opens.

Flinthart has arrived.

THE AWESOME POWER OF A FULLY OPERATIONAL DEATH STAR

Let me tell you about my friend Flinthart.

Flinthart, like the Decoy, is Canadian. But Flinthart, unlike the Decoy, looks like a pirate and when he speaks he prefers to do it standing on something – like a table full of barbecued boar. Or hanging from something – like a big chandelier. Waving a cutlass around if possible.

He is notorious for setting in train these calamitous chains of events, although he himself never seems to be around when the punches fly and sirens wail. He blows through town once every twelve months or so, loaded down by terrible drugs and bladders of fiery Turkish burgundy, roaring salt-encrusted tales of misadventure on the high seas and in the mountains of the Hindu Kush.

'Wake up, Birmingham!' he yelled at me. 'And dragged on by our pleasures we'll make a pup of this black night. We'll kick it before us, lest the dear sun never rise to kiss our brows again!'

My foam slab bounced violently as Flinthart leapt from a set of dresser drawers. I had feigned deep, implacable sleep when he burst into my room waving a bottle of something worrying and demanding I join him on some doomed carouse. But the sudden bouncing brought on waves of oily sickness and I squeezed my eyes shut to fight the gagging reflex. It was hopeless and after a few seconds I had to leap and run for the window to vomit. I let go like a water cannon.

'Bummer,' said Flinthart. 'Really shoulda opened that sucker before you hosed her down, JB.'

'Son of a bitch,' I muttered, belatedly forcing the window open in a panicky rush and leaning through to dry retch in the warm night air while foul droplets of recycled beer, carrot and corn trickled down on to my neck. By the time I'd recovered enough to push myself off the sill and confront the bastard he'd disappeared.

I staggered out to hear him kicking Taylor awake with some twisted Shakespearean arcana. 'Come, Taylor, come handsome cab man, you are known to me as one that loves a cup of hot wine without allaying Tiber in it . . .'

I heard Taylor groan tenderly. 'Oh Jesus . . .'

The house began to wake and rouse itself around me. The teev came to life as Jabba keyed the remote. The big screen filled with silent white noise, bathing the lounge room in its silver glimmer. Elroy was already up and fully charged. Missy's head popped over a carpet-covered office divider. Stace emerged from her bedroom in an over-sized tee shirt, her hair a dishevelled straw blonde mess.

'What the fuck is going on?' she croaked, swaying unsteadily.

The old curtain which guarded Taylor's sleepout swished to one side and Flinthart appeared in a puffy shirt, jodhpurs and riding boots. He was riotously drunk or stoned, or both, but on seeing Stace he tried to pull himself together. 'Ah. Fair Stacey,' he oozed. 'Will you join us on the town, perhaps to teach me terms, such as will enter a lady's ear and plead a love-suit to her gentle heart?'

'Oh fuck off Flinthart,' she sobbed. 'It's late.'

Taylor emerged, bleary-eyed as Flinthart suddenly staggered and fell across the hall to slam into the wall and slide down at Stacey's feet. 'Goddamn psilocybin,' he mumbled.

'Get up Pez-head,' said Stace.

Flinthart looked up with some difficulty. 'Ah, Stacey,' he said. 'You

 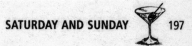

have witchcraft in your lips, there is more eloquence in a sugar touch of them than in all the . . .'

She turned and slammed her door on him. I leaned down and gripped his forearm as the safety chain rattled home inside Stace's bedroom.

'Up we get Sir Stupidhead,' I grunted. 'I don't think m'lady wants to come out and play. And frankly, who can blame her?'

Who indeed? The last time Flinthart had burst upon the stage of our lives Stace and Missy had been imprisoned for a horror weekend with a brain-damaged boxer. Flinthart had procured comps for some incredibly exclusive mid-winter rave and materialised on our doorstep looking for takers. Only Stace and Missy were interested of course – this was before Gay Phil's time – and thus they found themselves as Flinthart's guests with five thousand drug-fucked punters at a huge and unimaginably fabulous party in an old, abandoned power station crammed solid with industrial-strength blowheaters, bouncy castles, tattooists, clairvoyants, foam rooms, laser shows and tinsel storms. Flinthart seemed to know every serious drug lord there and by nine o'clock Saturday night the girls had consumed, free of charge, a gram of speed, four tabs of ecstasy and two Godzilla joints.

Eleven thirty Sunday morning their nervous systems were still lit up like giant Christmas trees. The party was slowly winding down but they were pumping, still making friends, feeling no pain, feeling very chatty, very dramatic, lots of speedy hand gestures and frenzied gum-chewing. Missy had lost ten or fifteen litres of sweat on the dance floor, boogeying so hard she made herself a little wading pool to splash around in. As the crowd thinned and lost energy, Flinthart insisted they all bale for a recovery.

Forty minutes later they squeezed into some sub-basement hell hole with about six hundred fags and one lone heterosexual male besides Flinthart in attendance: Theo the boxer, whose pick-up line was a

198   **SATURDAY AND SUNDAY**

simple invite back to his place for an orgy. It was a desperate, unsophisticated and fairly obvious gambit, which would have failed miserably had Missy not been slightly interested in him.

Whether it was the pick-up line, the lack of sleep, the exhaustion, or just that her synapses had been scraped raw, Stacey decided she was really down on this boxer. She could tell from fifty paces that he'd taken too many damaging head shots in the ring but she could also tell that Missy was seriously winning on with the guy. It was late Sunday afternoon by then. Stacey's tottering fuck-me boots had cut off all the feeling in her feet hours ago. She'd been awake for well over twenty-four hours and she wanted to go home. But Missy said the boxer was adamant they had to go back to his place for drugs. At which point Flinthart beams down from the *Enterprise*.

'Drugs. Did someone mention drugs? Aaah . . . music that gentler on the spirit lies than tired eyelids upon tired eyes?'

The three of them, Stace, Missy and Theo looked at him with eyes like fucking dinner plates.

'Think you can score, punchy?' Flinthart asked the boxer by way of translation.

Theo whipped a plastic baggie containing a Mars Bar's worth of white powder. 'This is great goey,' he said in his curiously nasal way. Against Stace's better judgment she was talked into a quick trip back to the warehouse apartment Flinthart had arranged for his stay in town. Theo was beside himself, babbling that he was going to buy them all a house because, *Youse girls, there's just something special about youse*. He assured them that if they ever needed any money they only had to call him because he was a millionaire, or would be when his grandfather left him three million in his will. I own sixteen houses, he said. *If youse ever need a house you can have one of my houses*.

It took them a while longer to get out of the club because while he might have had sixteen houses to fall back on, Theo didn't have his jacket, wallet, car keys or car with him. Some mate named D'Art had apparently made off with them. They settled on a Hellcab trip across the city after talking Theo out of trying to track down D'Art. Their chain-smoking Turkish cabbie had to listen to a Theo lecture on how fucked he thought the Kurds were, while he simultaneously used every corner as an opportunity to play a round of tit cricket with Missy's breasts. Stacey decided to remain stonily silent and concentrate on trying to unleash her pyrokinetic psychic powers to zap Theo into a charred and smoking ruin. With Flinthart and Theo both finding themselves 'a little short' the girls paid the fare.

It was 6 p.m. Sunday evening.

Stacey, who hadn't been to bed for nearly two days, was only interested in the speedball mix Theo had pulled out of his pocket. They flopped down on the kryptonite couch, the green, shiny horror couch that could drain the energy from Superman, and laid the powder out on a big old Coca-Cola mirror which had speed from Christmas Past caked into the cracks. Theo's bag gave them a jolt but it was gritty, nasty stuff which set the girls to twitching and scratching and generally coming on with the negative vibes about the quality of Theo's gear and, by implication, the microscopic nature of his willy. The result? A frenzied barrage of desperate but unproductive phone calls as this moron tried to make contact with the legendary Big Wednesday, the dealer of champions and Theo's close, personal friend. *Big Wednesday and me, like that mate, we're like that. We'd cut our arms off for each other.*

Flinthart suddenly sat bolt upright, sweating like a stick of unstable gelignite, mumbled something about 'the hounds', grabbed his keys and made for the door.

'Hey!' goes Stace but Flinthart waved back over his shoulder, yelled 'back soon', and disappeared out the door. Stace's blood froze as she

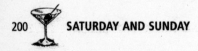

heard his cast iron security gate clang into place. They were effectively trapped. Theo didn't notice, preoccupied as he was with the where-abouts of Big Wednesday, and Stace took a few deep breaths, chilled herself out. Theo was big but very, very slow and she figured between them they could keep him under the thumb. Besides there was still a very real possibility Missy might just race him off for a few hours dalliance, leaving Stace to grab some sleep.

She put the kettle on and the girls sat on the couch, smirking and drinking endless cups of tea as Theo spent the next two hours trying to locate his electronic organiser, which contained all the phone, voice mail and beeper numbers for Big Wednesday but which had also disap-peared with the slippery D'Art. Call followed call, each rolling seam-lessly into the next, a Catherine wheel of distressed appeals which spun so quickly through the hours of drug-induced sleep deprivation that afterwards they could only remember one conversation, a mantra repeated endlessly within the crazed confines of a one-act play written, produced and directed by Andy Warhol on a bad brain day.

'Mate, mate it's me organiser. Me organiser! It's me life. It's got me special numbers that fucking organiser. Can you check your car? It's in your car. Yeah now! Oh come on, mate. Do me a favour. Oh, m-a-a-a-a-t-e, do me a favour. Yep Yep Yep. Okay give me a call back. Call me at this number. Well can you write it down? Well can you put some one on who can write . . . but m-a-a-a-a-t-e it's me organiser. Me organiser! It's me life. It's got me special numbers that fucking organiser . . .'

At eleven thirty on Sunday evening a big cartoon light bulb flashed on above Theo's head.

'Of course!'

Stace and Missy had tuned out at the far end of the couch. They'd been discussing whether a trip to the Hellfire Club might be in order if and when Flinthart returned. Monday was a public holiday. Stace had

 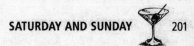

to pick a friend up at the airport but they could easy push on till the sun came up and still have time to recover. They could also ditch this terrible prat. But the prat had heard them laying plans. He quickly broke off an aggrieved phone conference with some reputed acquaintance in a limo hire firm.

'Of course! All right! If we're going out I can score on the street! I know everyone! They love me at Hellfire!'

And he started into some rambling drug-fucked delivery about how good he was in bed and how he's going to have them both and who needs Hellfire anyway they can whip him here at home. Theoretically, Stacey had eight hours before she had to drive to the airport. But sleep was not an option. And now Hellfire was not an option. Tying Theo to a chair and whipping him to death with a couple of extension cords was an option, but it was one she chose not to take. She and Missy decided they might as well just sit there, finish off his crappy speed and let him talk himself into the ground. They used a cocktail straw to hoover up the last traces of amphetamine crud from the Coca-Cola mirror, then switched over to that spooky completely non-verbal chick frequency and let Theo run away with a one-sided conversation about his Barcelona boxing gold, the gym he owned and how he didn't do real good at school because the others used to pick on him and he didn't know why, but he got a reputation as a good street fighter because he had to defend himself – his knuckles really were the size of golf balls and dislocated all to hell – and he really liked these girls, reckoned they could all go the movies together, every week, because he didn't get to go to the movies too much and he could learn from these guys because these guys were so smart and he really liked them, he trusted them, he liked and trusted them so much that he just wanted to tell them something. He just wanted to tell them that his first memory was of his parents in Portugal being shot, being assassinated because they were judges. Baddies in Portugal shot them because they hadn't made the right decisions. He was in the cupboard and heard the shots and the screams and the thing is mate, the thing is that he didn't remember any of that until three years ago. He'd blocked it out because it was so traumatic. But even more traumatic was that his uncle had brought him up as a son and never told him but he always knew because he was never treated as a son. The other kids they were always more special. Like, he had this pet dog called Prince and he loved Prince because he loves all animals. That's why he's a vegetarian. He loved little Princey to death. But his stepbrother and his stepfather decided they wanted a doberman and they had to get rid of his little doggy so they took it out and threw it over a high wall, miles away, so that it couldn't get home. They broke its leg. But because this dog loved him so much it dragged itself home, whimpering and whining with the pain, miles and miles with a broken leg, until it was just outside the front of their house when Theo saw it and ran outside, but too late! A speeding petrol tanker ran the doggy over and squashed him flat.

He had tears in his eyes. Assassinated parents, loveless uncles, troubles with the cops because he'd been shot in the hand with a Maxwell Smart-type pen gun. And a flat dog. Formerly known as Prince. Nobody understood him. Nobody cared. So he'd had to kill a few men in the ring to get it out of his system. He shook his head at the painful memories and Stacey noticed for the first time that his forehead was seriously concave. A big dip went in at least half an inch. In her mentally exhausted state she became transfixed by this bone depression, squinting and focusing on it through his stories until she couldn't hold back any longer. She reached across and touched his forehead. It gave in under the slight pressure and she jumped back. She asked Theo if he got it in a fight. But he said no, when he was a toddler his uncle drove a car over him on purpose.

Now it was four in the morning. Monday morning. Still sitting on

 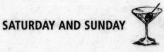

the kryptonite couch, gouging furrows in their arms, eyes hanging out on stalks. It was more than two days since they'd slept properly. Stacey was starting to fray along the psychic stress points, having acid flashbacks and unsettling hallucinations. Missy had curled into a tight foetal ball. But Theo was going strong, jabbering away like a madman, even though his stories were coming to pieces and remorphing like the liquid metal assassin at the end of *Terminator 2*. He was going to get the gold, going to fly his friends to Barcelona, and they'll be there, they'll be protected, he knows everyone, the houses, The Houses Will Be Okay, even if the Assassins come . . .

Stace could take no more. She decided to crash in Flinthart's room. He would not be needing it after she killed him. She shivered and launched herself out of the kryptonite couch. Big metal spikes of pain lanced through her calves and thighs and killer bees swarmed inside her head as she trudged off to the *en suite* where she turned the faucet to scalding hot, undressed, and slumped down to the tiles, legs splayed out and face turned upward. She stayed that way until the water went cold, forcing her to crawl out and towel off. She dressed in a track suit, about four sizes too big for her, which she'd dug out of a dresser. The aches and pains had died away a little but the killer bees hung around to party so it was a while before she realised the grunting she could hear was not her own. She shook her head like a dog emerging from a pool. The noise persisted, a sort of muffled *mmnnphing* sound. Kissing noises from the kryptonite couch. Stacey started laughing. She could not believe that Missy was going to fuck the guy.

'Oh Missy,' she whispered to herself. 'You are fishing in a very shallow gene pool.'

She figured Theo would have his hands full so it'd be safe to flake out for a while. But it was to be an unjustly short nap. Missy shook her awake after what seemed to be only a few minutes. It was, in fact, less than half an hour since she'd passed out. She felt even worse.

He was the worst fuck of my life! shrieked Missy in a stage whisper.

Stace blinked heavily, her head swam and it was a few seconds before she realised where she was.

'Is Flinthart back?' she asked.

'No no no,' said Missy, dragging her from the bed and over to the door so she could see Theo. 'The worst. Absolutely the fucking worst,' she said. Theo was oblivious to these reflections on his sexual prowess, having fallen asleep on the couch like a big smelly cat, arms stretched out, a majestic swathe of pubic hair exposed to the world, and dopey triumph smoothing out his crenelated forehead. The girls watched him out of the corners of their eyes as Missy told of their brief moments of passion. Theo had been rabbiting on about good clean sex, that's what it's all about and Missy had figured, what the fuck, at least he was built. While she was going down on him, giving him the headjob of his life, as she told Stacey, he asked in a less than steady voice, 'Have you brushed your teeth?' Kind of a mood killer but she carried on. Determined to pleasure herself with him. When they got down to business, he fumbled and thrashed about and eventually coughed and asked if she could put it in. Okay, she can do that. She lends a hand, gets him settled in, and starts to work on a rhythm but he shoots his load. There were a few hot and heavy moments where he could tell she was pretty disappointed so he made a charade of ploughing on but after another few seconds or so he arched up and yelled 'Oh me back, I've done me back!' and rolled off in alleged pain.

'Jesus Christ,' muttered Stace. 'Lets get out of here.'

'But how? We're locked in,' said Missy. 'It's two floors up.'

Stacey cast around for the tools. She found a bicycle lock at the bottom of a cupboard, searched for another minute without apparent luck, then came to a decision. She fetched her stockings out of the pile of party clothes she'd discarded for Flinthart's track suit. 'Chain his ankle to the couch leg with this,' she said, holding up the lock. 'And tie his hands with my stockings. If he wakes up tell him it's a sex game.'

Okay, Missy could do that. While she was immobilising Theo, Stace fashioned a rope from a couple of bed sheets, anchored one end to Flinthart's futon base, slid open a window, and dropped the rest of the sheet-rope out into the darkness. She flinched as she heard Theo wake up in the other room, momentarily disturbed to find himself chained up, but Missy murmured and cooed a few saucy promises into his cauliflower ears and he settled right down.

'I blindfolded him,' she whispered on returning to the bedroom. 'Oh, and now, he's got an erection.'

'You could always hang around.'

'Maybe not.'

Missy threw her stilettos and her purse out the window as Theo started up from the other room, 'I'm ready, youse girls. Ready for action. . .'

Stace tested the rope. It held firm.

'You go first,' she said to Missy. 'It's not far and it's grass below. Don't look down. Take it easy. You might have to drop the last five feet or so. Relax and breathe out if you do. And don't kick any windows. You'll have to lower yourself past them.'

Missy, in peak fitness from thousands of hours of dancing in night-clubs, had very little trouble letting herself down. As the strain went out of the sheets Stace walked briskly through to the living room to get her bag, which she'd nearly forgotten.

Theo laughed nervously, 'Here we go then.'

Stace shook her head, walked back to the bedroom and turned at the door. 'I've got two things to tell you Theo. First, I'm not going to fuck you. Second, I never was.'

'What . . . !'

Stace hurried to the window and climbed out, Theo's mournful cries following her into the night.

Little wonder then that Stacey wasn't leaping at the chance to spend another night on the town with our man Flinthart. I noticed Missy had also made herself scarce as I guided Flinthart through the kitchen. He was talking to himself about 'the mushroom shaman', muttering stuff like, 'One gram. Ground up. Less likely to vomit that way.' He seemed to be in the grip of a major hallucinogenic catastrophe.

'A dragonfly came to sit on my leg,' he told me, gripping my arm, his eyes blazing fiercely. 'I talked to the dragonfly in my head, and began to explain what it was like to be human. The dragonfly is an explorer, an ambassador from dragonfly land. They are curious creatures. It told me that dragonflies explore and what they discover is contributed to the collective dragonfly knowledge.'

'Jesus Christ,' I said, shaking my head. Elroy and Taylor had followed us through the kitchen. They were much more attuned to sudden disturbances in their biorhythms at the dead man's hour.

'Brew?' asked Taylor

'Three of them,' I said. 'I'll be back. I got to clean my room.'

That very unpleasant task taken care of I returned to the kitchen where Flinthart seemed to have made a complete recovery. He was still wired, but lucid now, reading from a note book for Taylor and Elroy.

'. . . and three capsules of powdered perganum harmala seeds to potentiate the D.M.T. and the psilocybin in the mushroom. Swallowed the first capsule at about 11.10 a.m. I noticed the first presence then, a bush turkey spirit, and interacted by dancing with it. Swallowed the other capsules at half hour intervals. Became aware of nausea. But I did not concentrate on this. Did some Tai Chi to move the energy through me . . .'

He looked up from his reading when he realised I was there.

'Flinthart's found a new drug,' said Elroy. 'It's bitchin'.'

'Gathered as much,' I grunted, collapsing into a chair and pulling a black coffee towards me. I noticed two cardboard crates of bottled wine by the table leg. Not cheap-looking gear either.

'Just a contribution in your hour of need,' said Flinthart. 'We're going into the Red Garter for a few pre-breakfast drinks. Care to tag along? I can tell you all about this marvellous discovery.'

'Actually I think I'd prefer to drive rusty nails through my penis . . . but . . . I guess I could do with a feed.'

'We could get a schnitzel at the Windmill,' said Taylor.

It was probably the only way the rest of the house was going to get any rest. We had a huge day in front of us and it wouldn't do to have this madman and his cronies getting out of hand before the sun came up. Plus, I really did have to eat something.

'Let me change,' I said. 'And keep the noise down.'

I left the kitchen as Flinthart resumed his reading on a slightly quieter note. 'Time had passed, but it was still quite light. The rapport with the plants started to creep on from this point, the shining white trees across the creek were actually shining. The trees were very . . . tree-like. I felt like a carrier consciousness and could see a future filled with hard, bright objects . . .'

I could see a future filled with Legal Aid lawyers. I shuffled down to Stace's room and knocked on the door. The house had resumed a wary slumber.

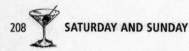

SATURDAY AND SUNDAY

'Just me,' I said. 'It's safe, for now.'

The door opened a crack at first, then a bit more, just enough for her to poke her head out.

'Has he gone?'

'Hey, J.B.' said Gay Phil, a bit dazed, from behind her.

'Hey, Phil . . . Nah. Afraid not. We're going to take him into town, get a feed and a drink. He's brought some terrible drug with him. And two big boxes of wine.'

'Monkey piss?'

'No. It looks okay. I think it's a peace offering for you and Missy.'

'It'd wanna be.'

I swayed a little and had to lean against the door frame.

'You look like shit, John,' she said.

'That's only 'cos I feel that way.'

'You sure you should go out?'

'Well there's not much of a choice is there? He's settled down for now but in five minutes he could be crawling around in the roof biting the heads off possums. May as well let him buy me a few drinks and a toasted sanger. You get some zeds. You're gonna need it for the *action* today.'

'Thanks,' she smiled.

'You'll owe me.'

'I know . . . big time.'

For the second time in a few hours I was awoken by someone rudely bouncing my mattress, less vigorously this time but with more than enough animation to shake me from the land of nod. Before I had any consciousness of being awake, I had a memory of a mad hand-over-hand scramble up the stairs of some strip club and steak bar where we finished up for breakfast beers. I recall there was a disagreement with some of the other patrons, initially over some point of snooker trivia, which soon blossomed into a full and frank exchange of views on matters of tariff policy and immigration. Anyway, some things were said about the perils of giving the vote to folks who like to play banjo with their toes and next thing I know Taylor had grabbed a hold of my collar, dragged me over the back of my chair while Elroy and Flinthart covered our retreat with a fusillade of well-aimed billiard balls; Flinthart roaring like Captain Ahab, *Haharr, lets have at them, JB!*

'JB . . . JB!!!'

Flinthart's guttural war cries grew softer and lighter, but with a more insistent note as I regained consciousness. It was Missy.

'JB. Get up, JB. You gotta come. There's cops at the door.'

Whoah! That did the trick. I forced my eyes open. Broke a pretty thick crust doing it too. If I'd ever read any Jean Paul Sartre this would have been the place to drop in a really appropriate quote from his book *Nausea*, which the girly swots told me is the definitive work on feeling a bit crook. But I skipped the lectures for *Intro to Existentialism* at uni – too busy drinking ten thousand beers and chasing this hot law student babe – and I never actually got around to the set reading. So you'll just have to imagine that I was feeling, well, more than a little unwell.

'They want to talk to you about Jordan,' said Missy, shaking me by the arm.

'Stacey,' I croaked. 'Where's Stacey?'

'Up the street. Setting up a table for the fair.'

'Okay . . . right . . . Jordan you say?'

'Yes.'

Okay, I blinked slowly. At least it was nothing to do with last night. Nobody killed by a cueball or anything. I struggled up onto my elbows. 'Missy,' I rasped. 'I'll make the bad men go away if you make me a cup of tea. Deal?'

'Deal,' she nodded and hurried away to the kitchen, calling out to

the cops, that I was on my way. I rubbed my face and rolled my feet
onto the floor. I'd crashed out in my boardies and an old, torn-up
Rolling Stone tee shirt. I figured that was good enough for company
and pushed off for a second bite of the cherry of that day.

The wallopers were in the living room, which was a bit nasty. I'd
expected to find them at the front door but there they were, a couple
of big, fat ticks, corruption oozing from every pore, one of them sport-
ing a righteous purple safari suit, while his mate strained the buttons
on at least a hundred bucks worth of primo lounge wear.

They were surveying the wreckage of last night's excesses. Elroy
asleep on the floor with his head hidden inside an empty beer carton.
Flinthart flaked out on the couch, face down, with three, maybe four
inches of buttcrack showing over the top of his jodhpurs. Leonard's
underpants on the march again, creeping across the floor towards
Elroy for feeding time.

'Fellas,' I nodded. 'What's the problem?'

They badged me. 'Detectives Eady and Belcher,' said the taller one
in the safari suit. 'What's all that bullshit out in the street for?'

'Sort of a fundraiser,' I shrugged. 'We're having a street fair to try
and save our place from being torn down.'

'Uhuh,' he said flatly, looking from Leonard's underpants to
Flinthart's buttcrack. 'I can see where that'd be something worth fighting for.'

'And who're these jokers?' his short mate asked, indicating Flinthart
and Elroy.

'That's Karamazov,' I said. 'And that's his brother. There's another
one around somewhere.'

'Oh yeah? What's their story?' asked Eady, fetching a packet of
Dunhills from one of the many pockets of his outstanding suit.

'A long story,' I yawned, rubbing my eyes. 'A thirst for life. The search
for meaning. You blokes want a brew?'

Eady shook his head and fetched a Polaroid from his shirt pocket. 'Recognise him?'

It was Jordan's face but there was something wrong with the photo. His eyes were unnaturally wide, his mouth distended in shock, as though the image had been snapped at the moment a firecracker went off in his bum.

'That's Jordan,' I said. 'He used to live here.'

'What d'you mean used to?'

'Sorry?'

'When's the last time you saw him?' he asked.

'A few weeks ago. He bailed on this place while I was away. Ripped us off pretty bad.'

'That so?' asked Belcher.

'Yeah.'

'So you weren't too happy with him?'

'Well it wouldn't be a million miles from the truth. Why? What's going on? Something happen to Jordan?'

'Did we say something had happened?'

Missy, wearing only a big white singlet, appeared with a mug of tea for me, momentarily distracting the cops with about twenty-five thousand watts of eyes, tits and teeth.

'Hello,' she beamed. They nodded.

'Thanks, babe,' I muttered before she hurried away. Eady and Belcher watched her go. I grinned at them quickly, conspiratorially, when they turned back to me. One of those bullshit guy things.

'So, Jordan, what's happened?' I asked.

'You home last night?' Eady asked in reply.

'No. We were all at the pub from about six till closing. My boss was there too. So what's the story?'

The safari suit drew deeply on his cigarette, stubbed it out on the wall next to Elroy's poster of Daphne fellating Scooby Doo, and blew out the smoke in a thin stream.

'Your mate's had a bit of an accident,' he said as Belcher tried to hide a smile.

Taylor swung the cab into Arthur Terrace. We could tell right away that something was wrong. Jordan's street was closed off where it curved around, about three hundred metres down the hill. An ambulance, four patrol cars and a couple of news vans were parked outside his place, although the word 'parked' would impose a sense of order on the scene which was absent in real life. They were all over the fucking place. Dozens of neighbours and onlookers had assembled at a perimeter guarded by uniformed police. Taylor pulled over to the kerb a safe distance away.

'What d'you reckon?' he mused aloud.

Neither Stacey nor I could help. We shook our heads.

'I don't know,' I said. 'But I reckon we might've come up short one fraudulator this morning.'

'The cops wouldn't give it up?' asked Stace.

'Not a sausage. Best I can figure it, maybe something's fucked up with a drug deal.'

'Well, let's blow this popsicle stand,' said Taylor. 'Whatever happened, it's got nothing to do with us.'

He threw the cab into a smooth turn and drove away carefully.

'Maybe they got some connection to that bullshit raid at our place. The one Jordan set up,' said Stace as we powered through the bends on Stuartholme Road, up in the hills out back of Toowong. Taylor steered down past the cemetery with one hand while he fixed himself a smoke.

'You didn't recognise either of them? I asked.

'One big fat copper looks pretty much the same as the next one to me,' he said around the cigarette. 'Twenty years of meat pies and

 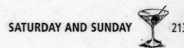

Fourex, scratching your arse and copping free blowjobs, you're gonna cut a fine figure of a man.'

'Sounds like taxi driver nirvana to me,' teased Stacey.

Taylor drew back on the smoke, 'We're here to serve, babe.'

'Well, whatever,' said Stace. 'I guess something went wrong for Jordan. But I doubt I'll be crying myself to sleep tonight.'

'I might,' I said. 'But that's only because I've got a filthy hangover and I'm a big wuss.'

'Well we can fix that,' said Stacey. 'Driver, the bottleshop.'

We returned to York Street with a carton of Coopers to find more cops there. Taylor pulled up under the baleful gaze of Pauline Hanson. Her giant, wolfine eyes looked down upon the world and they were pleased. Below her, in the street, a scene on the edge of chaos. Two hundred people, a dozen or so folding tables covered with food, barbecues on wheels everywhere, a marquee. The crowd, a gathering of the tribes. Dreaded folk, Mohicans, trad punks and goths mingled with indie kids, suburban surfies, skate boys, old hippies and ravers. There were plenty of families from the neighbourhood weaving kids in strollers and toddlers through a labyrinth of garage sales to join the crowd gathered in front of the abandoned house next to ours. Three police cars and a paddy wagon had pulled up there, surrounding a big red Mustang.

'Big turn-out you got here, Stacey,' I said.

'The Kremlin guys put a lot of leaflets up,' she answered, a bit distracted. 'Ran a few announcements on Triple Zed about the fair and the protest . . . What the hell is that?'

Both Taylor and I followed her line of sight and jumped, just a little, as we saw it too.

'That'd be a giant cockroach,' I nodded.

It was jogging from the Kremlin directly towards the knot of people

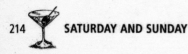

gathered outside number five, its useless stitched-on floppy roach arms flapping rhythmically, the identity of whoever was inside hidden by the slip-on bug mask. I thought at first it may have been the Decoy, because of the holes which had been cut in the costume, allowing the wearer to stick his own arms through so as to carry a protest banner: *This development really bugs me.*

But there's no way the Decoy would have been down for that. It had to be one of the lefties, and watching the lone roachman hustle across the road, frightening children, pushing and shoving his way into the crowd, we all recognised that awkward, jagged gait at the same time.

'The Singlet!' said Taylor.

We scrambled out of the cab, locked the doors and hurried down the hill, Taylor hauling the beer on one shoulder. It was a hot, fine day, with the sun already high overhead, baking the protesters. Nothing had happened yet, but I'd been to enough demos to develop a fine-tuned radar for bad vibes. As we approached, my screens lit up. At least eight uniformed cops and another two or three detectives were lined up protectively in front of the property. Brian and Debbie, our monster yuppie landlords, were arguing with Jhelise and the old guy from the street meeting, the staunchy Spanish Civil War vet, who sported an alarming beret.

Nobody from our house seemed to have bought into the encounter. Not directly anyway. Elroy and Flinthart were lurking in a worrying fashion just off to one side. I saw Leonard at the back of the crowd with Missy and Sativa, all three of them standing on tiptoe for a better look. And the Decoy was doing a very poor imitation of an innocent bystander at a folding table way across the street, inspecting a tray of fudge brownies or something. We moved up beside Brainthrust and the girls.

'Hey,' went Stacey. 'What's happening?'

They smiled, but only briefly. I could hear Jhelise shouting at Debbie, who was giving it back with interest.

'It's sort of confused,' said Leonard. 'Two coppers turned up at our place.'

'What, those guys this morning?'

'No. Constables,' explained Leonard. 'In uniform. About Pauline. They wanted to speak to Elroy. I think someone must have taken his number while we were up there. Anyway, they never got to him. We were talking to them on the footpath and they wanted to know what was going on so we told them about the yuppies and everything, but they just wanted to know if we had permits to run stalls and block off the street and so on.'

I looked at Stace.

'As if,' she gestured.

A few more voices joined the confrontation between Jhelise and Debbie and a ripple, a small wave of movement and energy ran through the gathering. Leonard continued, 'One of them got on his radio, was talking to his boss about the fair when a couple of Kremlin guys walked past and bought into it.'

'They told the cops this was a legitimate expression of the people's will,' smirked Missy.

'There was a bit of to and fro over that,' said Leonard. 'People were starting to notice. Then the yuppies turned up.'

Stacey sucked air through her teeth, 'Say no more.'

Sativa, who'd been eating raw chunks of meat off a wooden skewer, finished her snack and wiped her lips with the back of a hand. She closed her eyes and turned her face up to the sun. 'Do you think there is a dominant star sign amongst the police?' she wondered aloud. 'The sign of the pig maybe?'

'I wouldn't know,' muttered Stace before pushing into the crowd. I followed her through, emerging a few feet to the right of Flinthart, who was drinking dark liquid from a massive brandy balloon. He seemed to be enjoying himself enormously. He lifted his glass our way and winked when he saw us, leaning over and mock-whispering, 'For now sits expectation in the air, JB'. A detective in a sports jacket was trying to keep a safe distance between Jhelise and Debbie, who were going each other like yappy little dogs on speed.

'You might think you can roll in here and get what you want by throwing your money around,' shrieked Jhelise. 'But you don't own this street!'

'Not yet, maybe,' Debbie shot back. 'But I'm going to make it my mission in life to acquire the place you're living in you slack moll . . .'

The detective had one big, ham hock of an arm thrust out to separate them but even with his height and weight they gave him a real buffeting. At the same time the fiery old beret guy was jabbing a bony finger at him, yelling, 'I'm not frightened of you. I fought with the International Brigade!' Which drew a resounding cheer from all the lefties in attendance. He picked up on the vibe and plunged on. 'I faced down Nazi dive bombers in Guernica! And I saw off Generalissimo Franco's hired goons at Guadalajara with nothing more than a Webley pistol!'

More cheers from the crowd, including many of the home owners, the mums and dads. Two younger constables exchanged a worried glance. The rest of the uniformed cops, drawn up like the elite Republican Guard at the gates of Baghdad, simply gave us their stone faces. Brian, the wooden-headed pretty boy, was orbiting around behind the police in a series of tight figure eights, glaring at the more vocal protesters. Debbie decided to ignore Jhelise in favour of haranguing the detective to make use of Queensland's many fine, repressive laws banning public assembly.

'You know they don't have a permit,' she said fiercely. 'Just do your bloody job and clear them away.'

The cop had both his hands up by then, palms open and gently patting the air in a gesture of conciliation.

'I really don't think that would be . . .' he started. Only to be cut short by a roar as Red Mesh Singlet Guy, carrying his protest sign like a cavalry standard, broke away from the edge of the pack and charged around the police line.

'Cry freedom, giant roach!' yelled Flinthart.

All the cops turned to look. Their boss pointed after the Singlet with his walkie-talkie. 'Get that idiot out of there!' he shouted as Red Mesh Singlet Guy dipped his antennae and laid on speed for the front steps. Brian the yuppie jumped in front of him, legs propped wide in a martial arts stance, hands held ready to deliver a murderous combination of spear hand strikes and karate chops. The Singlet swept his feet out from under him with one deft scything motion of his banner.

Three cops peeled away from the line. The crowd in front of them surged forward. Flinthart suddenly leapt on to the small concrete fence waving his brandy balloon, sloshing red wine everywhere and yelling, *Into the breach, dear friends!*

'Remember Guernica!' cried the old beret dude, staggering after him.

'I don't believe this,' said Stacey. Maybe half the people around us suddenly moved as though a giant invisible hand had pushed them. A lot happened in the next ninety seconds. A lot of confused, chaotic stuff which would probably be remembered differently by everyone who was there. But I think I've established the critical event path: The Singlet, who had intended to chain himself to the steps, instead swerved and ran for our place as the police began their chase. With the attention of the sports-jacketed detective temporarily elsewhere, Jhelise and Debbie launched into a bitch slapping frenzy. The Decoy dived under a table full of fairy cakes and home-made toffees. McDoofus, the Kremlin's Spanish-speaking revolutionary from

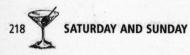

218   **SATURDAY AND SUNDAY**

Edinburgh University, threw a punch at a cop and got a baton in the guts. The Beret attempted to throw a punch at the same cop but merely overbalanced and fell on top of McDoofus who was writhing on the footpath. Parents scooped up their youngsters and fled in terror. A rumbling convoy of motorcycles turned into the street heralding the return of the karate dykes. The Singlet jumped our fence and evaded capture as his pursuers were swamped by the crowd. The karate dykes dismounted, waded into the fray and started swinging, looking for the Decoy. An overexcited Elroy was the first to notice their arrival and yelled, 'Lesbians! Lets get them.' Taylor, who loved the bar brawl scene in the opening credits of *F Troop*, handed Leonard his beer carton and joined Elroy. Their attack was repulsed with heavy casualties. People ran everywhere, some screaming, some whooping with delight. Flinthart, still atop the fence, splashed his wine around and made pirate noises. Sirens approached from all directions. Red Mesh Singlet Guy emerged at high speed from our front door, still dressed as a giant cockroach. He was immediately spotted by three vengeance dykes who mistook him for the Decoy. The Singlet was spear-tackled into the bitumen, and hustled away by his captors. The karate dykes fell back and left with their prisoner. Police reinforcements arrived. Game over.

Stacey, as usual, was right. We had all accepted the inevitable. Come Monday we would not have the money to pay off our persecutors or the power to resist them. Nobody doubted the tyrant Debbie's resolve. She would be on our doorstep with a dozen steroid-abusing nightclub bouncers at sunrise. We were fucked and there was only one thing for it. A Destructathon. If the yuppies were so intent on tearing our place down maybe we'd save them the trouble. Maybe we'd have an end-of-lease party that left nothing behind but a giant, smoking crater on their precious fucking land.

The police had terminated our street fair with maximum prejudice some hours earlier. It was late in the afternoon and, as so often in this house, we were gathered at the kitchen table. Except where once had lain bills and stale popcorn and cups of coffee there now spilled a debaucher's treasure chest of drugs. Most of the Kremlin guys and maybe thirty or so hangers-on from the protest had also descended on our place for post mortem cones, drinks and war stories. Flinthart and McDoofus, who had narrowly avoided arrest in the morning's melee, were busy ripping the corks from Flinthart's wine collection. Elroy was entertaining a couple of Spartacist League loons with tales of the many times he had been violently arrested and oppressed by the System.

Stace drew deeply on a joint, held the smoke, and, passed the butt to Leonard. She exhaled, 'Fuck 'em. If they can't take a joke.'

'What rein can hold licentious wickedness,' slurred Flinthart, already fucked off his nut. 'When down the hill he holds his fierce career?'

Or as Elroy put it while firing up a foot long doobie, 'Yeah! Stupid yuppies. Let them feel the awesome power of a *fully operational* Death Star.'

Sometime later, I came to in Hell's Disco Lounge. Hundreds of sinners everywhere. Loud music. A riot in our living room. Stacey was shaking me awake.

'You gotta come see this,' she yelled, trying to drag me into the land of the living.

I ran my felt-covered tongue around a sand-paper mouth and groped about for a beer I vaguely remembered abandoning on the floor by the couch in a previous life.

'It's Jordan,' she said, which got my attention. She pressed a stubbie of Coopers into my clumsy paws and pulled at my elbow to drag me up.

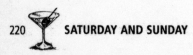

'S'okay. I'm coming,' I grunted.

We pushed through the crowd which I estimated had to be at least a hundred strong. Did we know that many people? We certainly didn't have that many friends. I suspected the work of Flinthart somewhere in back of this. Stace held my hand, lead me through to Elroy's room where I found all of my flatmates and Flinthart in front of the Bang and Olufsen. Jabba had to crank the sound right up because of the party noise and I stood leaning on Stacey's shoulder for a while trying to figure out why everyone was so keen to catch the local news. I had another revitalising swig of beer as some empty-headed blonde threw back to the station from a traffic accident. Then everyone was going 'quiet' and 'shoosh' as the weekend anchor gave us his 'concerned' look.

'Police are still investigating the bizarre death of a man in Red Hill earlier today . . .'

'That's Jordan's flat isn't it!' shouted Missy at a small graphic which had appeared above the newsreader's shoulder.

'. . . name has not yet been released,' the anchorman continued, 'but police are investigating a possible Asian crime gang link. The man, who was of Asian background, appears to have been killed by a bizarre sexual practice known as pumping . . .'

The room erupted into a raucous mix of cheers and whistles and disgusted shouts as the station cut to background vision of two giant tanks of compressed air being carried away from the scene by detectives.

'. . . police believe the man may have fatally miscalculated the pressure of the tanks, blowing himself to pieces in the search for sexual gratification.'

'Oh my God,' squealed Stacey. 'Elroy, what did you do when you were fucking around with those cylinders at Jordan's place?'

'Nothing! I didn't do nothing!' he said.

 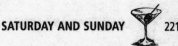

'. . . the body was discovered by a pair of visiting pastors from the Church of Scientology.'

The video cut to a grey-lipped, unsettled looking man and his frumpy female partner, who had found Jordan in half-a-dozen pieces, with his disembodied butt cheeks still firmly clamped around an industrial air hose. Then the station's police roundsman threw back to studio for a surfing dog story.

Jabba killed the power with his remote.

'Goddamn!' said Gay Phil. 'Wait till the boys at the bath house hear about this!'

Stacey moved to shut the bedroom door. She jammed a chair under the handle, cutting us off from the rest of the house. Everybody watched and waited.

'Elroy. You didn't touch those tanks. Understand me. You didn't go near them.'

'You don't need to tell me twice,' he said.

Stacey looked at each of us in turn.

'Did anyone see Elroy touch those tanks?' she asked.

'Not me,' I shrugged.

'Me neither,' said Gay Phil.

'What tanks?' said the Decoy.

'Nope,' went the T-Bird.

'I wasn't there but if I had been I wouldn't have', said Missy.

'Not once,' said Taylor. 'And I was with him all night.'

'As were we all,' nodded Stace. 'Which means there was no way, not a single fucking chance that he, or anybody else, had anything to do with what happened to Jordan.'

It seemed very quiet in Elroy's bedroom, in contrast to the party outside. Two seconds passed. 'Well, we have guests,' said Stacey. 'And we are being terrible hosts. I think we should mingle.'

Everybody smiled then. Stace removed the chair blocking the door and we filed out of the room. I waited behind until only Elroy and Stacey were left. He halted at the door.

'Thanks, Stace,' he said and quickly kissed her on the cheek before running off.

She blushed. I leaned on the door frame and offered her the last of my beer.

'Think I'll pass,' she said.

We stood, staring at each other for a long time. Finally, I couldn't take it any more.

'Stace,' I said. 'It's just . . .'

But nothing else would come. She touched me on the face, pulled me forward, kissed me lightly and said, 'I know.' And with that she spun away and disappeared into the party. I stood rooted to the spot. Why would she do that? I either didn't know, didn't want to know, or didn't want to deal with implications of knowing. I was reeling from sleep deprivation. My head felt like I'd been in a pillow fight, with sacks of potatoes soaked in poison gas. I tried to follow Stacey's progress through the mad crush of the party but she had already been swallowed up by the thousand limbed, thrashing, hydra-headed meat-monster which had squeezed itself into our place while I slept off Elroy's giant doobie. There was only one thing for it. I'd have to start putting away jugs of beer and pints of wine and lots of joints and more beer and more wine and maybe some of Flinthart's strange new drug until I was just this hopeless drooling grease spot of a boy in the corner. In the distance I spotted Leonard, Stavia and Jhelise alternating hits off a bong with helium balloon abuse. I tried to move to them but was jostled by a surge of dancing gay boys by the bar. I closed up like a prize fighter and set my course for the kitchen. I could just make out Flinthart and Taylor there, looming over some Kremlin trollop and drinking red wine from her filthy shoe. Flinthart made some pirate sounds and offered me the horrible thing but I took the bottle from him instead and poured a draught of burning cabsav down my throat. He leaned in close and shouted in my ear, something like, '. . . fragments have I shored against my ruins. . .' while pressing something into my palm. I gobbled it down. His eyes went wide and he said, 'Whoops.' I passed the bottle to the Kremlin chick. She wasn't so bad. She had jet black hair, a few unruly strands hanging down in front of her eyes. She was small and so pale skinned I wondered if she ever went out in the daytime. I . . .

Damn!!!

The sea of heads and shoulders around us became a real sea, a churning swell with long spools of colour and meaning blown back by the blacklight wind which came roaring out of Elroy's stereo speakers. Flinthart's drug was kicking in. Black canyons opened up in the press of people around me, snaking smooth-sided chasms of nothing. I reeled against the kitchen wall which had gone all spongey and soft. I reached one long, long arm out for the Kremlin babe. This arm just kept growing, like that stretch guy from the Fantastic Four. I think he was married to Invisible Girl; she had an invisible jet fighter and she was a hot babe. Oh yes. But not as hot as this Kremlin babe I had my rubber hands on, her dark green eyes, her purple lips a slash of lurid promise. I reeled her in as sludgy lust welled up from the bayou of my rubber groin. Yeah, this is good, I'm thinking. I'm gonna put the Move on her, that's right, the Move. And the thing is, she's cool for the Move. She likes the Move. She *wants* the Move. But Stacey? Would Stacey like the Move? I didn't know. I stared, baffled, at Flinthart, who was talking while his eyes sizzled and popped, eggs on the griddle, their golden yolks bursting and running down his copper cheeks. I checked inside the orbit of my mile long arm. The Kremlin babe was still there. But what would Stacey say? Maybe I should give this babe the Flick right now. Because the Flick was coming, we all knew that. Me. The babe. Old melty eyes Flinthart. We knew it. So why not just jump straight to the Flick. Save us all the hassle. A geyser of flame erupted from Taylor's hands. Neat trick Taylor, I said. The sea of people convulsed, a strange confluence of waves and tides. Taylor made the flame shoot from his hands again. He was . . .

Damn!!!

He was trying to kill a big roach. A real big one, six foot or more. He was trying to burn it with a flame thrower. Fashioned from his naked boobie lighter and a spray can of air freshener. Then the Kremlin babe had gone. So quickly. And now I had nobody to lean on so I fell down.

'Wake up. Wake up, JB!'

It was Missy. There'd been some sort of fight. Detectives at the door. Someone had been killed. Blown to pieces. In the Downunder Club.

'Wake up, JB.'

No. It wasn't Missy. That was yesterday. It was Stacey!

'It's Flinthart,' she said. 'He says he has a cunning plan.'

I forced my eyes open. Gyres of dizziness whirled inside my head. I was . . . where was I? I was in Stacey's room.

'How'd I get here?' I asked. It felt like coughing up fur balls.

'There're lesbians in your bed,' said Stace. 'It's okay though. They're like Page Three lesbians.'

'Oh boy,' I grunted weakly. 'Wait'll the boys find out I had a couple of good-looking dykes in my bed. I'll be a legend.'

'The boys already know,' said Stace. 'They've been peeking through the keyhole for two hours.'

I yawned massively, involuntarily. I felt very weird, very strange, but not in a bad way. Stacey was kneeling at the edge of the mattress. She reached behind her and brought forth a cup of tea.

'Oh thank God,' I muttered.

'You should get up,' she said. 'We may have to leave soon.'

 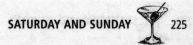

'What is it, Monday or something?'

'No. Sunday. Early Sunday morning. But Flinthart has a plan.'

'A plan?' I went suspiciously. 'What sort of a plan?'

'A fairly desperate one,' smiled Stace.

'Right,' said Flinthart. 'I suppose you're all wondering why I've gathered you here today.'

Nobody answered. We were a sore and sorry fucking Team York Street that morning. The house was a disgrace; broken furniture, holes in the roof, a whole section of the back wall missing – big enough to ride a motorcycle through. And below that on a burned patch of grass, the motorcycle itself. Taylor and Elroy had bandaged heads and no eyebrows; burnt off when Taylor's can of air freshener exploded as he had tried to exterminate a roach-suited Elroy. Leonard had taken a little walk down the boulevard of broken dreams after he found Sativa making out with Jhelise in the shower. Gay Phil had an amyl hangover. The T-Bird was so sick he'd vomited his breakfast protein shake straight back up. The Decoy expected another Vengeance Dyke raid at any moment. Missy was wearing sunglasses and sitting very still.

Flinthart, who seemed completely unaffected, ignored the silence. He paced slowly and deliberately back and forth across the lounge room. 'We find ourselves cut off, surrounded, fucked by the fickle finger of fate' he said. 'But my friends we are not in virgin territory. When Gordon was surrounded at Khartoum, or when the Nazis bore down on the 101st Airborne Division at Bastogne or when Her Majesty's 2/24th Regiment faced a whole Zulu army at Rorke's Drift did they break and run, squealing like a bunch of sissies? No. I think not. Perhaps they wanted to. Perhaps they even thought about it. But come the day they carved their names into the bus seat of history with the flick knife of boldness and derring-do.'

Elroy, who was sitting on the couch between Taylor and Stacey, tried to lean over for an explanation but the effort caused him to wince. Flinthart placed a giant riding boot atop our shattered coffee table and one hand upon his hip. Before we could stop him he was bellowing away with Kenneth Brannagh at Agincourt.

'To suffer woes which hope thinks infinite, To defy Power which seems omnipotent, to love and bear, to hope till hope creates, from its own wreck the thing it contemplates . . .'

'The plan, Flinthart?' interrupted Stacey somewhat testily.

'Well,' he said in a calmer voice. 'We'll be selling drugs to school children and gambling with the profits.'

'Schoolies Week!' exclaimed the T-Bird, the first to catch on.

'That's right,' said Flinthart suddenly disappearing around the corner then reappearing with a cardboard box full of party leftovers; bottles of bourbon and vodka, assorted beers and a considerable stash of marijuana, acid and DMT, the last donated by Flinthart himself. He asked Stacey how much money was left from Jordan's stuff and she estimated about four hundred dollars.

'Then I propose the following,' said Flinthart. 'We remove ourselves to the coast with all dispatch. We make our way directly to those venues which clueless, private school types from Sydney are known to frequent. We sell them our leftovers at ridiculous prices. Combine the profits with the other four hundred dollars and prevail upon Mr Howard 'Three Fingers' Hunt to work his magic on the blackjack tables at Jupiters.'

The silence which greeted this announcement was more contemplative than before. After some consideration Stacey was willing to try. The T-Bird of course, was keen as mustard, simply because it would move him that much closer to large numbers of nubile teenage girls who hadn't had unsafe sex with any gay men yet. Only the Decoy was sceptical.

'I know Fingers is a great card player,' he said. 'But a gamble is a gamble.'

'Oh we don't intend to gamble,' Flinthart explained. 'That's for schmucks. We're going to cheat. What d'you say?'

Stacey stood up, fetched a can of beer out of the box and popped the top. 'I say *Viva Brisvegas!*'

Man, I get shivers just thinking about my first Schoolies Week. A clueless newbie, I'd caught a Greyhound to the coast. Rode that pooch from Ipswich to deliverance with half-a-dozen mates and forty-two bucks to my name. Seeing as how every one of those dollars was earmarked for beer and drugs we had no money for food or shelter – so we slept in the dunes and cruised McDonald's dumpsters. I somehow blundered in on the tail end of a three day pool party under the shadow of the Magic Castle at Nobby's Beach. This orgy was the work of some Catholic school girls who'd trashed themselves with one pint of cheap wine and thrown their parents' expensive holiday house open to the world. When they announced that the third day of their bacchanal was officially Topless Swimming Day I remember thinking that This Was It. I was definitely getting some this time. But even then you know, I wasn't lightning quick on the uptake. Some Marcia Brady type paddled over to me and slurred that I had something she wanted. I looked at her, uncomprehending. 'Uh, right, beer's in the fridge,' I said. She gave me a funny look, and after a while I clued in.

'Oh right. Oh yeah. Great.'

Sadly as she was leading me to a second storey bedroom we encountered this huge statue, one of those buried Chinese warriors those archaeologists keep digging up. This thing was about eight foot tall, and I guess it was just an imitation, but it looked like it was worth about three million bucks to me. I followed this girl up the stairs, held in a slack-jawed trance by the magical, fleshy rhythm of her butt as she ascended, a little unsteadily, a few steps in front of me. I was so completely drawn in that I missed her stumble at the top of the stairs, just caught the drunken lunge for support as she tripped, grabbed at the giant clay warrior for balance and reefed him right off his goddamned feet. He came down like one of those ten storey grain silos they like to show being blown up on the news. Slowly at first, then all at once in one great crashing catastrophic explosion of debris and destruction. Standing amongst the shrapnel and dust clouds, my heart sank. I knew I wasn't getting anywhere that afternoon, 'cept maybe into a taxi to make a quick getaway. So after that first time I didn't struggle with a lot of second-hand bullshit and filtered mythology about Schoolies Week. Not like the T-Bird, or even Elroy, who'd never been to Schoolies; since you really have to graduate from high school first. Being repeatedly expelled up to the age of fifteen doesn't count.

I rousted the dykes out my room, dragged my crusty old dinner jacket from the cupboard, had a quick shave and put my head under the shower for ten seconds. We split into three groups for the trip to the Gold Coast. Elroy took the T-Bird and Jabba in the milk van. Stacey drove myself, Missy and Taylor in the cab. (Taylor was incapable of controlling a vehicle.) And Flinthart ferried down Leonard, Gay Phil and the Decoy in his old purple Charger. I headed out early, making the empty freeway on the outskirts of town before seven and driving like bastards for the blue Pacific. I'd called Fingers' room at the casino but they said he was down on the floor so I left a message that I'd be through with a few friends and some more money. Just after nine we pulled into the Casino car park and split into two teams. Flinthart, Missy and Elroy took the Charger back into town to scout for recovery bashes where they could unload our merchandise. Everyone else drifted into the casino in dribs and drabs.

Another Kodak moment: Flinthart and Elroy in Hawaiian shirts and ridiculous 70's style reflecto sunglasses. Missy fleshing out some sweaty, wet-dream Suzy Wong outfit. A beer garden. Four teenage schoolboys with too much money, gulping and ogling the big bag of dope and DMT stuffed down between her breasts.

'I'm telling you, boys,' leers Flinthart, surreptitiously waving a joint around. 'One puff of my lady here, it'll pour rainbows through your eyes and punch out the seven veils of consciousness separating this world from the next.'

'What about chicks?' asks the bravest of the lads as Missy gives him a lurid smirk.

'Ha!' goes Flinthart, clapping him on the shoulder. 'Son, you don't want to even *think* about letting chicks near this stuff. It's too *dangerous*. The Virgin Mary got a taste of this and she'd be chompin' on your teeny weeny breakfast sausage before you knew what hit you.'

Uhuh, nods Missy.

'Oh boy,' says the youngster.

I walked into the casino with Stacey, who was tricked out in her cocktail dress. It was perfect for a Sabbath morning on the coast. We presented as a couple of third generation leisure class reptiles who'd breezed in to hazard the family silver after a night at the disco. Jupiters' atrium was crawling with a full array of rebounding wedding guests, itinerant party animals and a couple of dozen gullible-looking ostrich farm investors.

'Jeez,' I muttered. 'If we'd known these guys were gonna be here

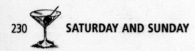

we coulda just dressed up as Big Bird and had 'em empty their wallets.'

Stacey bit her lip and cast around for any sign of Fingers. 'Well don't write it off as a plan,' she said. 'We might need a fall back position . . . let's check the tables.'

We entered the cavern of the main gaming room. About half the card tables were active. Nobody was jumping in the air or kissing complete strangers like in the commercials. The incessant *bloop bleep bloop* of the machines overlaid the shrapnel clatter of occasional payouts while hundreds of punters bent to their task of slowly and methodically feeding every dollar they had into the jaws of the Beast. Over near the two-up pit about twenty tables had been roped off for the Blackjack tournament. Abandoned at the moment, they awaited the resumption of play after lunch. I recognised a couple of faces here and there. Old pros keeping their hands in. Friends of Fingers. Brett 'The Chin' Cheney, Alan 'Blackjack' Herman and Mr Striptease, a Tasmanian with the disconcerting habit of progressively shedding his clothes during a good run.

Stacey and I made our way over to Cheney's table as he split a pair of eights for twenty/twenty-one, raking in a big pile of chips after the dealer drew a ten on fifteen.

'Hey, Brett,' I said. 'Seen Fingers?'

'JB, my man,' he answered without ever taking his eyes off the felt. He pushed a small stack of hundred dollar chips out, pulled an eight, then a nine, to square off with the house which sat on seventeen. He pushed his hands through his short, blonde buzz cut, rubbed his eyes and signalled to a waitress for another cup of coffee. He looked like he'd been awake for three days and possibly he had. It was not unknown for some of the tour's heavy hitters to develop urinary tract infections from refusing to leave the table.

He spun slowly on his seat, opting out of the next two or three hands. 'Fingers took a bath,' he said. 'About three in the morning.

Clubbed to fucking death. This dealer? He was a fucking killer, man. It was like the hand of God Himself was pulling those cards. Fingers'd make twenty, this guy'd make twenty-one. Fingers pulls twenty-one. This guy lays down a Little Richard.'

'A what?' asked Stace.

'Queen of hearts and ace of spades,' I explained.

'Man, it hurt to watch,' shuddered Cheney. 'Fingers musta dropped twenty large for sure.'

'Twenty thousand dollars?' gasped Stacey.

'On the grave of my mother,' nodded Cheney.

'Chinman,' I said, 'your mother's selling swampland in Florida.'

'Hey man,' he shrugged. 'It's a kind of death.'

'You know where Fingers is now?' I asked.

'Could be hiding in his room. We all got freebies. There was a bad scene at the bar about four or five. I wasn't there but I heard Fingers and some other guy really went at it. They turfed the other guy of course. But I ain't seen the big man since.'

Cheney gave us Fingers' room number. Stacey set off to round up the rest of the crew and I hurried upstairs. Philippino maids with linen trolleys haunted the otherwise deserted corridors. One of them gave me a look as I pulled up outside Fingers' room and started hammering on the door. She jabbed a finger at the Do Not Disturb sign hanging from his door knob but I kept knocking.

'Hey, Fingers! Open up. Cavalry's here.'

I couldn't hear any movement inside the room and the maid looked like she was getting ready to call the bouncers when the door swung open. I didn't even see Fingers' face, just his hairy butt. He was already headed back to bed, shoulders stooped, hair a mess, wearing one black sock and nothing else. I smiled at the maid and slipped inside.

'Hey, Fingers,' I said. 'The Chin tells me you had kind of a rough one last night. Dropped twenty K in the hole.'

232 **SATURDAY AND SUNDAY**

'Twenty-two,' he croaked, already swaddled in his blankets again. 'Ouch, that's gotta hurt.'

He merely sighed, 'They gave me a serial killer instead of a croupier.'

'The Chin says you had a little excitement down the bar too.'

'I don't really remember,' said Fingers, rubbing the back of his head. 'Some crazy motherfucker said I was moving in on his woman.' He sighed again, a heavy, world-weary sound. I wandered over to the bedside table and picked up the room service guide. 'You still on a comp?'

'Uhuh,' he grunted. 'Why? You want some breakfast? Call it up. Have 'em send a whole buffet cart if you want. Fuckers owe me. Gonna be a hell of a job to amortise my costs on this one.'

'Cheers,' I said, picking up the phone and punching in the number for room service. Fingers lay staring at the ceiling as I ordered scrambled eggs, bacon, sausages, toast and coffee for twelve. When I rang off Fingers had stopped staring at the ceiling and had taken up staring at me instead.

'That'll learn 'em,' he said flatly.

'Got company coming,' I explained. 'Stacey and the others.'

'Oh right,' he nodded. 'How's that business going at your place? You can't stay here you know. I gotta disappear by Monday. I crashed out of the playoffs. This room's just a sympathy fuck. To keep me coming back for more.'

I filled the kettle with water and fetched a couple of powdered coffee sachets from the fixings by the mini-bar. 'You mind?' I asked, grabbing a handful of tea and coffee stuff to cram in the pockets of my dinner jacket. 'We're kind of short at home.'

Fingers shrugged. He nodded at the mini-bar. 'If you're making a brew there's some of them little bottles of bourbon in the fridge.'

I cracked the seal on a miniature Jim Beam and poured it in. We drank the coffees black and sugarless.

'So you wanna get back in the game?' I asked about halfway down my mug.

'Ha. You gonna stake me a twenty K buy-in?' he said a little sourly.

'No. But I can probably spot you a lazy grand.'

He shook his head. 'Minimum buy-in's ten.'

'Well you wouldn't buy into the main game. Not at first. You could use our money on the sucker tables. Work it up till you got what we all need. Ten for you. About five for us.'

He looked at me like I was a little slow. 'I could lose a thousand bucks just getting the feel of the table.'

'Yeah, I know. But you know we can massage the odds. Hit that table with a flying wedge.'

'The Wedge,' he laughed. A tired little laugh. 'You want to run the Wedge in this place? Man, I oughta slap you down for a crazy man right now. This ain't no fucking one-deck burn joint you know. They got the Eye in the Sky. They got spooks haunting the floor. Guys with scanners checking for guys with computers. Wires and mikes in the lifts. You can't run no Wedge in here.'

'We got a team,' I said, pressing the issue. 'The Decoy's here. You played with him before. You know he can walk with the King. And Leonard, he's a walking, talking human pentium. You could teach him the numbers, in half an hour, he'll be kicking your hairy arse all over the house.'

'JB, he could be Hewlett fucking Packard . . . he ain't gonna be flying no Wedge through here.'

'And we got Flinthart too.'

Fingers stopped mid sip.

'You got Flinthart here? . . . Shit, negro! Why didn't you say? . . . find me my cummerbund.'

*

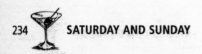

Fingers, fully and formally dressed, sipped from a strong cup of brewed coffee. No instant crap this time. He replaced the cup on the trolley which was already piled high with breakfast leftovers. He addressed the room, now crowded with my flatmates.

'In 1962 an event took place which reverbs down through the years to this very day. In 1962 Professor Edward Thorp, from the Department of Mathematics at the University College of Los Angeles, published Beat the Dealer, a systemic analysis of changing probabilities in the game of blackjack.'

Fingers paced to and fro across the room. He had everyone's attention, although Leonard and the Decoy were probably concentrating hardest of all. Flinthart was compulsively rolling a fifty dollar betting chip around his fingers like a cut-rate magician. Taylor, Elroy and the T-Bird were over-eating on Fingers' tab.

'The essential thing to remember about blackjack,' he continued, 'is that unlike other games the cards are not shuffled after each and every hand. The dealer works his or her way through a shoe containing up to six decks. Therefore, each hand played and discarded affects the probability of the same cards appearing again. Thorp also proved what generations of card players already knew intuitively. Certain cards improve a player's chances against the house. For the trained player, this renders blackjack as much a game of skill as of chance.'

The Decoy gave Fingers a searching look. 'Are you leading up to what I think you are?' he asked. 'Because far as I recall they ban card counters from these places.'

Fingers smiled indulgently.

'My friend,' he said. 'Right now, below us, in the gaming room, there are maybe one hundred blackjack tables in operation. They're all dealing somewhere between ninety and a hundred hands an hour. Some folks are strutting away from the tables like Elvis in flares because they took the house for three hundred dollars. They're winners. They're

Players. They're sitting at the right hand of the Lord. And they're gonna come back here in a few hours and lose it all, and then some, because every single game in this place is loaded in favour of the Man. If it wasn't, the Man would go out of business. In the case of blackjack the motherfucker takes an advantage of about two percent. That is, for every hundred dollars pushed across the table he only gives back ninety-eight. Every minute of every day.'

The Decoy shrugged noncommittally. This wasn't news to him.

'But by applying your skill as a card player,' said Fingers, 'by remembering that certain cards have gone, and others are yet to come, and by playing in tandem, as a team, we can turn that advantage around so that three quarters of the way through a shoe, the advantage ceded to us can be as high as two or even three percent. We're not changing the outcome of a game, we're just making our best estimate and backing it with our money. If we estimate wrong, we're out of the game.'

'We hit them like a flying wedge,' said Flinthart from his perch by the window. 'Just like in football. We combine and focus our strength on a single point.'

'The flying wedge was outlawed in football,' said the Decoy.

'Well, lets not take the analogy too far,' smiled Fingers. He picked up a small pile of cash from the coffee table and riffled through it quickly. 'So what are we playing with here? A grand or so?'

'Nine hundred dollars,' said Stacey.

'Yeah, we would have had more,' said Flinthart. 'But Schoolies has been running a week and the kiddies cash flow has dwindled somewhat.'

'This'll do fine,' said Fingers. 'Now, JB and Flinthart have both flown the Wedge before. But Decoy, Stacey and Leonard, you got some hard study ahead of you. We're not going to hit the floor until later tonight. There'll be a lot more action then and they're less likely to tumble us. You just gotta learn some basic rules and hand signals. I'll do the

playing for you. You just watch me, without being obvious, and we'll be cool.'

'Well I don't know about this,' said the Decoy. 'This sounds like trouble to me. I don't know that I want to be in this.'

Finger shook his head in exasperation. 'Decoy,' he said. 'We need you out there. I need someone who knows how to play as a point man.'

'I'll go point man!' said Elroy. 'I wanna be a point man.'

'No offence son,' said Fingers. 'But the point has to be a sharp operator and you're dumber than a sack of hammers. You look kinda weird too, with all your eyebrows burned off like that. I figure to put you and Taylor on the two-up pit with the lovely Missy here to make a lot of noise. Kind of draw the attention away from us. If that's all right with you.'

'I guess so,' mumbled Elroy, a little hurt.

'Right then,' said Fingers, warming to his topic. "We good to go, Decoy?'

'I don't think so,' he said quietly.

Late night Sunday.

The gaming room is pumping. Hundreds of spectators watch the pros at the tournament, telling themselves they would make the same moves if they were sitting there with thousands of dollars in chips stacked in front of them. At a single table on the edge of the tournament crowd I sit with Stacey, Leonard, Fingers and two strangers. We are six grand up, mostly through Fingers who has a stack of black, hundred dollar chips in front of him. A few metres away, at the two-up pit, Elroy, Taylor, Missy and the T-Bird are roaring and cheering as a new spinner lets the coins fly. Between them and the blackjack championship only one pit boss has wandered over to watch our game and only for a few minutes. He smiles at Fingers, who is well known in these parts. 'Good to see you back on the horse Howard,' he says. 'Good to see you doing so well again. Keep it up guy.'

Fingers smiles tightly at him as the dealer turns over her hole card. A three on a ten. She draws another from the shoe. Three of hearts. Sixteen. She draws again and busts. Pays out four hundred.

'Thanks,' smiles Fingers as the pit boss ambles away. 'Put the evil eye on me will you, you sonofabitch?' he mutters.

Stacey thanks the dealer and leaves the table. Two minutes later Gay Phil replaces her. They do not acknowledge each other. As far as the croupier is concerned, only Fingers and I have met before. Stacey returns to Fingers' room to add her winnings to the pile.

The hands come and go. Sometimes we win, sometimes we lose. But more often, under Fingers' tutelage, we win. Over the arc of the night, through dozens, then hundreds, maybe a thousand hands, we slowly accumulate capital. For every one hundred dollars we push out, a hundred and two come back. It's hard at first. We drop three hundred. Stacey is nervous, Leonard a little too intense, a little too obvious. Our croupier deals a lot of shit. Twos and threes for us. Aces and eights for herself. But gradually, as we chew through the shoe, Fingers starts amping up the bets. With three quarters of the first shoe gone he suddenly starts laying down stacks of black chips. The cacophony around us makes concentration difficult and at one point Stacey makes everyone laugh by nearly splitting a pair of queens. Even the dealer smiles. 'Sorry,' grins Stacey ingenuously, 'I guess I don't really know what I'm doing.' Exactly what a casino likes to hear. But Fingers is watching. He knows that most of the crap cards are gone and we've got a run of tens, jacks and queens waiting for us.

Bang! Gay Phil and Leonard both score blackjacks. The dealer busts on twenty-two, twenty-three. We are at eight thousand dollars and counting. Fingers is incredible. Vengeance personified. It's almost like you can feel the heat coming off him, he's working so hard at tracking aces and high cards through the six deck shoe. But he doesn't look like he's concentrating. That's the thing. He's flirting with the croupier and some spastically drunk American woman who's pulled into one of the sucker seats at the table. He's flipping and jiggling his chips at light speed. In the flurry of hands and fingers, though, are a series of embedded codes for the rest of us. Double down, get heavy, split those eights. You can tell Leonard has had a revelation. The shifting integers of the Ten Count system are a natural for someone trained to think in long string digital sequences. We are killing them, hammering them, slamming them into the ground with the Flying Wedge.

Then it all comes crashing to a halt.

'You sonofabitch, you done it again!'

The dealer looks up and her face registers shock. None of us has time to turn. The drunken American woman yells, 'Harold! No!' But it is too late. Her loud, check-jacketed, even-drunker companion, hauls off and king hits Fingers with a roundhouse punch to the back of the head that starts somewhere out near Saturn. You can hear the bones in his hand crack as his fist impacts on Fingers' skull. The croupier screams. Flinthart, just arrived at the table, cries out, 'Ye gods!' I jump to one side and fall off my stool. Leonard protects the chips and Gay Phil leaps on Harold, wrestling him to the sticky carpet and keeping him there with an arm lock and knee in the back of his neck. Security teams come running. At least two hundred people, in a crowd ten or fifteen deep, watch them grab Harold, the guy Fingers had been fighting with earlier that morning. They frog-march him out of the room. Again. Casino goons fuss over Fingers, apologising profusely, offering all sorts of inducements to take the matter no further. But it is all lost on him. He is unconscious and will remain so for the next ten hours. When he is finally carried away Gay Phil, Leonard, Flinthart and I are left at the table with a few thousand dollars worth of chips and nary a clue between us. We are thinking about leaving under the cover of the confusion. But if we leave we lose. We are still thousands short of what we need. We can't even discuss it openly for fear of tipping off the casino to the fact of the Wedge.

Then the Decoy, who has refused to participate up to this moment, appears at the table wearing a ridiculously large stetson and chomping a fat cigar. 'Evenin' boys!' he cries in his thick American accent. 'Make room. Make room. The cat in the hat is back!'

'I've never seen this much money in one place,' says the Decoy.

It is five in the morning. We are all in Fingers' room. He is semi-conscious and incoherent. Jabba is watching MTV on the in-house cable. The T-Bird is asleep in a chair. Taylor has curled up under a table. Flinthart is asleep in the bath, covered in warm water, breathing through a snorkel. Everyone else is awake. The Decoy is counting our money again. Twelve thousand dollars. Elroy rifles through the bar fridge looking for any stray alcohol he may have missed. Leonard and Missy are sharing a club sandwich. I am perched at the end of Fingers' bed, next to Stacey.

'So what's the plan?' asks Leonard, slobbering mayo everywhere.

We stare at the cash, a small miracle revealed on the shag pile rug of a casino hotel room.

'We got four hours before those yuppies turn up at York Street,' says Stace. 'What does everyone think? We going to see it through or bail?'

'You know they're not going to give up,' says Gay Phil. 'Do you think it'll matter if we pay them this morning? They're going to tear that place down, one way or another.'

'Yeah, they got a lot of money tied up there,' I concede. 'I don't want to lose, but, you know . . .'

I trail off. Nobody speaks for a while.

'Well,' says Stacey, at last. 'I guess we could just divide our winnings. Give Fingers his cut if he ever comes out of that coma and, you know, get on with our lives.'

'You really want to do that?' I ask, putting a hand on her shoulder.

'No,' she says.

The room falls silent again, for a long time, until the Decoy speaks, 'I know a great place we could stay.'

All eyes are on him.

'My place, at the coast,' he smiles. 'It's big enough, especially now that Roger's run off. And this would pay the rent for two years.' He picks up a fistful of money.

We all look at each other.

'What d'you reckon?' I ask Stacey and she shrugs and says, 'Maybe.' Just maybe. Then she smiles and Missy smiles and Elroy finds a couple of mini-bottles of vodka at the back of the freezer and the Decoy raises an eyebrow and plucks a cigar out of his pocket and lights up and cries out, 'Looks like we got us a convoy!'

DIRK FLINTHART'S CASK WINE TASTING NOTES

We of the Wine Review Team are going to review EVERY SINGLE CASK WINE that we can find! Fasten your seat belts and brace your brain cells, because here come the whites!

ORLANDO RHINE RIESLING

Comes in a lovely metallic green and gold carton; promises all sorts of things like delicate floral bouquets and crisp dry finishes. Mind you, it's lying through its long, sharp, pointy teeth – this wine is a vicious predator, gleefully disembowelling anyone foolish enough to ingest it. Overall, though, it isn't too bad.

ORLANDO SPAETLESE LEXIA

'Late-picked lexia grapes . . . light, fruity wine . . . pronounced floral bouquet'. What twaddle. Floral bouquet my bottom: this is the kind of floral bouquet I wouldn't send to Saddam Hussein's funeral! Mind you, the sickly-sweet flavour kind of grows on you after a few glasses. Maybe I'll try this one again when I'm feeling really suicidal.

STANLEY RHINE RIESLING

What the hell is 'lifted fruit'? Did they steal the grapes? If they did, they got ripped off badly! Andrew swears he once licked a pig's under-arm on a dare – and that this wine brought the experience back to mind in Technicolor. I guess you can't argue with that!

STANLEY COLOMBARD CROUCHEN

'Whale urine filtered through cinnamon and castor sugar,' says another taster as he sways on the stairwell. Why is he swaying? Could it be the vast quantities of wine, or is it just the instability of the foundations of this place. Bloody coast houses – they're all built on sand. Don't drink this wine. It'll make your house collapse.

MORRIS OF RUTHERGLEN RIESLING

Sour and villainously industrial. Cathy was prepared to praise it for its dryness, but when the racking gut cramps overcame her, she changed her mind. Volume-Test Animal claimed he wouldn't even poison a cat with this stuff – so we tried. The cat wouldn't have a bar of it.

STANLEY LITE WHITE

I must confess that we didn't actually drink this. The prospect of drinking a wine with full nausea value but reduced ethanol content was so totally horrifying that we simply didn't buy it, despite its exciting white box.

GOLDEN GATE RIESLING

The end . . . surely this is the end. Nobody can walk straight anymore, and there are some who cannot even crawl straight. It tastes sort of bad, like the grape-stompers were still wearing their socks when they stomped the grapes. But I'm glad the grapes got stomped, 'cause they deserved it.

STANLEY WHITE LAMBRUSCO

White Lambrusco? I kind of like this stuff, normally – but normally it's red, comes in a bottle, and is lightly carbonated. Carbonating anything in a bladder would be stupid – it would create an effect not dissimilar to that caused by the build-up of gases in the stomach of a decaying corpse. And coincidentally, decaying corpses is the image which springs to mind when confronting this horror of a wine. Not your average decaying corpse either, but a huge, maggot-ridden elephant corpse, liquefying in the sun. Ewww, yuck!

BURONGA RIDGE RIESLING
Barnes suggests that this stuff tastes like it has already been used as enema fluid before it was encasked. That remark was enough to set poor Wounded Andrew off again. I don't blame either of them, frankly.

COOLABAH MOSELLE
I don't believe it. Barnes is up and swilling again. This is beyond comprehension. Why does his liver continue to consent to live with him? The Coolabah Moselle is kind of nice, by the way, in the way that all wines become nice after the first two litres or so.

STANLEY CHABLIS
Who really gives a shit anyway? It tastes much the same coming up as it does going down. Yes – I admit it . . . I've been talking to God on the Great White Telephone. Oh Lord, when will this punishment come to an end?

STANLEY FESTWEIN
Fuck all of you. I've had enough of this . . . I saw this Chihuahua the other day. It was mounted upon the back of a very somnolent and fat Labrador, humping away like crazy. I'm not even going to try to relate that to wine – though perhaps it is significant that I remembered this embarrassing sight during my attempts to swallow the Festwein. Raggedy Andrew is nearly comatose. Wounded Andrew lives, albeit in a horrifically crippled fashion . . . why do we do this?

DE BORTOLI PREMIUM SEMILLON
Nice box. Zlpkjk jeezus I can't keep doing this what are we trying to drink now? I don't think I candf keep this up anymorem. Help, help, help.

Why does Barnes still keep moving? He should be dead.